MANDRAGORA

A sailing ship leaves Scotland, headed for South Australia. For the passengers, the voyage offers a fresh start in a promising land. But on the way they meet sudden malice and inexplicable danger and at the end of their voyage, the ship is wrecked in a wild winter storm.

There are only two survivors—a seventeen-year-old girl and a young seaman who take shelter in a cave to wait out the storm and there they find warmth, security and love. When they finally emerge, there is something left behind. Something evil.

A hundred years later, another young couple uncover the place where the lovers found sanctuary.

But some things are best left undisturbed . . .

Here are four of them.

Mandragora

David McRobbie is a full-time writer and lives in Brisbane.

Also by David McRobbie

Flying with Granny
The Wayne Dynasty
Waxing with Wayne

MANDRAGORA

David McRobbie

MAMMOTH
AUSTRALIA

First published 1991 by
Mammoth Australia
a division of the Octopus Publishing Group
22 Salmon Street, Port Melbourne, Victoria 3207
Reprinted 1992

Edited by Maryann Ballantyne
Designed by Andrew Cunningham
Typeset in 11/13pt Times by Bookset Pty Ltd
Printed in Australia by Australian Print Group

National Library of Australia
  cataloguing-in-publication data:

McRobbie, David.
  Mandragora.
  ISBN 1 86330 101 1.
  I. Title.
A823.3

For Kay

Mandrake. Any plant of the genus *Mandragora*, having very short stems, thick, fleshy, often forked roots and fetid lance-shaped leaves.

The mandrake is poisonous, having emetic and narcotic properties. Its forked root was thought to resemble human form and was fabled to shriek when plucked up from the ground. [SOED]

. . . the root of the mandragora often divides itself in two and presents a rude appearance of a man. In ancient times human figures were often cut out of the root and wonderful virtues ascribed to them. It was used to produce fecundity in women (*Genesis xxx. 14–16*). Some mandrakes cannot be pulled from the earth without producing fatal effects, so a cord used to be fixed to the root and round a dog's neck and the dog being chased drew out the mandrake and died. Another superstition is that when the mandrake is uprooted it utters a scream. Thomas Newton, in his *Herball to the Bible*, says: 'It is supposed to be a creature having life engendered under the earth of the seed of some dead person put to death for murder.'

[Brewer: *The Dictionary of Phrase and Fable*.]

Chapter One

From high on the cliff path, Adam Hardy looked down at the line of footprints dotted along the edge of the surf. Even from that distance he could tell they'd been made by bare feet and in what direction they were heading, which meant if he kept walking he'd find her further along the beach and she'd be alone.

He smiled to himself and thought about how he'd approach her.

'Hi, Catriona. Doing a bit of beachcombing, eh? Mind if I walk with you?' Just like that. Cool. Then to keep the conversation going he could ask what she'd found at the water's edge and maybe he'd discover something too, which of course he'd hand over to her. After all, Catriona was the one doing the beachcombing; Adam would have found what *he* came for.

He was aware that his private and one-sided feelings for Catriona Chisholm were threatening to take over his entire life. He'd been busy with his school work and his reading and model electric railways when all at once he found himself taking an interest in girls—in particular Catriona. Instead of getting on with work in class he spent a lot of time looking in her direction and the interest often carried on even when he wasn't in school. At spare moments Adam found himself thinking about her and wondering if she ever spared him a thought in return. Girls were funny that way; they could tell what you had on your mind but they were much better at hiding their feelings. He'd once read an article that said girls were more mature than boys of the same age which is why they went for older guys. That way they met their intellectual equal, which was all very interesting as a theory but it sort of left him out in the cold.

Now, his first private meeting with Catriona was working to plan. He knew he'd find her around the next headland and from the single line of footprints at the water's edge, he could tell she was alone so there'd be no one from school hanging around to make a big deal of it.

If she expressed any curiosity about how Adam knew about her solitary expeditions, then he'd be able to say he got the information from her mother. By chance, he had found out that Catriona went beachcombing in the afternoons, bringing back bits of driftwood or sometimes, if the weather had been rough, fragments of sodden timber or even pieces of crockery given up by the drowned wrecks of sailing ships that lay along the coast.

He had dropped into the souvenir shop in Dunarling to buy a tin of Humbrol enamel to touch up the paintwork on one of his model locomotives, although he had a guilty feeling that, compared with his new interest, playing with model trains was becoming distinctly juvenile. As Barbara Chisholm gave him his change, Adam had admired a small and brightly painted wooden carving of a sailor which stood on the counter with a sign saying it was hand made.

'Who's the sailor?' he asked.

'That's Jamie Ramsay,' Barbara teased him. 'Our local hero. I thought *everyone* knew that, Adam.'

'Sorry, I should have guessed.' He hated being caught out like that.

'He's carved out of driftwood,' Barbara went on. 'Could even have been a part of one of the old sailing ships. Catriona collects the wood, I dry it and decide what it's to be, carve the figure, paint it and put it on sale and between us we've got a nice little cottage industry.'

'Where does Catriona find the driftwood?'

'On the beach, of course,' Barbara smiled. 'Where do you think you'd find driftwood? She's out at Dunarling Rocks right now, looking for whatever turns up. She goes beachcombing most afternoons.'

'Oh, I see.' Adam considered this information.

As he moved along his high position on the cliff path, he rounded a bend and suddenly saw Catriona down at the water's edge, barefoot and long legged with her skirt tucked up, picking her way up the beach. He smiled and increased his stride to catch up with her.

In the final year class at Dunarling High School, Catriona sat two desks in front of him so he was able to look at the back of her head and her neat dark pony tail for most of the day. Whenever he answered a question from the teacher, Catriona had a disconcerting habit of turning around and looking directly at him. Most of the other kids looked to see how the teacher was accepting the answer, but not Catriona. She always spun around and looked at him frankly and when he finished she'd raise an eyebrow or give a faint smile as if rewarding him for what his answer was worth.

It was as if there was a little private thing going on between them—somehow as if she was the one making the overtures. But you had to be careful with girls. He knew that. Read the signposts the wrong way or make your move too soon and it could be all over school. The year before he'd made an ill-timed approach to an older girl and she'd let him think he was getting somewhere then knocked him back. But what was worse, she'd gone and told everyone about it which caused him a lot of embarrassment all round.

Once bitten, and all that; softly, softly next time, he told himself.

Down on the beach, Catriona stopped and kneeled to examine something she'd found in the sand and the wind caught her long hair and blew it about her face so she turned her head slightly to let the breeze put it in place again. She examined the thing she'd found, turning it over and over in her fingers as if making up her mind whether or not it was worth keeping.

The only impressions Adam had of Catriona were the ones he'd picked up at school. He could tell she was clever and serious, also much more mature than the other girls in the class, which made it doubly difficult to chance a move in her direction. There was also that tantalising rumour about her.

Last summer holidays she'd been seen out late at night with some second year university students who'd arrived from Melbourne to work on a project at the museum. Adam had heard there'd been some sort of 'incident' with the two students; Catriona had been in it just as much as the older ones and the police had caught them all red-handed. The university students' parents had whisked them back to the city; a big shame job it was. Some of the townspeople said it was nothing but harmless high spirits. Others took a more serious view and asked what Dunarling was coming to. But what had Catriona done?

When the new school year began, several versions of the escapade began to circulate, each becoming embroidered into a whole tapestry of intimate detail, with evidence and names of witnesses, 'she said's and 'that's what I heard anyway'. Faced with such a maddeningly seductive mystery, two other girls, Mairi and Megan, tried to edge closer to Catriona to get the inside story, but they drew a blank.

'She only goes for sophisticates,' Mairi sniffed.

'Yeah, thinks she's too good for us,' Megan added and they left it at that.

All this time, Catriona seemed aware of the stir she'd caused but kept up an air of amused detachment, making it plain she wasn't interested in telling anyone what had happened. She'd always been one of the quiet girls in class but suddenly at the start of the new school year, here she was with a reputation—which prompted a couple of boys to chance their luck with her but they got nowhere. Adam was pleased about that part of it but at the same time he couldn't help wondering what she had got up to in the holidays.

Down at the water's edge, he saw her straighten up and continue to examine the object until a wave rolled in, covering her feet and ankles. The sudden shock of that seemed to help make her decision for she threw whatever she'd found back into the water and picked her way further on, looking out to sea where heavier waves surged into Dunarling Rocks sending white spume flying.

Catriona made things even more difficult for Adam because she never went to local dances and at school she kept to herself so it was hard to get her alone, even to talk to or go down to David Riccio's new coffee shop for a milk shake.

So with all that on his mind, Adam was about to meet Catriona on her own. At any rate, that was the plan.

As he rounded a bend on the cliff path, so absorbed was he in gazing down at the surf he failed to notice a little way ahead, two boys with their backs to him, crouched behind a large rock which stood on the seaward edge of the cliff path. They were like a pair of hunters who'd tracked their quarry, seeing without being seen. Now they were looking down on Catriona where she walked on the beach.

When Adam realised who they were, he stopped dead in his tracks and suddenly felt his heart sink, but it was already too late. Of all the people to meet, this pair were the ones he least wanted to see.

Richard Vernon and Mike Carter were well known to Adam and to everyone else at Dunarling High, especially to some of the kids from the junior school. Keeping his eye on them, Adam began a delicate retreat, hoping to get back to the bend in the cliff path before they realised he was there. But Mike Carter suddenly sensed his presence and nudged Richard and they both turned around to face him.

'Well, well, well. Look who's here.' Richard stood up and dusted the knees of his jeans. 'If it's not Laurel N Hardy. Out for a backward stroll, eh?'

'Backward stroll,' Mike sniggered. 'That's good, Richard.'

'Yeah,' Adam said. He knew from experience that to say too much gave Richard a chance to make some smart comment at his expense.

'Sneaking up on us like that,' Richard's voice was mocking yet without humour. 'Planning something, were you? Spying on us, eh?'

'No, just walking.'

'Backwards?' Mike said. 'You always walk in reverse?'

'Forget it,' Adam said.

'Well, lose yourself.' Richard's lip curled. 'We don't want you here.'

Mike and Richard moved back to the rock, ignoring Adam for the moment.

'She's some looker, eh, Richard?'

'Yeah, Mike. I reckon.'

'Spot the legs, willya.'

'Yeah. I heard she comes across,' Mike said.

'Fair dinkum?'

'Yeah. That's what they say. It's what a coupla guys at school reckon.'

'And what do you reckon, Laurel N Hardy?' Richard walked slowly back to Adam. 'You reckon she comes across?'

'I dunno.' Adam burned inside. 'I don't think she's the type.' He hated having to *allow* this conversation. It was as if they were making public property of her.

'They're *all* that type,' Mike sneered. 'Some of them take a bit longer getting round to it, that's all.'

'Yeah, and some of them don't know it,' Richard added. 'But they all come across in the end.'

'You didn't get very far with her,' Adam said. 'I saw her give you the big freeze when you tried.'

'Oh, is that what you reckon, creep?' Richard sneered.

'Yeah, it was all over school—*Vermin*.' Almost instantly, Adam wished he hadn't added Richard's nickname.

'Living dangerously are we, creep?' Richard's voice went down to a whisper.

For the last two years, the smaller kids at school had privately named this pair 'Vermin and Garbage'. They sometimes referred to Richard as 'Vermin Vernon', which made them feel better but they made sure they only used the names in their own company. When one of the kids carelessly wrote the word 'Vermin' on a chalk board, Richard knew what it meant and spat on the writing and rubbed it off with the sleeve of the first small boy he grabbed. In this way he let it be known it was instant grief for anyone to use that word again.

As if acting out a well rehearsed strategy, Mike circled behind and suddenly pinned Adam's arms and when he was safely held, Richard drew his arm back and gave a short twisting punch to the stomach. Adam gasped in pain and doubled over. In that instant, he caught sight of Catriona down on the beach. She had turned around for some reason and started back the way she'd come and now she looked up sharply to witness this moment of humiliation.

There was worse to come. Richard suddenly spun him around and sent him sprawling head first off the edge of the cliff path! As he fell, Adam tried to grab hold of the short scrubby gorse bushes but he was moving too fast. He managed to twist his body and began to roll sideways down the bank, kicking up curving billows of loose sand as he went. Instinctively he closed his eyes and hoped there were no rocks waiting for him below.

Halfway down the bank, he came to a rolling stop in a small depression and lay for a second, spitting out sand and thinking he'd come as far as he could. Suddenly the ground opened up under him and he began slipping into a crevice where he landed in an awkward bundle, face up and winded. He opened his eyes and realised he was at the bottom of a fissure in the sand bank with the blue of the sky somewhere overhead. Warily, he tried to get up but at that moment, from the bank above, another wall of sand dislodged itself and slipped down on him with a dull whoomp! Adam felt it coming, closed his eyes and was covered.

He tried to struggle free but he was pressed down by the weight of the sand. It was in his clothes and his hair. Sand blocked his mouth and nostrils so he kept his eyes tightly shut and began to panic. There was no way he could call out or move and it was impossible to breathe. This was a visit from death!

Then a hand found his face and he felt someone scooping sand away from his nose and mouth. He took in a huge lungful of air while the hands kept digging him out. Before long, he could crack his eyes open a millimetre and saw it was Catriona.

'Are you all right, Adam?' she said. Her voice was anxious.

He spat out a mouthful of sand and managed to croak an answer although his tongue was thickly coated. Catriona kept scooping with both hands using strong determined strokes and throwing the loose sand to left and right.

'Don't move too much or you'll bring more of it down on you,' she said and worked steadily until Adam managed to free one arm then the other. As Catriona gathered the sand on each side of her, he felt able to move his body.

Richard and Mike came on the scene, their expressions all genuine concern.

which twisted and turned. They held their candles in one hand which slowed their progress but at last the tunnel opened out into another, smaller cave which contained nothing but evidence of a small fire having been coaxed into life at some time in the past.

'Place is empty.' Richard held up the butane lighter and looked around. He spat on the sandy floor and they heard it land. The silence was total.

It was Catriona who found the only feature of real interest in the cave. On the floor in a dark corner furthest from the entrance, she discovered a small pyramid of sand, too regular in shape to have been formed by nature.

'This could be a grave,' she said in a hushed voice and knelt beside the pyramid, staring intently at it. 'Perhaps there's a baby buried here.'

'Or treasure.' Mike knelt and put his candle on the floor beside the small mound. 'Yeah, what about jewels and stuff, eh?'

'Could be,' Richard said.

'That's why they made it a pyramid shape. To show it's full of treasure.'

'The pyramids were *tombs*,' Catriona spoke scornfully.

'Yeah, but they were still full of treasure,' Mike argued.

'Honestly, we shouldn't disturb anything,' Adam said. 'I mean this has got to be Jamie Ramsay's cave. Okay, so we found it, that's great, but it doesn't *belong* to us.' The other two ignored him and even Catriona knelt with her hands in her lap, staring at the pyramid of sand as if she'd suddenly become entranced with it.

Richard dropped to his knees beside Mike so Adam made a small mound for his candle to stand on and knelt alongside Catriona. It was Richard who leaned out and gently chopped his hand into the pyramid and slowly cleared off the top of it to left and right. The sand was dry and trickled away in front of them. He sliced his hand in again and pushed more sand away and this time, they saw the tops of five small, oblong wooden boxes.

'Coffins,' Mike whispered. 'That's what they are. Little coffins; it's a grave for midgets or something.' In the light from the candle, his face was pale, his eyes wide.

Four of the coffins were grouped together, with a fifth one a little way apart from the rest, towards the door of the cave.

'But what's in them?' Richard said. '*Who's* in them?'

'Maybe it's jewels or something,' Mike said.

Very gently, Richard prised one of the coffins out of its bed of sand. He tapped it clean with his fingers then placed it on his upturned palm where it fitted exactly. The coffin was made of rough, unpainted wood with small, rusty tinplate triangles fastened to the sides. On the lid was another piece of tin, as if forming a nameplate for the tiny occupant.

For a moment they didn't speak but stared at the coffin in Richard's hand. It was Catriona who broke the hushed silence.

'Adam's right,' she said. 'We should leave everything and report it. I mean, it's history and we've got no right in here.'

'Yeah, we might do damage.' Adam was glad to have her support.

'That's bullshit!' Richard said, suddenly breaking the almost reverent mood that had settled on them. 'Whatever's inside's dead, so what damage can you do to a dead thing just by looking at it?'

'I saw a program on TV about archaeological sites and stuff,' Adam persisted. 'Before they touch anything, they take pictures of it. You know, they make notes and sketches and take photographs and then go to a laboratory to open whatever it is.'

'That's right.' Catriona's voice was almost a whisper. 'We shouldn't touch anything.' He looked at her and was surprised to see how pale she was.

'Are you all right, Catriona?' he said.

'We shouldn't disturb them,' she repeated in such a low undertone Adam almost had to read her lips. 'I mean, who knows?'

'Crap!' Richard snapped his fingers and held out his free hand to Mike. 'Scalpel!'

Mike produced a pocket knife and opened the main blade and slapped it into Richard's palm as if they were in an operating theatre. Still looking for a reaction from Catriona, Richard slipped the blade under the lid of the coffin and flicked it up. The wood splintered and sand fell away.

Inside the broken coffin they saw a tiny wooden figure dressed in a knitted black jersey and canvas trousers. It had a painted face with open eyes and a tight lipped grin that held no mirth. Its arms were folded in front of it in a proper attitude of burial.

'It's a doll,' Mike said. 'That's all—a bloody wooden doll!' Relief was evident in his voice. 'Who'd go burying a doll? Some weirdo?'

Richard flicked the doll out of the coffin and held it to the side of his face and pretended he was a ventriloquist.

'Hello folks,' he said with his mouth to one side. Adam found himself looking not at Richard but at the doll's face and he shivered briefly. Its expression seemed to have changed to one of triumph.

Mike laughed as he delved into the sand for another of the coffins.

'Come on, fair's fair,' Adam protested. 'We've got to preserve these just the way they were.' He stretched out his hand to protect the nearest coffins but with sudden venom Richard snatched up the knife and pointed it in his direction.

'You're boring, creep!' His eyes flashed in the candle-light. 'These are mine, okay?' His voice was hoarse.

Adam managed to pull away the coffin nearest to him and shake the sand off it before tucking it inside his shirt while Richard gathered up the rest.

'I reckon we can sell these, eh Rich,' Mike said.

'The name is Richard,' Richard said quietly, still looking at Adam as he spoke. 'Haven't you learned that yet? It's always Richard. Got it?' His eyes flashed.

'Yes, Richard,' Mike said in a low voice. 'Sorry, I forgot.'

'Then don't forget.' There was a tense, uneasy silence and Adam even felt a brief touch of pity for Mike.

'Come on, there's no way you can keep those things,' Catriona said.

'Yeah, let's get back and report it.' Adam stood up.

'Who you gonna report, creep?' Richard said, stroking the blade of the knife with his fingers as if wiping off some blood. Then he took the candle from Mike and held it high.

'Yeah, creep,' Mike chipped in. 'You gonna report me as well?'

'You've got one doll,' Richard said. 'So that's the one you report, Hardy. You never saw any others. That's your story. And we weren't here. Okay? Now, memorise that, creep, and get lost. Mike and me still got some business here.'

Without a word, Adam picked up his own candle and made for the low tunnel entrance and Catriona rose from the sand to follow him.

'Hey, hang on a minute, creep.' Richard looked at them both as if calculating his next move. 'The doll stays behind.'

'But you just said . . .' Adam protested.

'Not *that* doll,' Richard's voice had dropped to a whisper and he turned the knife blade slowly so it glinted in the candlelight. 'You can keep the one in your shirt, Hardy, but the other one— *she* stays behind.'

Adam felt his mouth go dry and stood, uncertain, with his candle held high. It spluttered and wax dripped. Even Mike was startled and glanced with disbelief at Richard before taking a half step away from him into the shadows. In the edgy silence, it was Catriona who acted. She suddenly dropped to one knee and scooped up two handfuls of sand and threw one straight into Richard's face and with the other, she doused his candle then pushed Adam towards the low entrance.

'Come on, let's move,' she said. Adam ducked into the tunnel and holding up the candle, he began to crawl. In the darkness behind them, he heard Richard shouting but not in a voice he'd heard before nor in words he could understand.

Soon Adam and Catriona were able to move in a half crouch and then stand fully upright as the tunnel widened around them. The most difficult task then was to shield the delicate flame from the draught of their movement but soon they found the large outer cave still lit by fading daylight and scrambled up the slope to the exit.

Outside, in the evening air, they tumbled down the bank to the firmer sand of the beach where Catriona took Adam's hand and they started to run from Jamie Ramsay's cave.

Chapter Two

As they walked in step along the beach, it grew dark and the air became chilly. From time to time, Adam looked back anxiously in case the others had found their way out of the cave and were following them but there was no one in sight. They kept up their pace until they saw the lights of Dunarling winking ahead of them; then Adam felt easier. He glanced at Catriona and sensed that her tension had slipped away too.

'Look, I think we'd better work out what to say.' He was distinctly itchy and uncomfortable from the sand that had covered him.

'We just tell the truth.' Catriona seemed to have made up her mind. 'We report what we found—the cave, the dolls, end of story. I mean, come on, Adam, all that stuff's important.'

'Yes, well,' he began and hesitated.

'Well what?' There was a sharp edge to her voice.

'What about *them*—Richard and Mike?' he said. 'What they said. You know, about us keeping quiet about the four coffins they took.'

'You only agreed to that because they had us baled up.' Catriona sounded scornful. 'I mean, you're not going along with it, are you?' He was silent and she looked at him and sighed and shook her head slowly. Adam knew he wasn't making a good impression.

'It's difficult,' was all he said.

'Oh, all right.' They had reached the main street. 'So what are you going to do?'

'Well, I'll just say we found the cave, and the one coffin I've got.' Adam was relieved. 'We'll hand it over to Hamish Leckie at the museum.'

'Look, Adam, you've got to stand up and fight,' she said sharply. 'It's the only language their sort understand.'

'Yeah, easy to say, Catriona.' His voice betrayed his reluctance. 'But they're the *worst* sort.'

'Honestly, it makes me sick to think of that Richard Vernon swaggering around the place,' she said. 'And Mike Carter's nearly as bad only he's just easily led, that's his problem.'

'There was all that business with Richard and the two kids from the junior school,' Adam said. 'Remember?'

'And he got away with it,' Catriona said. 'With his solicitor father on his side; but everyone *knows* he did it.'

'Okay, then we just let it go?'

'Please yourself,' she said. 'But honestly, I wish I were a boy. I wouldn't let him get away with it!'

☆   ☆   ☆

Barbara Chisholm cleared a space on her crowded workbench and switched on a low overhead lamp to get a better view of the tiny coffin. Catriona had insisted Adam come into the shop and show the find to her mother.

'I'll be extremely gentle with it,' Barbara said. 'After all, it's a piece of history.' Like the other four coffins, this one had tiny triangles of tinplate set into the sides and on the lid. Catriona and Adam knelt side by side at the edge of the pool of light and watched as Barbara carefully brushed away traces of the sand that had buried the coffin for so long. She took up a thin bladed knife and gently inserted it under the lid and levered it off.

Inside they found a dark brown wooden doll, dressed as the first one had been in a grey jumper and canvas trousers only this one had a cheerful painted face.

'It's just the same—' Catriona started to say and by way of warning, Adam pressed his knee against hers. She looked at him with a half smile, rolling her eyes and he gave just a hint of a cautioning frown in case she said more.

'The same as what?' Barbara asked, concentrating on the doll.

'Oh, the same as . . . same as I imagined it to be,' Catriona ended her sentence limply and bit her lip as if just waiting to be found out.

'Oh, Cat,' Barbara said calmly, without looking up. 'What a strange way of expressing yourself! *The same as I imagined it to be!*'

'I'll give it to the museum tomorrow,' Adam moved in to cover their brief moment of confusion.

'Well, nowadays you have to give things up,' Barbara said. 'It's not like finders keepers —if you hold on to things you're really breaking the law.'

'I know about that,' Adam said and thought of the other four dolls.

'But it's marvellous if you've really found Jamie Ramsay's cave,' Barbara went on. 'All these years everyone said it was a myth, and now you two have discovered it. Just how did it happen?'

'I went down the sand bank off the cliff path and that caused a sort of landslide and suddenly, there was the entrance,' Adam said. 'The sand must have covered it over the years.'

'You were out together?' Barbara asked casually.

'No, I was down on the beach,' Catriona said in a rush, 'and Adam was up on the cliff path and he . . . came down. Sort of tumbled.'

'Ah, he *fell* for you?' Barbara had a smile on her lips. 'There's nothing *wrong* with being out together, you know.'

'Do you mind if I ring Hamish Leckie to report it?' Adam asked. It wasn't the questions that were tricky. It was the answers; convincing liars they were not.

He telephoned the number only to hear Hamish Leckie's answering machine tell him the curator was in Melbourne attending a regional museums conference and would be back on Saturday. Since that was still two days away, Adam left a message to say they'd found Jamie Ramsay's cave and he had an artefact to show him.

Hamish Leckie was a relative newcomer in the community. When he arrived in town, the *Dunarling News* ran a feature story, describing him as a 'hero of the Falklands war', which didn't please Hamish at the time. As a sergeant in the Royal Engineers and an explosives and demolition expert, he had been one of the first ashore and later, sickened by the carnage of that brief war, he had quit the British army and come to take up a post in this quiet little backwater museum. A complete change of scene, the newspaper said.

'I'd keep quiet about finding the cave till Hamish gets back,' Barbara Chisholm advised. 'The last thing we want is clumsy amateurs messing around with whatever's in there. You never know what damage they could do or what they might take.'

Catriona and Adam kept their eyes on the doll and said nothing.

☆   ☆   ☆

Adam paused at the dining room door. His parents hadn't waited for him and were well on with dinner. When his mother looked up and saw him she pretended to recoil at his wild, dishevelled state.

'Adam, dear,' she said. 'I'd prescribe a shower before you eat.'

'And before you clean up,' his father put down his knife and fork and turned to regard Adam, 'perhaps, just the smallest word of explanation would be in order.' Nothing ever seemed to ruffle his parents. They were the calmest people he had ever met. Adam had a theory it was because they were medically trained they didn't get into a flap about things the way other people did. His mother was in general practice in Dunarling and his father was surgeon at the hospital.

'Sorry, Mum, sorry Dad,' he said and explained what had happened, once again, carefully omitting the part Richard and Mike had played. It was an accident, he claimed. He'd slipped and fallen down the bank and that's what disturbed the sand that revealed the cave entrance. Then they'd gone inside and found the coffin and one or two other things. He showed them the small coffin he had brought home.

'Who was with you?' his father said.

'Catriona Chisholm.'

'Ah,' said his father and resumed eating.

'Then have your shower, Adam dear,' his mother intervened, 'and come down for dinner. I've kept it hot.'

He was amazed at the amount of sand that washed off his body and how it persisted in sticking to him, making his skin itch. But at last, he felt clean enough to put on some fresh clothes and go downstairs.

Outside the door of the dining room he paused to read a post card which had come for him in that morning's mail. It was from Charlie Rexford, one of his friends from school who was on a Rotary Exchange Scholarship in Kansas. Inside the dining-room, his parents were lingering over their coffee and Adam heard them mention Catriona's name.

'Barbara Chisholm never married, you know,' his mother said. 'Just took herself off to Melbourne, quite deliberately I believe, and came back pregnant. She never named the father and I don't think she ever told him she was expecting his baby. She brought Catriona up on her own.'

'And how do you know all this gossip?' her husband enquired.

'Well, I delivered the baby of course,' Adam's mother went on. 'The year after Adam was born. Barbara shared a few confidences with me, both before and after she had her baby. But Catriona was lovely and she's grown up dark and beautiful, just like her mother was in those days. Maybe a bit wild too. You know, independent.'

'An unwed mother and now our boy's mixed up with the daughter,' his father said.

'Well, he has to get interested in girls at some time, Gordon,' his mother replied. 'Besides, he could do a lot worse than Catriona Chisholm. She's extremely intelligent and very pretty in case you hadn't noticed.'

'And a bit too free and easy,' his father rumbled. 'A wild one, so I've heard, with a bit of a reputation already. I suppose that comes from not having a father's influence.'

'Gordon, you're a sexist pig!' his mother said mildly and poured herself more coffee.

'And Jean, you're matchmaking with my son!'

'Our son,' Adam's mother corrected him.

Adam made a noise outside then walked into the dining-room and took his place at the table.

'Feeling better, Adam dear?' his mother was calm as she put a heated plate in front of him. There was a casserole on the electric warmer so he lifted the lid and helped himself.

'Now, Adam, time for a little talk,' his father began while his wife raised her eyebrows and shook her head slowly as if to steer her husband off the topic. 'What were you doing on the beach with the Chisholm girl?' his father said.

'Catriona, Dad. Her name's Catriona.'

'Yes, Catriona. Well?'

Adam felt he should come out and say he'd gone there knowing he'd find her alone. It would be one way of saying:

'I like Catriona and I think she's nice and I want to be with her and share things with her and find out if she feels the same about me.' Instead he kept his eyes on the plate in front of him.

'I only met her by accident, Dad,' he murmured.

☆   ☆   ☆

The doll lay in its coffin on Adam's bedside table. He took the lid off and looked at the face. It had quite a nice expression; the mouth was painted slightly off to one side, as if whoever made it wanted to give it a wry, cheerful look. The eyes seemed to hold a smile and Adam smiled back at it. It wasn't at all like the one Richard had held up in the candlelit cave; there was a brightness about this one. Perhaps it had been the dull light of the cave that added to his impression of Richard's doll but at the memory of that face Adam still felt ill at ease and shivered suddenly.

The body of this doll was carved from a single piece of dark wood, a root of some sort, which branched to form the legs. The doll had no feet so it could only stand by leaning against something. It's sweater was knitted from rough grey wool and the trousers were made of stiff canvas. The arms were fashioned out of a twig which had been bent so they crossed in front of its body.

Adam took the doll out of its coffin and propped it against the bedside lamp and looked into it's cheerful face.

'I wonder what Scottish kid on that ship played with you?' he said aloud. 'And come to that, why were you buried in a grave with the other four?' Well, Hamish Leckie would probably know the answers so he would have to be patient.

Adam lay back on the bed with his hands behind his head and stared up at the circle of light thrown on the ceiling by the bedside lamp.

'What'll I call you?' he said, glancing sideways at the

doll. 'What's a good Scottish name for a wee lad like you?' As he stared at the small figure under the bright light, it seemed its expression had changed. There was a keenness about the eyes, almost as if the doll was anticipating something.

'I think I'll call you . . . Tam Dubh,' he said and instantly, there seemed to come a flash from the eyes as if the doll approved of the name. Adam smiled and lay back and looked at the ceiling again. Tam Dubh; he laughed aloud. Where had *that* name sprung from?

He felt comfortably drowsy and his thoughts drifted to Catriona. At least he had moved closer to her and yes, she'd certainly responded but it hadn't been in the way he'd expected. But still, they had broken the ice and it would be easier to talk with her at school, especially now they had something to share. He began to feel heavy and lethargic and he knew sleep was not far off. His eyelids started to droop and at one point he dozed then suddenly opened his eyes and on the ceiling, in the circle of overhead light, he saw Catriona's head and shoulders, hazily outlined as if she were a cameo brooch. Then it seemed everything else in the room was slowly fading until there was only the circle with Catriona in the centre.

She looked down at him and her face was troubled and full of concern, just the way she'd been that afternoon when she dug him out of the sand bank. He smiled slowly up at her, then noticed how strangely she was dressed.

It was an old fashioned, dark red gown of a velvet material, cut to a V at the neck. Catriona's hair was done in a different style, with two dark ringlets falling forward over her shoulders. He'd never seen her like this and he wanted to ask her about it, although he knew by now he was held fast in a dream.

'Catriona,' he said, and she made no response but kept looking steadily down at him as if something was troubling her. She shook her head slowly.

Suddenly, over her left shoulder, Richard Vernon loomed into view, his jaw working and his expression cold and hostile. As if to claim ownership of her, he put his right hand on Catriona's shoulder and she froze at his touch and seemed unable to pull away from him. Still looking at Adam, Richard casually slipped his fingers around Catriona's neck and Adam saw the fear grow in her eyes as the fingers moved caressingly upwards to her chin. Richard then turned her face slowly to left and right, as if showing her off to Adam as he would a prized possession. His expression changed to one of sneering triumph.

Concerned yet fascinated by these dark images, Adam let the dream roam on unchecked while he took in details of what he saw. Richard wore a dark, rough woollen sweater and somewhere, vaguely in the background there lurked a second figure, like a sailor dressed in blue, with wide trousers. Behind that one and even further back, there was another figure and beyond that only a shadow, but it had movement in it.

This can't be right, Adam thought. On the cliff path, Richard had been wearing jeans. He wondered why he was dressed in that fashion and why Catriona should wear such a gown. He continued to watch as Richard stroked Catriona's neck briefly then slowly his hand dropped to the V of her dress and he let his forefinger rest there lightly, all the while looking at Adam as if testing how far he could go. Catriona froze as Richard fished up a golden chain that encircled her neck. A locket came up from between her breasts; it was a golden heart which Richard began to finger.

'*Stay your hand, Swith,*' Adam said and was briefly surprised at the words he used and how deep his own voice had become. '*Awa', Swith!*' He reached out and took the golden heart locket from Richard's hand and gently let it settle around Catriona's neck once more. He was surprised at how close he was to her. He grasped Richard's fingers and pulled his hand away from her neck. '*Thou hast neither business nor fight wi' this lady. Tak yersel' awa'!*'

'*Tam Dubh*,' Richard said in a voice as deep as Adam's, '*dae ye no ken thy man is curset? He is curset wi' fire, he is curset wi' mischance and he is curset wi' foulness. He canst loup and jink but thou canst dae naught for thy man. He cannot escape the curses laid upon him. Tak ye heed, Tam Dubh!*'

Richard backed away and with the other figures, shrank into the dark haze of the background. Catriona stayed looking down at Adam, with the marks of Richard's fingers still red on her neck. Her eyes looked into his and he knew her distress. He gazed at her face but she only shook her head sadly then slowly faded from his sight and Adam lay for a long time gazing at the empty circle of light until he became conscious that the things in the room were all around him once more. He was fully awake.

He reached up and snapped out the light then at the window he saw a red glow in the sky and realised it was morning so he rolled over and pulled the counterpane about him and closed his eyes to snatch a few extra minutes sleep.

Some time later he woke to find it was still pitch dark outside and he was cold because he hadn't slept under the blankets. He clicked on the bedside light again and noticed that Tam Dubh had fallen on his side on the table so Adam placed him in his coffin and put the lid on. He looked at the time on his alarm clock; half past two. He was chilled and stiff so he dived under the sheets and was soon fast asleep.

☆　☆　☆

In the morning, the alarm clock woke Adam from a deep sleep and he staggered out of bed as if he'd been drugged. Both of his parents had already left the house so he showered, dressed and ate breakfast in a mechanical fashion. All the while he thought of Catriona, not as she'd been on the beach but as he'd seen her in his dream.

It *had* to be a dream. What else could it have been? Yet as it unfolded, he remembered experiencing a sense of wakefulness. With a dream, you're in it and part of it but with this thing last night, he'd been more of a spectator, almost as if it had been put on for his benefit. He could still recall every detail of what he'd seen, which he never could do with a real dream, no matter how vivid it was.

'Tak ye heed, Tam Dubh! Dae ye no ken thy man is curset? He is curset wi' fire.'

Was it a message or a vision or some kind of hallucination? Then came a more ominous thought—was there something about the doll that had affected his mind? Did it carry a disease? Was *that* why it had been buried?

Adam slammed the front door, got his bicycle from the garden shed and started out for school. He got as far as the main street of Dunarling before remembering that he'd cycled past two sets of traffic lights without stopping. Had they been green or red, he wondered.

'Take a grip on yourself, Hardy,' he said and cycled on, trying to pay more attention to what he was doing.

On the road ahead, there was some sort of hold-up. Firemen clumped around in their heavy gear, rolling up their hoses and stowing them in their fire engine while a policeman kept the early morning traffic moving past a roped-off area. Adam slowed when he came to the spot and saw the burnt-out shell of the Dunarling Hardware Store. Just then Catriona came along on her bike and stopped beside him to look at the blackened ruin.

'It was quite a blaze,' she said.

'I saw a glow from my window,' he commented.

'Down here it was like a fireworks display,' she said. 'The store was full of paint, turpentine and thinners, not to mention gas bottles and it was exploding everywhere. It's a good thing the place stands by itself or the whole street could have gone up then it would have been farewell to lovely historical Dunarling.'

'I missed it all,' he said. 'Living up where we do, we're a bit out of things.'

Adam saw the owner of the store reach down and pull up a charred ruin of a sign on which were still visible the words: *A. Calhoun, Proprietor*. There were tears in the man's eyes.

'Catriona, are you feeling all right?' Adam asked suddenly.

'You mean after what happened yesterday?'

'Yeah.'

'Well, I'm fine, but you're the one who got all the shock and the bruises.'

'How's your mother? I mean, is *she* okay?'

'Barbara's fine.' Catriona looked at him keenly. 'But I think she suspects there's more than one coffin.'

'Oh, well, I just hope she doesn't make anything of it.'

'She might. Come on, we don't want to be late, Adam.' They cycled past Dunarling Railway Station and the town museum where Hamish Leckie lived and worked.

'Catriona,' Adam said suddenly. 'Do you own a gold chain and a heart shaped locket?'

'No,' she said. 'Are you going to give me one?' Adam swerved to avoid Mrs McKinley's terrier as it dashed out to snap at his heels.

They reached the school gates and waited for a gap in the oncoming traffic then turned in off the main road and cycled past the throng of kids from the junior school. Mairi and Megan raised their eyebrows when they saw Adam and Catriona arrive together then put their bikes side by side in the rack. It would be all over Dunarling High School by lunch time.

Richard Vernon was standing on the verandah of the computer room with Mike Carter a pace or two behind.

Mike whispered something to him and they saw Richard's lip curl in a sneer. He nodded slowly.

'They seem to have recovered from yesterday,' Catriona observed.

'Yeah,' Adam agreed and privately wondered what kind of night Richard had spent. Had he been affected by his doll?

☆ ☆ ☆

In the afternoon Adam sat in the computer room gazing at the glowing screen in front of him. Beside the disc drive there lay a pile of stained and mildewed sheets of paper. This is what comes of getting involved, he thought.

A few other students were in the room, hunched over their screens working quietly on assignments. On the booking sheet he was only down for half an hour on the computer, then someone else would come fidgeting around, looking pointedly at their watch to remind him his time was up. He tapped at the keyboard and called up a new document then typed the title on the top centre of the screen:

> *The Diary of Ewart MacColl, Esq. Farmer,*
> *lately of Maybole, Ayrshire.*
> *On board the barque* Dunarling, *Saturday*
> *6th March, 1886.*

It was going to be a massive job transcribing the diary of Ewart MacColl, Esq. and Farmer; many of the pages were damaged and torn and some were badly water stained making the words faded and almost unreadable. As for the handwriting, it was old fashioned but neat in its own way, with little curly decorations on the capital letters. He began to copy the first paragraph into the computer.

In the normal course of events, I am not one to keep a diary however the circumstances in which I find myself are sufficiently unusual for me to set down my thoughts and experiences in these pages. I am aboard ship direct for South Australia.

Briefly, Adam wondered about the man who'd written these words so long ago. He imagined him writing with a scratchy steel nib and every two words or so, dipping it in ink from an open bottle—and all that on a sailing ship rolling on the ocean. He pressed return and typed the next paragraph.

. . . The vessel upon which I am sailing is the Dunarling *of Glasgow which her owners advertise as a stout, seaworthy ship promising a safe and swift passage. All my worldly goods are in my baggage, together with some tools and implements specially purchased, for I am advised that such necessities are in short supply in Australia. Upon arrival in that far colony, I am promised to receive a grant of land to the value of £20 and informed there is plenty of willing labour to be had.*

The whole town revolved around that sad broken ship, the *Dunarling*. There had been a small settlement a few kilometres down the coast from the submerged rocks where the ship had foundered in the night. Because of the storm few local people had ventured out so they had no idea of the tragedy so near at hand until fully three days later, James Ramsay and Margaret Colquhoun knocked on the door of the first house they came to.

In the aftermath of the wreck of the *Dunarling*, people came from Melbourne and beyond, eager to get their hands on whatever the sea gave up. Some did so well out of it, they stayed and formed a bigger settlement which grew and prospered. Residents, looking for a name for their growing town, chose *Dunarling* in memory of the ship that lost its way.

For Adam it was an eerie feeling to read the hopeful

words in the diary; everyone who'd gone to school in Dunarling knew the story off by heart and thanks to various salvage operations over the years there were reminders of the ship throughout the town. One of her anchors formed part of the memorial in the cemetery overlooking the sea and the museum held various personal items, with neat cards to say what they were and how they had been used by their original owners. The ship's starboard navigation light glowed nightly behind the bar in the Dunarling Tavern flanked by a couple of brass lanterns; the polished hub of the steering wheel was on the wall of the dining-room.

The Diary of Ewart MacColl was another example of an artefact that had been in private hands since the days of the wreck. Mrs Chisholm, at seventy-eight, Dunarling's oldest resident and Catriona's grandmother, had died the year before, bequeathing to the museum a steamer trunk containing the old diary, a sheaf of papers and documents and a family Bible, all recovered from the wreck after the tragedy. When Hamish Leckie saw the state of the trunk's contents, instead of greeting them with joy, he showed his disgust.

'Och, people who treat things like this should be put in jail or severely punished, so they should,' he fumed.

'Hamish, I had no idea my mother had these things,' Barbara Chisholm said. 'If I'd known she'd have passed them on sooner.'

'That doesn't make me feel any better,' Hamish said and stamped out of the museum.

'But Hamish,' Barbara called after him. 'Surely my mother's beyond reproach—after all, she'd dead.'

'Aye, well that's no excuse. What good are these to us now?' Hamish shouted back to her from the footpath. 'That so-called diary is unreadable, the Bible's green with mildew and rot, and a wee moose has been making a nest in the papers. Some bequest!' He stormed into David Riccio's coffee shop and found a table in a corner so he could brood in private.

From this incident was born the Museum in the Community Project.

The idea was simple. Dunarling Museum didn't have the time, the money or the staff to study and preserve all the documents in the Chisholm Bequest, let alone catalogue them, so he asked various community groups to share the work. The senior students at the high school, scout and guide groups, members of the Dunarling Historical Society and interested citizens received parcels of letters and papers and careful instructions on what they were to do.

Three university students from Melbourne came to spend their summer vacation, preserving and repairing what they could of the bequest, and incidentally providing Catriona with that reputation for some sort of naughtiness which bothered Adam more than a little. Meanwhile, the main task was to transcribe all the documents in the bequest so they could be studied at a later date. Adam delicately turned a fragile page of the diary which was his project and began copying more of the words of Ewart MacColl.

This morning, we sailed down the River Clyde from the Broomielaw on the steam tender Hero *to meet up with the* Dunarling *at the Tail o' the Bank. I stood upon deck, observing the bustle of our departure and casting an eye over my fellow emigrants. Oh what a sight greeted me! On the quay stood a group of people, come to farewell their friends and relatives or just to witness our leaving. Mingled among them were dock workers who attended to gangplanks and ropes and baggage while in the background, a lone piper played a lament.*

Catriona came into the computer room, sat at a desk near Adam and placed a folder of dusty, yellowed papers beside her. She smiled at him and he nodded. What a difference a day makes, he thought. Catriona took up the first paper and studied it then recoiled.

'Yuk! Little cockroaches!' she said and dabbed at the desk top with a tissue.

'I've got mildew and water stains on mine,' Adam told her and turned to the diary again.

. . . *Many on the dockside called out to friends on the* Hero *and there was more than one eye with a tear blinding it. Some passengers cried out in Gaelic, for they were High-landers and spoke little English; most were honest, thrifty Scottish working folks, husband, wife and young ones, off to a new life in South Australia.*

For the husbands, the voyage seems to offer hope and a new life; for the bairns, judging by the way they ran about the deck, hiding among the baggage, it's an adventure.

Looking at the worried faces of the wives, I could see these next four months at sea will give them little to relish. At this moment, it pleases me I have remained a bachelor for I'd not like to put a wife to such travail. Still, many women are compelled to make this voyage and all credit to their fortitude.

'Catriona, what's a bairn?' Adam asked, eager to maintain contact with her.

'I think it's a child,' she answered, intent on her own papers.

How easy it was to talk with her now, Adam thought and turned again to the diary.

. . . *On the dockside, however, there was one woman who remained a little apart from the rest of the milling crowd. She stood looking at the* Hero *and its passengers; a thin figure, wearing on her head a dark shawl from which protruded strands of fiery red hair. It was not her bare feet nor the wild Gypsy look of her that caught my eye but the expression on her white face. It was a look of triumph yet tinged with such a mixture of hate and venom that for a full moment, I shivered.*

At that instant, some other activity took my attention and when I turned back to the Gypsy woman, she had gone from her spot on the dockside and I could no longer see her, but still she left me with a feeling of ill ease.

'What are you up to, creep?' said a voice in Adam's ear. It was Richard Vernon, with Mike a step or two behind.

'Working,' Adam said shortly, not turning around.

'I can see that, creep. What are you working on?'

'Transcribing this diary. Written by some passenger on the *Dunarling*.'

'Call that a diary?' Mike said. 'It's a heap of garbage.'

'You'd know about that,' Adam said without looking up.

'How'd you get that job, creep?' Richard said.

'Hamish Leckie asked me.'

'You didn't happen to say anything else to Leckie?'

'Such as?'

'Such as a whisper about one or two small items.'

'Dolls, you mean?' Adam raised his voice so that others in the room heard him and looked around.

'Yeah. You remember what I said?'

'I haven't said anything, if that's what's got you scared.' He turned to face Richard squarely. 'Now, I want to get this done, so rack off, Vernon.'

Richard looked at him and a flash of hate came into his eyes, but Adam held his gaze and it was Richard who had to look away.

'Yeah, just watch it, swot!' he contented himself with saying.

'And keep your nose clean,' Mike added as they

sauntered off and began badgering someone at another computer. Adam glanced across to see if Catriona had witnessed this exchange but she was absorbed in her own work. He tapped at the keyboard again.

. . . Then all was bustle; the Hero's *engines began to throb and we moved slowly away from the dockside as if the collected will of all her passengers was reluctant to start out on such a long voyage. We will be sailing at least a hundred days until we reach our destination. Already the word has gone out that the captain desires to make good speed to South Australia, which suits me fine for I am a fair weather sailor.*

Little by little, we pulled out of sight of the crowd of wellwishers and soon left the skirl of the pipes behind as our small steam vessel took us down the River Clyde to join our sailing ship. I must confess myself to a heaviness of heart at the notion of leaving Auld Scotia, perhaps forever, but directly turned my thoughts to more cheerful prospects of the life awaiting me in my new home.

Adam sat back and read over the diary again. There was more of it to do—a lot more, but it had waited over a hundred years to be read so it could wait a few extra days. He ejected his disc, packed up the diary into its folder and looked across at Catriona who was still working.

'Is your stuff interesting, Catriona?'

'Some of the writing's hard to read.' She frowned at the papers on her desk. 'Looks like nothing but newspaper reports and old letters and there's such a stack of it. It's going to be boring.'

'My job's interesting,' he said.

'Lucky you.'

'I'll share it with you if you like,' he said. 'You know, let you read it as I do it.'

'Yeah, okay, Adam.' She turned again to her keyboard. 'And you're welcome to any of this stuff.'

'If you're heading home soon, I'll ride with you.' He kept his voice casual.

'Okay.' She tapped at the keys without looking up. 'I'll get this page finished then I'll be with you.'

Adam walked over to her desk and drew up a chair and sat beside her, looking at the papers in front of her as she worked. From that angle, he could see her face reflected in the screen and it pleased him just to look at her. She turned briefly and smiled when she saw him there, then finally she packed the papers into her school bag and stood up.

'Let's hit the road,' she said and smiled again.

Just like that.

Chapter Three

On Saturday morning at half-past-nine, fresh from his visit to Melbourne, Hamish Leckie returned by the fast train to Dunarling Railway Station and went next door to the museum. He looked at his accumulated mail and then, as a matter of routine, checked to see if there were any messages on the answering machine. At a quarter to ten, he hurried up the three stone steps to Adam's front door where he rang the bell and almost at the same time, rapped impatiently at the heavy door knocker.

'Jamie Ramsay's cave,' Hamish said in a rush when Adam appeared. 'You left a message to say you found it.'

'Yes, Catriona Chisholm and I—' Adam started to say but Hamish cut him short.

'I always knew someone would discover it one day. Och, I knew it, I knew it. The story that pair told was too convincing to be made up.'

Adam's parents had gone their separate ways to work leaving him in peace to finish a late breakfast. He invited Hamish into the kitchen and to a place at the table where he helped himself to a cup of tea from the pot. The fact that the tea was barely warm didn't appear to bother Hamish.

'And you talked of finding some artefact, Adam.' He took a gulp of tea.

'It's a doll sort of thing,' Adam said and showed Hamish the small coffin with Tam Dubh nestled inside.

'Oh, look at this now.' Hamish handled the coffin almost with an air of reverence. 'I've not seen one of these wee fellas outside of Scotland.'

'But what is it?'

'It's a doll made out of a mandragora root. That's the mandrake to you and me; *Mandragora Juss*, poisonous actually.'

'Poison?' Adam said. 'Would it still affect people? I mean, even after all this time?'

'It could do but I don't know much about toxicology.' Hamish pulled a small magnifying glass from the top pocket of his coat and examined the figure as it lay in its coffin. 'I'd better not handle this wee lad too much. I believe it's a kind of good luck talisman that old sea captains used to carry with them on their voyages.'

'If it's from the *Dunarling* it didn't do a very good job, did it?' Adam said.

'Ay, that's true enough.' Hamish made a short bitter laugh. 'Now, how'd you find it and what else was in the cave?'

Adam began his carefully rehearsed and delicately edited account of finding the entrance to the cave and of how he and Catriona alone had explored the interior and discovered the small grave which they'd opened to find the doll in the coffin.

'Och, you really should have left everything undisturbed,' Hamish said. 'I mean, the pair of you attended the lectures on the care and preservation of artefacts. As soon as you knew the cave was of historical significance you should have left it to me.'

'Yes, sorry, Hamish,' Adam tried to explain. 'But we didn't want to leave anything in there in case other people found it.'

'Catriona Chisholm should have known better,' Hamish cut him off. 'I wonder what was she thinking of?'

'Sorry, Hamish,' was all Adam could say.

They left the house and drove to the museum in Hamish's old grey Holden utility. He collected a camera, a notebook, two powerful torches and a fluorescent lantern and headed off towards the cliff path.

'We'll pick up Catriona on the way,' Hamish said. 'If she was in on the discovery I'd like to hear her side of the story too.'

'What did you do with the doll, Hamish?'

'I locked him in the strong room out of harm's way.'

'I called him Tam Dubh,' Adam said.

'Did you now?' Hamish was thoughtful. 'And why that particular name?'

'On the night I found him it just sort of came to me. Why do you ask?'

'Oh, no reason. Tam is the Scottish way of saying Tom or Thomas, while Dubh is Gaelic for black. Tam Dubh— Black Tom, not bad at all. I just wondered where you got such a name.'

They drove the rest of the way in thoughtful silence. Adam knew the name hadn't just come to him. *Tam Dubh had introduced himself.*

Catriona was already dressed for cave exploring in old jeans and a faded windcheater. She carried her own torch and crowded into the utility and slammed the door. Adam was pleased to have her so close to him on the front seat. Her leg carelessly pressed against his and he felt the warmth of her and wished the journey to the cliff path could be a hundred times as long.

Under the strong mid-morning light from the entrance, the outer cave looked different. Hamish Leckie switched on his fluorescent lantern and carefully examined the wooden spars and declared them to be from the wreck of the *Dunarling*. The metal parts were in surprisingly good condition and Hamish said they'd make a worthwhile addition to the other bits and pieces of the ship already in the museum. He also spent some time examining the bottles, the packing case and the empty basket. However he tutted angrily over the discarded candle stumps when he found them lying on the sandy floor of the cave.

'These things stay here untouched for a hundred and ten years,' he said severely, 'then you two come along and just light them up as if it didn't matter.' He carefully dusted the sand off the candles and put them into a small case he carried with him.

'It was my idea to light them,' Adam said and saw Catriona raise her eyebrows at him and look away.

'Now, where did you find the mandrake doll?' Hamish asked abruptly.

The inner cave still held the same hushed air it had when they first entered it. Hamish inspected the place where the fire had been then went to the ruins of the grave and put the fluorescent lantern on the floor beside it. Adam and Catriona knelt opposite him.

'And how high was the mound and how was it shaped?' Hamish demanded.

'Sort of—like a pyramid.' Catriona demonstrated its height and general shape with her hands. The remains of the plundered base were still evident.

'And the coffin,' Hamish went on. 'Just where was it placed?'

'About here.' Adam pointed to the outline that had been left after he plucked the small coffin out of its grave.

'I wish you'd left the whole thing the way it was,' Hamish muttered and took the lantern and closely inspected the sandy devastation without speaking. They watched him work and Adam's apprehension began to rise when he saw him pause at another coffin shaped indentation in the sand.

Hamish took a small brush from his case and flicked gently at some loose grains of sand and grit. Adam caught his breath when Hamish exposed a clear impression of one of the other coffins.

Under cover of the semi darkness, Catriona pressed her knee against Adam's and he glanced at her briefly but her face was expressionless. She merely nodded downwards to indicate what the small brush had uncovered in the sand.

Then from different angles, Hamish began to take photographs of the remains of the pyramid, setting off flash after flash that lit the walls of the cave with eerie shadows. At last he was satisfied and packed up his gear.

'All right.' He stood up and dusted the sand from his knees. 'We've done all we can here so let's get back to the museum.' His attitude had changed and Adam knew he'd found out about the other coffins.

'What will happen to this place?' Catriona said.

'Oh, we'll clean it out, make sure it's safe then let the public loose on it,' Hamish answered. 'That's about all we can do. The Council doesn't have the money to protect the place from graffiti artists and vandals.' He moved towards the low entrance. 'Grave robbers too,' he added as a bitter afterthought. 'No protection against them either.'

Catriona followed Hamish along the tunnel then Adam crawled miserably after them.

☆　　☆　　☆

In Dunarling, news of the discovery of Jamie Ramsay's cave caused a great deal of comment. Over the weekend, Hamish Leckie removed the spars and other bits and pieces to the safety of the museum and made sure there was nothing left in the cave. Then on Monday he went on local radio to talk about the discovery and attributed it to a couple of local high school students.

A reporter from the radio station found out who the students were and on Tuesday after school he invited Adam and Catriona to the local studio to tell about their discovery. Catriona left most of the talking to Adam, who made such a mess of the interview the reporter could only use about fifteen seconds of the recording.

'I felt such a nong,' he fumed as they left the studio together. 'A complete ding-a-ling! Um, ar, ar, ar um, that was me. I thought I could speak.'

'You were only tongue tied because you had a lot of things on your mind,' Catriona said.

'Such as?'

'Such as being super careful not to dob in your mates,' she went on. 'You're protecting Vermin and Garbage.'

'They're not my mates,' he said. 'Anyway, you didn't help much, did you?'

'I didn't fancy varnishing the truth,' she said and turned towards the shopping mall. Adam almost had to run to catch up with her.

'But we agreed, didn't we?' he said.

'No, *you* agreed, Adam. And look where it's landed us. We're the ones copping the blame for taking the other four coffins.'

'Nobody knows about them.'

'You're unreal. Leckie's got the *evidence*. You saw what he found in the cave, Barbara *suspects* there's more than one coffin and I already *know*.'

'But you don't count,' Adam said and instantly regretted it.

Catriona regarded him for a few seconds before replying.

'Excuse me, I'm having coffee with someone.' She turned and walked into the shopping mall to David Riccio's coffee shop leaving Adam standing miserably on the pavement.

The rest of the week was like being on a slowly sinking ship. Catriona seemed to avoid him at school and it was almost as if they'd never shared the experience of the cave.

To make matters worse, two of Adam's mates, Trevor Ross and Phil Hunter, had heard the interview on the radio and made a joke of it. They declared Adam celebrity of the week and asked for his autograph. The fun lasted a long time.

At night, Adam started having dreams, real ones this time in which disturbing sounds and images came and went. Bells rang and there were cries and shouts in the darkness, and he saw flames and smoke and heard the roar of a fire over which the deep voice of Richard Vernon became clear: '*Tam Dubh, dae ye no ken thy man is curset wi' fire?*' A burning sensation touched his arms then he saw Mr Calhoun from the hardware store hold up his charred and blackened sign and shed tears over it and Adam woke up with his pyjama front sodden with perspiration and his heart pounding, convinced he was either deranged or infected with something, or maybe he was *possessed*.

He didn't sleep again that night.

☆   ☆   ☆

On Friday afternoon, Ailsa Robertson, the cadet reporter from the *Dunarling News*, rang him at home to say she'd like to do an article on the discovery of the cave and the things he had found in it. She called at the house next morning with a photographer, all ready to get a picture or two.

Adam wasn't in any particular awe of Ailsa; after all, only two years before she'd been a senior student herself at Dunarling High. With more warning this time, he worked out a carefully edited version of the discovery and was able to field Ailsa's questions and sound reasonably intelligent.

'That's fine.' Ailsa closed her notebook when she'd written all the answers she wanted. 'Now, what do you think about coming out to the cave so we can get a picture of you pointing out the entrance?'

Adam agreed.

'We can collect the girl on the way,' the photographer

said as he started the engine of the car.

'Her name's Catriona Chisholm,' Adam said.

'Fine.' Ailsa jotted it down in her notebook.

Ailsa sat in the front of the car beside the photographer and talked to Adam over her shoulder about ideas for the article. She planned to dress two store dummies as Margaret Colquhoun and Jamie Ramsay and photograph them in the inner cave sitting by a small, glowing fire.

'Pity we couldn't set it up like that all the time,' she said.

'The inner cave's a bit hard to get into,' Adam said. The car slowed and stopped at the souvenir shop and Ailsa went in to talk to Barbara.

Catriona came out of the shop and pointedly got into the front passenger seat with the photographer, leaving Ailsa to raise her eyebrows and smile as she took the vacant seat beside Adam. Catriona stared fixedly ahead as they drove in silence down the street to the start of the cliff path.

Carefully, the photographer posed Catriona on one side of the cave entrance and Adam on the other then prepared to take the picture.

'This time, try not to behave like a ding-a-ling,' Catriona whispered as she held her pose.

'There's a nice angle for this story,' Ailsa said as the photographer pressed the button. 'Romantic young lovers shelter in a cave. A hundred or so years later another young couple find it. You two aren't going steady or anything, are you?'

'There's no chance of that!' Catriona spoke with such an air of finality that Ailsa turned away with a smile and said, 'Oh dear.'

'She prefers university students,' Adam said and for the second time regretted his hasty words.

'You'll keep.' Catriona smiled sweetly as the button clicked. Adam looked into the camera lens as he waited for the photographer to focus for another shot.

'This'll be on the front page,' Ailsa remarked. 'Next Saturday's edition.'

But the following weekend their photo wasn't where they expected it; the article about the cave was relegated to page five while the entire front page of the *Dunarling News* was taken up with another story under large headlines, accompanied by a series of photographs.

Arson Attempt Fails

Late last night an attempt was made to set fire to Dunarling Museum. Mr John Morrison, a night shift baker on his way to work, discovered the fire in the alley between the railway station and the adjoining museum.

Mr Morrison raised the alarm and the fire brigade arrived soon after and managed to bring the blaze under control.

Mr Hamish Leckie, curator of the museum said that the damage was superficial and confined to a small area of the museum near the brick wall which formed the back of the strong room. 'Had the fire been lit against the wooden part of the wall, it might have been a different story,' Mr Leckie said.

Dunarling Station-master Mr Charles McKew said damage to the station was slight and would not affect preparations for the Railway Centenary Re-enactment which would go ahead next month as scheduled.

A police spokesperson stated that this is the fourth case of arson in Dunarling in the last two weeks. Forensic experts have been called in from Melbourne to assist with the investigation. [See Editorial page 4.]

☆ ☆ ☆

'Did you see our photo in the paper on Saturday?' Adam said.

'Yes, I saw it.' Catriona was making a great show of being absorbed in her computer.

'Well, what do you think?' Adam persisted. He had decided to set things right by tackling her head on.

'What was that?' Catriona looked up as if he'd interrupted her train of thought. 'Did you say something?'

'Forget it,' he said and turned back to his own computer and the Diary of Ewart McColl, Esq.

Friday 12th March, 1886
The weather has turned rough and the ship heels first one way and then the other, depending upon which tack we are on. It is difficult to sleep because of the changing angle of my berth and the constant shouting and clatter of the sailors as they tend to the sails above our heads. Being the month of March, I am thankful for my great coat which I pull about myself whenever I go on deck for it is very snell.

'Catriona, what does "snell" mean?' Adam said.

'How should I know?'

'Sorry, just asking. I think it means cold.'

'Whoopee for you!'

'As in frigid,' he added under his breath, turning a page of the diary.

Monday 15th March, 1886
Having a cabin to myself in the after part of the ship, I am luckier than most of my fellow passengers, of whom I have had little sight since our departure. I fear many are laid low with that cursed affliction, mal de mer or seasickness. Fortunately I am spared this, being able to take my place at mealtimes quite regularly.

There is but a bare handful of us travelling in saloon

*class and consequently, we take our meals with the captain
and some of his officers, which means we receive first hand
intelligence of the day to day running of the ship. Captain
Stewart is a man of little conversation so it helps him to
have ship matters to talk about.*

*The surgeon, Mr McWalter, is an affable man who keeps
the conversation at meal times lively for he has made many
voyages to Australia and provides us with numerous small
items of intelligence about Adelaide, of which he has a
great store of knowledge.*

*Of the other passengers, I fear there is little to report.
There are two maiden ladies, the Misses Cameron, going
out to join their brother in Sydney who is a major in the
militia. There is also a merchant and his wife, both of whom
have barely shown face in the saloon because of the seasickness. A servant takes to them a daily diet of cold boiled
potatoes, which is his own patent cure for that malady.*

The next few pages of the diary were gummed together with
mildew and grime. It would take a greater expert than Adam
to separate them. He found another page where the writing
was legible again.

Friday 2nd April, 1886
We have met fine weather at last!

*Oh what a joy it is! The sea is calm and blue yet there is a
good breeze which speeds the* Dunarling *along at a brisk
pace. Porpoises keep us company and provide excitement
for passengers one and all. I wonder that we are not taking
them out of their way for it seems the same porpoises have
been with us these several days past. Many are the cries and
exclamations that greet these frolicsome creatures as they,
for hours at a stretch, loup over our bow wave.*

Adam paused when he typed the word 'loup'. He had heard
it before and then he remembered it was in the dream or

vision he'd had when Catriona had been there: *Tam Dubh,
he canst loup and jink but thou canst dae naught for thy
man. He cannot escape the curses laid upon him.*

'Loup and jink?' he mused aloud. 'I'll need to ask
Hamish.' He tapped again at the keyboard:

Sunday 4th April, 1886
*It was a balmy night and I was fast asleep, dreaming a
dream of great pleasantness. In my dream, someone began
to ring a bell and I thought, no, these are not the bells of
our Parish Kirk back in Maybole, for I knew it not to be
the Sabbath.*

*Then I heard a call and that is what woke me up to the
realisation that someone was tolling the ship's bell with
great urgency and calling that dreaded word, "Fire!"*

*I hastily tumbled out of my berth and donned my breeks
and a shirt and rushed up on deck where I saw the ship hove
to in the moonlight. The sails hung slack and there was
thick smoke drifting about the deck.*

*Sailors began rushing hither and thither, carrying buck-
ets and axes while worried looking passengers began to
keek out of doorways and alleyways.*

*All was confusion on deck; sailors gathered around a
hatch and began removing the covers and as they did this,
more smoke billowed out, hiding the scene from view. Three
men began working a pump, and above the noise, I could
hear the regular "slush-bump, slush-bump" as they plied
the handle.*

*Then there was flame and more smoke and sailors poured
water on the spot and before long, the air began to clear but
the reek of burning hung about the ship and stayed in my
nostrils for many hours.*

*After the fire was dowsed, sailors remained on watch to
keep a lookout for any fresh outbreak while passengers
began to slip below to resume their night's rest.*

In the saloon, somebody made coffee and offered me a

mug of it, which I accepted gladly for the smell and taste of the smoke tarried in my throat. Still wearing his sea boots, Captain Stewart came clumping in and took a mug of coffee then sat frowning at nothing in particular.

"This time we were lucky, Mister McColl," he informed me after an interval. "Had that fire started in the for'ard hold, we might not have got off scot free."

"Why is that, Captain?" I ventured to enquire.

"Why? Because in that hold we carry naptha, turpentine and paraffin wax." He made a gesture of suddenly opening both hands outwards and said "poof", as if to signify an explosion.

He nursed his mug of coffee for a few minutes as he continued to frown, then stood up and left the saloon without another word.

After the fire the captain and his officers held an enquiry among the crew. How had the fire started? Had anyone been down in the hold? Had anyone seen anything to account for it? To all these questions, there was no clear answer. The fire had just started near some baggage.

Adam had been typing the entry at a furious pace but now he stopped and read it over then pushed his chair back from the computer terminal and looked around for someone to share it with.

'Catriona, they had a fire,' he said.

'That's old news,' she replied absently, still absorbed in what she was doing.

'No, I don't mean at the museum,' he said. 'I mean on the *Dunarling*. Bet you didn't know that.'

'I never bet.' She had a maddening answer for everything.

See if I care, Adam ground his teeth and stared at the screen for a full minute before turning to the next page of the diary.

Monday 5th April, 1886
One crewman, by name Buchanan, received severe burns
on his forearms so he was given light duties and an extra
rum ration. This morning, I saw him on deck bandaged to
the elbows, staring at the hold where the fire had been. He
had a strange, puzzled expression on his face as if he were
trying to make sense of what had happened in that place.

Adam remembered his dream—there was fire and smoke,
bells and noise and a burning sensation on his forearms. For
a moment, he felt it again and wiped his hands down his
arms as if to rid himself of it but then the sensation passed
and he realised he was running with perspiration.

☆   ☆   ☆

He found Hamish Leckie in his office in the museum,
talking on the telephone. Hamish held up one finger to
indicate he'd only be a minute and Adam backed out of the
office to wait.

'No, there was no real damage,' he heard Hamish say.
'Yes, it could have been serious but the fire brigade got
there in time. Mind you, just because all those members of
the Railway Hysterical Society have tarted up the station
with fresh paint and a lick of Brasso, they're getting all
the glory.'

At these words, Adam grinned to himself. His father was
a leading light in the Railway Historical Society and had a
lot to do with refurbishing the station and planning the
Railway Centenary Re-enactment.

'Yes, I'll send a full report,' Hamish concluded and
hung up and called out to Adam. 'Young Hardy, now it's
your turn.'

'Hello, Hamish,' Adam said. 'Just popped in to say I'm
getting on well with the diary.'

'Here, are you all right, Adam?' Hamish was all concern.

'Yes, fine.'

'You look a bit sort of—wabbed out. Are you sure you're all right? Not overdoing it?'

'I'm fine, Hamish,' Adam assured him. 'I've brought you a printout of the diary entries.' He pulled out a sheaf of papers. 'Did you know they had a fire on the *Dunarling*?'

'Did they now?' Hamish said. 'Any damage or loss of life?'

'No, they found it in time.'

'I'll read this, Adam.' Hamish took the papers and leafed through them. 'A timely discovery, right enough.'

'Like the fire outside the museum,' Adam observed.

'Aye, and talking of discoveries, young Adam Hardy, I've been meaning to have a serious word about that one you made.'

Hamish reached into a drawer and took out a bundle of colour photographs and set them out in an accusing line on the desk. They were of the ruined pyramid from the inner cave.

'See here.' He pointed to a small impression in the sand. 'That's where you say you found the coffin.' Adam nodded. He could sense what was coming.

'Now, over here,' Hamish indicated another part of the sand mound. 'I can clearly see the impression left by another coffin. And there, if I'm not mistaken is the outline of yet another one. So what I want to know is, just how many coffins did you find?'

Adam looked at the evidence in front of him.

'Five,' he said and hung his head.

'Where are the others then?' Hamish waited for a few seconds. 'Come on, Adam. I've already spoken to Catriona.'

'Oh,' Adam said and began to tell the whole story of his meeting with Richard Vernon and Mike Carter, of the way Catriona discovered the cave entrance and what happened once they went inside. 'That's the truth,' he ended.

'Ay, well, we'll see what a bit of Commonwealth legisla-

tion will do for Master Vernon and his solicitor father,'
Hamish said. '*The Historic Shipwrecks Act of 1976*. That
ought to do the trick.'

☆   ☆   ☆

Catriona was about a hundred metres ahead of him, pedalling along on her way to school. Adam increased his speed
to catch up with her.

'Hamish Leckie knows about the other coffins,' he began
and was breathless.

'It was bound to happen,' she said.

'But he says you dobbed me in.'

'Me? I haven't spoken to Hamish Leckie. Not since that
day we went to the cave together.'

'But he says . . .'

'Oldest trick in the book,' she laughed. 'Play one suspect
off against the other. Don't you watch television?'

'Anyway, he's going to see Vernon and Carter.'

'Good. It's about time too.' They cycled along together
for fifty metres or so.

'Do you mind if I ride with you?' he said.

'You can do what you like, Adam.' She tossed her head.
'The road's free.'

'Oh,' he said and taking this as a rebuff he touched the
brake and fell back. She went on ahead of him then looked
back and shook her head sadly and cycled on.

☆   ☆   ☆

Thursday 8th April, 1886
We have a mystery man aboard the Dunarling *who provides
a rich banquet of speculation for the Misses Cameron. He is
a steerage passenger who keeps very much to himself and
only rarely shows his face upon deck. The man is accompanied on this voyage by his son, a lad of about seventeen
years whom I have seen only twice.*

Passengers in steerage generally live in cramped accommodation below decks therefore it is a particular joy for them to meet fine weather so they can escape the confines of their berths and pass the time on the open deck. But not so our mystery man and his son. They spend their days hiding away from God's good sunlight and indeed, as Mr McWalter went round on his weekly inspection, he had to order them both up on deck for the good of their health.

On that occasion, the man and his son skulked away by themselves into a remote corner of the ship where they sat staring at the sea without speaking. I was sketching at the time and therefore able to observe them in reasonable detail. The father I would judge to be a respectable clerk of some description, perhaps lately employed in one of the mercantile houses of Glasgow.

Since they sat in the general subject area that I intended to sketch, I included them in the picture. I drew the father as a man with a tall, thin stooped frame. He wore glasses and a wide hat pulled well down over his eyes. He seemed a gentle enough soul and from time to time, murmured a word or two of conversation with his son.

I drew the son as a slender, fine featured youth, with small delicate hands. He too wore a hat, well pulled down over his face, but despite it, I was able to observe a stray lock of long dark hair. Young man, I thought at the time, what are you going to make of Australia?

'Hey, creep!' It was Richard Vernon with Mike Carter not far behind him. 'Why'd you go blabbing your face off to Leckie?'

'He found out for himself,' Adam said without looking up from the computer.

'I thought I told you to shut up about what we found,' Richard went on. 'Now along comes Leckie and makes a big deal of it.'

'Yeah, he fronts up to me as well,' Mike added. 'Where's the coffin, he says.'

'So come on, creep.' Richard tapped Adam's shoulder. 'I don't like people running to my father saying they're going to do this or do that. It's time you and me got things sorted out, eh?'

Staring at the computer screen, Adam's face burned. This was the confrontation he had dreaded. He knew Catriona was over in the far corner of the room and she had stopped tapping at her keyboard so she was probably taking everything in.

He took his time pressing the keys to save the last entry then pushed the chair back from the workstation and swivelled around in Richard's direction. Slowly, he stood up and looked him in the eye.

The effect was almost electric. Richard backed away as if he'd received a sudden shock and Mike quickly averted his eyes. In the corner of his eye, Adam saw Catriona watching.

'So, let's settle things then,' he said.

'Yeah, so just watch it, creep.' Richard turned away and made for the door of the computer room. 'We'll sort it out, soon enough.'

'Yeah, real soon,' Mike added and spat on the floor.

Adam stood and watched them leave. He turned to look at Catriona but she had her head down and was busy with her work. He sat down again and turned a page of the diary and with hands that still shook, began to gather up his things to go home.

☆   ☆   ☆

'What do you think of that?' Hamish Leckie spoke in triumph and held up another doll. It was the one Adam had seen Richard with in the cave and he shivered slightly at the memory. There, it had been evil looking with a triumphant expression on its painted face. In the brightly lit museum it looked almost pallid and emaciated as if somehow it's inner spirit had been burned out.

Tam Dubh on the other hand seemed to glow from his coffin with dark good health and cheerfulness.

'There's quite a difference between them,' Adam said.

'That sad wee fella's probably much older,' Hamish said. 'Mind you, it's a pity about the others.'

'Why, didn't you get all of them?'

'No, Masters Vernon and Carter said they pelted the others into the sea,' Hamish said. 'Can you believe the wantonness of that pair?'

'I can believe it.'

'I've a good mind to report it to the police,' Hamish went on. 'Let them prosecute.'

'People have tried that before,' Adam observed. 'And they didn't get very far.'

'That's true. Still, we did manage to get two of the dolls out of five, so that's not bad.'

'What are these dolls?' Adam leaned over and examined Tam Dubh closely.

'That's a big mystery,' Hamish said. 'Some of them were supposedly made for good purposes—they were a sort of ship's spirit, carried by the captain and looked after, you know, bedded down in the captain's cabin and given a box to live in, even food to eat and the captain would talk to it and consult it on ship matters. In return, the wee mandrake would protect the ship against dangers.'

'Worked their passage,' Adam said.

'That was the belief,' Hamish went on. 'Then there's another theory that says these little figures were revenge dolls. Bought and sold to people who believed in such things and set to work in retaliation for real or imagined grievances.'

'And there were five of them on the *Dunarling*,' Adam said.

'Yes, so it seems. Still, I'll try to find out more about

them and we'll put these two on display in the museum soon. Oh, and you'll have to think of a name for the newcomer, Adam.'

'What about "Swith"?'

'Well, Swith will do nicely.' Hamish Leckie looked at Adam keenly. 'Where are you getting these names? Tam Dubh, now Swith.'

'Don't know,' Adam said.

'It's the old Scots word for "swift".'

'Maybe I got it from the diary of Ewart McColl,' Adam suggested. 'There's a lot of Scots words there. Bairn, snell, loup and jink. I know what bairn and snell mean—but what about loup and jink?'

'Loup is to jump or leap,' Hamish said. 'And jink is to dodge, so I suppose it means to duck and weave, to jump about and dodge.'

'To avoid what's coming to you?' Adam said.

'Yes, something like that.'

'*Stay your hand, Swith.*' Adam heard again his own words from the vision. '*Thou hast neither business nor fight wi' this lady. Tak yersel' awa'!*'

Then the other voice came back to him, the one that came from Richard Vernon but didn't really belong:

'*Dae ye no ken thy man is curset? He is curset wi' fire, he is curset wi' mischance and he is curset wi' foulness. He canst loup and jink but thou canst dae naught for thy man. He can not escape the curses laid upon him. Tak ye heed, Tam Dubh!*'

Adam shivered.

☆   ☆   ☆

The page of the diary was watermarked and difficult to read so he had to trace over some of the words with a pencil. As soon as he began to make sense of the entry, he typed it into the computer.

Tuesday 13th April, 1886
The father and son have obviously had a great falling out
with each other. The son sits off by himself and refuses to
talk with his father although the latter tries many times
to coax the boy into conversation.

All this I observed as I sat sketching some sailors who
were busily intent upon making dollies out of stray ends of
rope for the amusement of some children.

It amazes my how dextrous the sailors are and with what
little material they can fashion these dolls. The children are
wide eyed with wonder at their new treasures and spend
many an hour, as if they were little mothers themselves with
bairns of their own, nursing the dolls, braiding their hair
and generally cosseting them.

The boy appears to be interested in the sailors and their
doll making activities on behalf of the children; yet towards
his father he maintains a stiff and sullen silence.

Catriona gathered up her things and left the computer room
without as much as a glance in Adam's direction.

Stiff and sullen silence, Adam thought. *That'd* be right.
But he had an uneasy suspicion that any move to put matters
right between them would have to be his.

He ejected the disc and packed up his things to go home.

Chapter Four

Wednesday 14th April, 1886
After the excitement of the fire on the Dunarling, *conversation in the saloon turned to more regular subjects and it was not long ere the Misses Cameron turned their curiosity full bore upon our man of mystery.*

"All I am willing to tell you of the fellow is his name and previous occupation," said the captain.

"Well, what are they?" the older Miss Cameron demanded.

"Name, Mr A. Colquhoun, Christian name, Adam," said the captain. "Shipping clerk of Glasgow, emigrant to South Australia."

"And the son?" Enquired the younger Miss Cameron. "What of him?"

"A lad of seventeen years, Ma'am," the captain informed us. He was not a great fount of knowledge, except about the ship. Ask him to talk about staysails, spankers and topgallants and he would hold forth all through one meal and half way through the next; about passengers he was less than voluble.

"The other morning, I ventured to speak with the boy," the older Miss Cameron persisted. "But the lad only smiled at me and moved away. Such a sweet smile though."

"Perhaps he is mute," the other Miss Cameron suggested, but I was able to discount that theory for I had often seen the boy engage in conversation with his father. I had not heard clearly what he said, but at least the boy had spoken some words, that is until they had their falling out, which is strange for a son to be so at odds with his father.

I wonder what could have driven them apart?

Adam sighed deeply as he read over those last words he had typed. Driven apart summed up his own situation very neatly. As the days passed he worried more and more about the state of his mind, not that there had been any more dreams, at least none of the vivid, disturbing ones but at odd times during his waking hours he gained the eerie impression that someone was watching him.

As he moved around the school or as he did things at home, he'd sometimes catch a tantalising glimpse of a tiny furtive movement but the moment he turned to look at the spot, the thing had gone leaving him with an empty feeling. Rolled into one it was *deja vu* and that uncanny 'just there' sensation of having a word on the tip of his tongue. It was almost there—and yet it wasn't.

The experience made him jumpy and irritable and on one occasion, it nearly came to a fist fight with Trevor Ross which took a week to get over. Another time he snapped at Phil Hunter and caused a sullen exchange of insults. Driven apart, that was it.

At the breakfast table at home, he brought up the general subject with his mother but his father came into the room, demanding immediate attention and made some throwaway diagnosis that Adam needed to get out and play more sport.

'Yes, Dad,' Adam said and left the table.

'Adam, hang on a minute,' his mother called. 'Just let me sort your father out first.' But Adam was already on his way to school.

It would have helped if he'd been able to share his concerns with Catriona. After all she had been in the cave discovery from the beginning and the weirdness had all started with that. But she went out of her way to avoid him and in class barely glanced in his direction and pointedly confined her sessions in the computer room to the times Adam wasn't booked in. In the mornings she started out for school earlier than usual and when Adam decided he'd also leave home before his regular time, Catriona suddenly changed tack again and began arriving much later, sometimes cutting things so fine she risked being reported for it.

The two girls, Mairi and Megan, who'd noticed Adam and Catriona's friendship develop, also observed the obvious coolness between them. At general assembly on a warm Monday morning, they passed remarks loud enough for Adam to overhear.

'They tell me they're getting a divorce,' Mairi said in a mock serious manner. 'Such a shame. Lovely couple.'

'Was it irreconcilable differences?' Megan asked.

'Yes, tragic,' said Mairi and they heaved deep sighs and shook their heads sadly. Catriona was nowhere in sight so Adam pretended he hadn't witnessed this little by-play; still, it was hard.

He began to find solace in the stained and frayed pages of Ewart McColl's diary. At least it was one part of his life where he could make progress and knew where he stood.

Sunday 2nd May, 1886
The weather stays fine. The days are warm and the nights balmy. Many passengers sleep on deck for it is hot in the accommodation. Two nights ago it became very still and oppressive with clouds so heavy the stars could not be seen.

The captain sniffed the air and ordered the sailors aloft to shorten canvas for he feared a tropical squall. The men had hardly gone above when there came a sharp gust of wind and the ship heeled over and began to gain speed.

Passengers gathered their bedding and scurried below out of harm's way as the sailors aloft, stepped out on their slender foot-ropes and began to drag hand over hand at the buntlines as they reefed in the heavy sails.

Rain began to fall in torrents and the sea around us became turbulent. In the midst of this there came a sudden crack and a noise as of a great whip being wielded. A metal cable which secured the upper mizzen mast had parted! There came a further snap and a second cable on the same side parted and flew upwards.

Far aloft, two of the sailors attending to the mizzen royal fell from their perch. With a cry one of them dropped into the sea and was lost behind us in the foam and there was nothing to be done for him. The other sailor was more fortunate although he was caught by the leg in a clutter of rigging and dangled precariously in mid air as sails, spars and loose gear swung and tumbled about him.

From his position on the mizzen upper top'sl, a young sailor, Ramsay I think his name is, climbed further aloft. He made himself secure and managed to catch his shipmate as the roll of the vessel sent the man swinging in towards the mast. Ramsay held fast to him until two other sailors clambered up to complete the rescue.

The after deck was a tangle of ropes, loose sails and broken spars yet within a space of only twelve more minutes, the sea had abated and returned to its former serenity. The stars looked down upon us once again and a light breeze blew but in such a short space of time, we had been cruelly visited by destruction and sudden death.

In the morning, we counted the toll. One sailor lost overboard, McDermott by name and another with his leg so badly crushed he will never again be able to put weight upon it. The upper part of our mizzen mast has been carried away and the remaining sailors were even then aloft, intent

*upon securing a jury rig to see us through the Roaring
Forties which is yet to come in our voyage.*

Adam shared this latest information from the diary with
Hamish Leckie who read the computer printout through
without speaking.

'Y'see, Adam, no one ever knew there had been a fire on
the *Dunarling* or that there was gear failure like that,' he
said at last. 'That's why it's important to get these papers
into a form we can read.'

'It's hard work but I'm enjoying it,' Adam said.

'And what does Catriona say about it?'

'Well—we don't actually talk much.' Adam turned away
and pretended to be busy with some papers in his bag.
He really wanted to say they weren't saying *anything* to
each other but he let it go. After all, it wasn't Hamish
Leckie's problem.

'Oh, but you should talk,' Hamish said. 'Y'see, by
sharing things you encourage each other. I mean, you're
both looking at the same slice of history. Did she tell you
about the passenger's Bible she's working on?'

'No.'

'It's a family Bible,' Hamish went on. 'A real heirloom
with details of the births, marriages and deaths of the family
members written in the front. You should get her to show it
to you.'

'Yeah, sometime,' Adam said. 'But I've got my own
study to think about.'

'Well, it's a good idea. Get together with Catriona and
tell her what you're up to.'

'I'll try,' Adam said.

'Don't just try. Do it!'

☆　　☆　　☆

Monday 3rd May, 1886
This morning some sailors reported to the captain that the loss of the upper part of the mizzen mast was not a mischance nor had it directly resulted from the squall. To back up their assertion they had certain evidence.

It was the severed end of an iron cable which had been cut half way through. They showed a hacksaw which had been stolen from the carpenter two weeks ago and was found in McDermott's gear—the one who was lost overboard.

He had been acting strangely for some days before the event and spent a deal of his free moments on deck instead of asleep below. When he did sleep, which was rare, he was heard muttering as if in argument with someone. He seemed to be talking with a person named Agley, which we Scots know as a word which means "awry" or "disordered".

If the severed cable was McDermott's doing then he certainly did make things go agley and he paid the price for it so amen to that.

'Catriona,' Adam said and waited for her to look up from the keyboard. He had found out when she'd booked a session in the computer room and made a point of coming in at that time.

'Yes?' She kept her eyes on the screen.

'Look, Hamish Leckie thinks it would be a good idea for us to swap information.'

'Hamish Leckie thinks, does he?' she typed rapidly as she spoke. 'Don't you think for yourself?'

'I think he's right.'

'Do you?' she said and stopped typing.

'You've made a lot of mistakes.' Adam leaned closer to the screen then turned to look into her face and just caught the tail-end of a smile there. 'You were going too fast and not paying attention.'

'Was I?' She recovered her composure but it made him bolder.

'Hamish says you're working on a family Bible.'

'It was in with a lot of old papers and letters,' she began to sound more reasonable. 'You can have a look at it some time.'

'Yeah, I might do that.' He kept his voice casual. One step at a time, he reminded himself. 'Do you want to read this?' He put a printout beside her keyboard. 'It's what I have got from the diary so far.'

'Oh, thanks.' She ignored the printout and started typing again, frowning at the faint writing on the letter she was transcribing. 'Damn! Sometimes this is so hard to read.'

'Yeah, I get that too,' he said and lingered, hoping this shared problem would bring them closer.

'Look, the Bible's at home,' Catriona said. 'So pop round and have a look, that's if you really want to.'

'Yeah,' he said. 'Some time next week then.' He backed away but Catriona swivelled around in her chair and looked into his eyes without smiling.

'That'll be fine.' It was as far as she was willing to relent at this time, but Adam took it as a sign that things were improving between them. He went away with a smile on his lips, found a free computer and started work on the diary.

Thursday 6th May, 1886
There is such a clacking of tongues today. Such a twittering and clucking and cooing from the Misses Cameron for we have yet another mystery to fill the hours.

The Dunarling *has been constantly plagued with sickness of one kind or another—fevers and sundry disorders, frequent injuries, scaldings, burnings, bruises, broken limbs and the like, all of which keep the surgeon busy.*

Indeed, we have already had five deaths aboard our gallant barque with three burials at sea, sombre occasions which cast a great gloom over the entire ship. The sailor McDermott was apparently lost by his own hands. Another who died in this way was Buchanan, the hero of the fire.

One morning, he was not found to be in the hospital where he should have been, whereupon the ship was searched stem to stern, ending with the conclusion he had either fallen to his death in the night or had jumped; no one can be sure.

We have also had births—a boy born to one of the Highland women and a set of twin girls born into a Liverpool Irish family.

Added to all of these has been a certain "transformation" in our midst.

One of those afflicted with a fever was the son of the mysterious Mr Colquhoun. Apparently the father tried to nurse the boy himself without calling upon the services of Mr McWalter, but some other passengers got wind of the situation and, despite loud protestations from the father, fetched the surgeon to examine the youth.

When Mr McWalter cleared the cabin in order to inspect the boy, a certain conversion was revealed and he ordered the patient instantly transferred to hospital; not to the male section but to the women's!

The "son" has been revealed as a daughter! Master Colquhoun has become Miss!

The captain quizzed Mr Colquhoun about this deception, whereupon the latter staunchly refused to give reason for it although he declared he had one. It was a personal matter, the father insisted; he had broken no law and the reasons for his subterfuge were now left far behind in Scotland; beyond that, the man refused to comment.

"Just so," said the captain. "Indeed you have broken no law, Mr Colquhoun, sir, however, this is a God-fearing ship and whilst I am captain of it I declare it is not rightful that a father share accommodation with his daughter!"

"Then where is she to sleep?" enquired Mr Colquhoun.

"Arrangements will be made," the captain said.

True enough, when Miss Colquhoun came out of hospital, quite mended I am happy to report, she found herself sharing a berth with two single young women, who seemed happy to have a change from each other's company for the rest of the voyage.

So, the mystery remains—why the deception on Mr Colquhoun's part? Oh, on that little issue, the Cameron tongues were active indeed.

Miss Colquhoun began to spend more time on deck to enjoy the fine tropical weather. Since she had no clothing appropriate to her sex, some women passengers searched their baggage and soon had her attired in more suitable garb, to wit: a dress of deep russet colour, a shawl and bonnet.

The Cameron sisters have been active on another enterprise; they have found Miss Colquhoun's name. It is Margaret.

'Wow!' Adam said when he finished typing. He looked around to share this new information with Catriona but he'd been so absorbed in transcribing the entry, he'd failed to notice the others had gone. The rest of the computer screens were blank and the covers were on the keyboards.

He read the words over again as he waited for the dot matrix printer to churn the paper out in neat folds.

☆   ☆   ☆

That day after school, and quite by chance, he met Ailsa Robertson from the newspaper in the street.

'Hello, Adam,' she said. 'Did you like the article about Jamie Ramsay's cave?'

'Yes, pretty good.'

'Making any more significant discoveries?'

'No more caves,' he said. 'But I've been working on an old diary, you know, transcribing it, and there's all sorts of stuff we didn't know about the *Dunarling* and that last voyage.'

'I'm all ears and notebook,' she said. 'And since we're almost there, let me wheel you into David Riccio's and fill you up with coffee and cream cakes and you can tell me all about it.' Flattered and glad to share the information with someone, Adam let Ailsa take him in hand and before long he had disclosed to her all the details of the fire and the storm damage. Last of all, he revealed the information that was uppermost in his mind; the way Margaret Colquhoun had started out on that voyage pretending to be a boy.

For the price of a cup of David Riccio's coffee and a slice of cream cake, Ailsa Robertson received excellent value. She went away with a well filled notebook and a copy of the printout of the diary of Ewart McColl, promising to let Adam know when the next article would appear.

☆ ☆ ☆

'Adam, you've hit the big time again!' his mother called from the foot of the stairs in a newsboy voice. 'Read all about it!'

He was already dressed so he came downstairs to find his father reading the article on page three of the Saturday newspaper.

'You little publicity seeker,' his mother said. 'Here, Gordon, let the boy read what Ailsa Robertson's made of all his hard work.' She plucked pages of the newspaper from her husband's fingers and passed them to Adam.

'If you've got all that spare time,' Adam's father said, 'I'd like a hand with the Railway re-enactment. That's local history too. Painting to be done, varnishing, polishing, cleaning up. Willing hands needed.' He shook a piece of toast free from the rack and buttered it.

'Yeah, soon, Dad,' Adam said and found page three.

As soon as he saw the headline, he began to feel uneasy:

Lone Student Takes on a Mammoth Task

They had used a picture of Adam standing at the entrance to Jamie Ramsay's cave. Somehow Catriona had been excluded altogether and the article gave the impression that he was the only member of the Museum in the Community Project. It didn't mention Dunarling Museum or Hamish Leckie, who had started the idea. Worse than that, it said nothing about what Catriona and the other people were doing and as if to hammer a final nail into the coffin, it suggested that Adam was also working on a large family Bible.

There was a separate article which talked of the *Dunarling* being a ship of bad luck and mystery. Ailsa Robertson had used selected portions of the diary which described the fire and the loss of the upper part of the mizzen mast. When it came to the revelation of Margaret Colquhoun's sex, Adam's heart sank. Ailsa's style of journalism had cheapened it and made it sensational:

> . . . when the doctor ordered the patient to strip, startled passengers found the slightly built 'boy' was actually a beautiful young girl.

Mid-way down the text there was a small cartoon sketch showing a rear view of a voluptuous, semi-naked woman smiling over her shoulder as she revealed herself to a startled doctor. The doctor stood with stethoscope in hand while in the background, a couple of smirking male passengers looked on.

'It wasn't like that!' Adam said. 'She's got it all wrong! I mean, what doctor would behave like that?'

As he read the rest of the article, his mother had been watching the changing expression on his face. She patted his hand.

'Come on, Adam,' she said. 'You're not the first to be disappointed by the media way of doing things. The truth sometimes spoils a good story, it always did.'

Adam leaned forward on the table with his head in his hands.

'Oh no,' he said but he was thinking mainly of how Catriona would react to this new disaster.

☆ ☆ ☆

The following Monday morning, and for more than just that reason, things were not good. Adam arrived at school to a complete barrage of leering comments.

'Hey, Adam, let's have a squiz at the dirty bits, eh?' Trevor Ross said.

'Any pictures?' Phil Hunter asked. 'Come on, let's have a read of the sports page.' Some of the girls were just as bad with their comments and Mairi and Megan greeted Adam by striking seductive poses the way the cartoon figure had done. One of the teachers asked if he could have a transcript of the diary. The only good thing was that Catriona hadn't arrived at school to say what she thought of the article.

Before the assembly bell rang, there was yet another sensation that took the heat off Adam. Richard Vernon drove in through the gates in a small red sports car with Mike Carter in the passenger seat. Instead of parking, he drove around the school yard scattering those in his path. He did a circuit of the older stone buildings, reversed into the new area where the portable classrooms stood then shot across the playing field with a crowd of cheering kids in hot pursuit. He did a final three point turn then reversed into a shady part of the bicycle shed and got out and was instantly surrounded by a crowd of kids from the junior school.

'Some car,' Phil Hunter said.

'Pity about the nut that holds the wheel,' Trevor Ross commented.

The assembly bell cut short the excitement and there was a dash for the main hall with the smaller boys making 'vroom, vroom' noises and changing gear as they ran. If any teachers noticed Richard Vernon's spectacular entry into the school yard, none of them said anything.

Mr Grant, the deputy principal, advanced into the assembly hall with a visitor half a step behind him. It was the sergeant in charge of Dunarling Police Station.

'Sergeant Balfour has something important to say,' Mr Grant announced. 'So if you'd all please try to pay attention.' He yielded the floor.

'Thank you. Look here, boys and girls,' the sergeant began. 'You've probably read in the papers about a series of arson attempts in town over the last few weeks.'

'Lot of arson about,' Mike whispered to Richard and suppressed a snigger.

'I'm sure you've also seen the story about the break-in down at the railway works department,' Sergeant Balfour went on. 'The thing is, as part of that incident a quantity of explosives, detonators and other material was removed.'

'Boom!' said Richard loudly and Mr Grant took a full step forward and frowned in that direction. The platform creaked loudly under his foot. One or two people laughed.

'Not funny,' Mr Grant warned. 'Bereft of even a modicum of humour.' As he glared around, the back door of the assembly hall clicked open and Catriona slipped quietly inside, which was unfortunate timing on her part. Mr Grant slowly turned his attention full bore upon her.

'After assembly, the late Miss Chisholm will present herself in my room,' he said and a few people laughed again. Sergeant Balfour raised his eyebrows impatiently then looked pointedly at his watch.

'You should know,' he went on, 'that explosives and detonators are dangerous. We don't think they were taken by professional thieves which is why I've come here. So if you know anything about this business, or if you suspect one of your school mates, then come forward and tell us.'

'Dobbers!' Mike muttered.

'Dobbers, yes.' Sergeant Balfour nodded towards Mike as if to acknowledge a good suggestion. 'If some idiot shows you gelignite or detonators, then be a dobber and ring the emergency number.' He nodded briefly then spoke a quiet word to Mr Grant and was off.

Adam turned to see if he could catch Catriona's eye but she sat with her head down.

'All stand,' Mr Grant decreed, and the school week started.

☆   ☆   ☆

Catriona made her feelings very plain. She stopped beside Adam's desk during the morning science lesson.

'I don't mind you hogging all the glory,' she said quietly. 'If that's what you're like then it's your problem.'

'Catriona, I didn't want it to be like that—' he started to say but she cut him short.

'That business about Margaret Colquhoun starting out dressed as a boy—couldn't you have shared it with me before going to the newspapers? I mean—we *were* in it together.'

'I tried,' Adam began. 'But Ailsa—'

'Oh, Ailsa! What did she do? Bat her big brown eyes at you and turn you into play dough?' Before Adam could say a word, Ms Mullins, the science teacher, cut the conversation short.

'Look, if you two are having some sort of lovers' tiff,' she said reasonably, 'could you keep it for the boudoir?' Mairi and Megan heard the remark and tittered into their hands and Catriona shook her head and moved away with her face burning.

In the middle of the morning, an ancient bus from the Dunarling Bus Company rolled into the school yard and pulled up with a squeal of brakes and stood with its well-worn diesel engine ticking over noisily.

'Now, when you get on the bus,' Ms Mullins said to the class, 'I want you to act in a civilised manner. When we get up to the water pumping station, at least make an attempt to ask a few intelligent questions. Right?'

Laurie Sinclair, the elderly driver, opened the bus door to let the senior year students in and they came up the steps with their clipboards, information sheets and list of questions. Laurie had been on these science project trips before and preferred them to trundling around town taking money and punching tickets.

Adam saw Richard Vernon stop Catriona and nod in the direction of the bike shed where he'd parked the sports car. She shook her head and moved past him and got on the bus. Richard stood looking at her briefly then went away. When Adam caught up with Catriona, she'd already found a window seat and Mairi had taken the one next to her.

'At least give me a chance to explain,' Adam hissed before moving further down the bus.

'Ooooh!' Mairi rolled her eyes. 'Adam's got something to *explain!*'

'Move on!' Ms Mullins ordered.

From the bike shed, there came a sudden 'vroom' as Richard started the motor of the sports car.

'What's *he* up to?' Ms Mullins said, ducking her head and frowning through the bus window.

'Going up there in his car, Miss,' Megan said.

'Is he now?' Ms Mullins showed her annoyance but it was too late to do anything about it. The car backed out of the shed and roared past the bus with Richard and Mike laughing and gesturing as they went. The little red sports car went out of the main gate, turned right and accelerated away. With something like envy in his eyes, Laurie Sinclair watched it go then engaged first gear.

They made a slower, more lumbering journey up the long twisting road to the water pumping station where their science project was to examine the way the town handled water treatment and reticulation.

Adam sat alone and stared at the town spread out below with the blue of the sea in the background. The feeling of unease returned. Something was at the corner of his eye but when he turned, it was gone but you can take in a lot in a fiftieth of a second. After all, cameras do it all the time. This time he'd seen a face.

A gleeful face. *Ugly and gleeful.*

When they finally turned in at the pumping station, the red sports car was already there. Mike had his head down, fiddling with the stereo while Richard, wearing dark glasses, leaned back in his leather seat casually surveying the bus as it pulled up with a squeal of brakes and a death-like shudder as Laurie cut the diesel motor.

Ms Mullins was first down the steps and went over to Richard's side of the car.

'Okay, Vernon,' she said. 'Out! Confrontation time.'

Casually, Richard opened the door and got out and stood with his head to one side, waiting for her to speak.

'I don't recall giving you permission to drive up here,' she said. From behind their clipboards one or two people in the senior class raised a muffled cheer.

'You tell him miss!'

'As long as I'm in charge of this class,' Ms Mullins went on, 'you'll do things my way. Got that?'

'Yeah,' Richard said.

'So from now on, for you it's the bus like everyone else.'

'Okay, so what am I to do? Leave the car up here?'

'Obviously not. But next time leave it behind. And take off those ridiculous sun glasses when I speak to you.' She turned and walked back to the group. 'Right—everybody inside.'

There was nothing unusual about Dunarling's water supply. The lower part of town was fed from a water main which didn't have enough pressure to reach the upper town, so there was a pumping station and a concrete overhead supply tank. The pump room was small and the group from the school filled it to capacity. They gathered around, all ready to ask the intelligent questions they'd rehearsed. Even Laurie Sinclair came in with them, saying he was never too old to learn.

Andy Gibson from the council was on hand to show them around, not that there was much to see; a blue painted electric pump, some pipes leading in and out, polished pressure gauges and an electric switch board with a digital clock above it.

'The pump's automatic,' Andy Gibson explained. 'Turns itself on four times a day. Six am, noon, six pm and midnight.' He went to the switchboard and overrode the automatic switching gear and let them hear the sound the pump made as it ran then he switched it off and undid a couple of handscrews and swung a metal cover plate aside to show them the filters at the suction end.

'We could stick some laxative in there and give everyone the trots,' Mike said and giggled.

'Hey! We get our water from this pump,' a girl protested. So did Adam's household, but he let it go.

'Pretty mind numbing stuff,' Richard commented loudly and Ms Mullins shook her head in disbelief while Andy Gibson smiled.

Questions followed: How many megalitres a day does it pump? Is there any form of water treatment? What pH level do you maintain? Andy Gibson patiently replied and people dutifully wrote what he said. The session was interrupted when there came another burst of engine noise from the car park.

'Richard Vernon!' A boy called. Some people laughed while Ms Mullins only raised her eyes. The sports car took off with a blast of its horn.

They filtered out into the sunlight and climbed aboard the bus where Catriona still avoided Adam. When they were inside the pump room, he had tried to move closer to her but the crowd made it difficult, besides which he'd had enough of other people's jokes and remarks. As he passed to the back of the bus, Catriona had her head down, writing something in her clipboard. Ms Mullins took a seat beside one of the boys and Laurie counted heads then started the motor and engaged first gear. He turned left out of the car park and began to tackle the first downwards incline.

'*Adam*,' a voice said. '*Gae ye forward now!*'

As if expecting to see the speaker, Adam turned around but Trevor and Phil in the seat behind only gave him a vacant stare. The brakes squealed as Laurie stood on the pedal at each bend in the road.

'*Gae ye forward now*,' the voice said again. '*There is danger to come. Tis thou must put it right. Dinna delay!*' It was sharper and more urgent but this time he recognised the voice from his dream. It was Tam Dubh!

Adam stood up and steadied himself against the lurching of the bus. Without knowing what was expected of him, he moved along the aisle to the front. As he passed Catriona she glanced up at him in a puzzled way but he kept moving forward.

'Excuse me,' Ms Mullins said as he reached her seat. 'Who are you and what are you doing on this bus?'

Adam ignored her and kept going towards the front. In the wide rear vision mirror he saw Laurie Sinclair glance up at him as if surprised at his appearance. Adam waited, not certain of what to do next.

Then he saw what was wanted of him. Laurie pressed the clutch pedal and flicked the gear lever into second and the bus began to slow for a long downhill run combined with a sweeping bend to the right. Laurie touched the brake pedal to slow the vehicle even more, but there was no answering squeal. A sudden frown came to his face and he pressed harder and the pedal went right to the floor and the bus gathered speed on the downhill run.

Frantically now, Laurie pumped the brake pedal then snatched at the handbrake but that only produced a futile grinding noise from the rear. The bus picked up speed. One or two of the others realised there was a crisis and somebody began to scream. Laurie tried to change down into first gear but in the middle of this action, he suddenly clutched at his chest and fell backwards, leaving the engine out of gear and the bus surging forward freely.

'*Now, Adam,*' Tam Dubh's voice said. '*Dae ye no' see why I sent ye? Dinna be afraid.*'

As if in a dream, Adam stepped forward and grabbed the wide steering wheel and wrenched the bus to the left.

'*What are you doing, man?*' he heard Ms Mullins scream. The vehicle bounced then tilted sharply to the left as its wheels dropped into a grassy ditch which ran along the side of the road. Inside the bus, people fell violently against the windows and the ones sitting on the right grabbed hold of seat backs as the vehicle ploughed along at that crazy angle for fifty metres or so until it came to a grinding halt. The motor cut abruptly and in the silence, somebody moaned and a boy sobbed. Laurie's face was dark grey and he was having trouble breathing.

Ms Mullins stood up rather shakily then began to claw her way along the sharply tilted aisle towards the back of the bus.

'Pull the rear window in!' she ordered. 'Then get out and move well away. Come on, pull yourselves together!'

Adam found a lever near the floor and tugged it and the driver's seat slid away from the steering wheel. Laurie fell towards him and Adam lowered his body to the floor. He heard one short, strangled gasp. Mouth to mouth resuscitation, Adam thought, and tried to remember what he knew of that technique. Having checked that Laurie's airway was clear and his head correctly tilted, Adam gripped Laurie's nose and began.

'That's it,' he heard Catriona say. 'Go on, Adam, you need to keep it up.'

'Yeah,' he said and pressed on Laurie's chest a few more

times while at the rear window Andy Gibson suddenly appeared and began to help the stream of dazed and silent people out of the bus.

'I was following you,' he called to Adam. 'I used the car phone. Help's on the way, mate.'

Laurie's eyes were open and he lay gazing up at them blankly and a voice came to Adam:

'*Tam Dubh, dae ye no ken thy man is curset? He is curset wi' fire, he is curset wi' mischance and he is curset wi' foulness.*'

Chapter Five

'I suppose after this you'll be in all the papers again tomorrow.' Catriona held up her hands and dramatically stretched them apart to make giant headlines in the air. 'Dunarling's Schoolboy Hero!'

'Go easy,' Adam said.

'This time, Ailsa Robertson will make a *really* big fuss of you,' she said. 'That last effort was nothing, Adam. This time it'll be the works.'

'I didn't know she'd write an article like that,' he said. 'I'm sorry I ever met her.'

Catriona picked up a small pebble from the roadside and tossed it at another one and missed.

Following Andy Gibson's call on the car phone, Dunarling's two ambulances had come up from the town, followed by three police cars and a heavy breakdown truck from the bus company. News of the accident spread rapidly through the community and it wasn't long before concerned parents dropped whatever they were doing and got in their cars and utilities and hurried to the scene.

With the main door of the lopsided bus blocked with ploughed up earth and undergrowth, two of the ambulance men climbed in at the rear window and made their way

79

along to the front. They took over from Adam and Catriona who'd stayed comforting Laurie Sinclair until he'd made it clear he was all right.

'By the looks of this old rogue,' the senior of the ambulance men said, 'you've done a good job. I reckon he's fit to run a hundred metres.'

'A bit less of the old,' Laurie growled from his position on the sloping floor. The ambulance men cheerfully ushered Adam and Catriona outside to be cared for by their colleagues from the other ambulance. They made sure Laurie Sinclair was stable enough to be moved then ferried him out of the rear emergency exit of his stricken bus and took him away in the first ambulance to leave the scene. With siren blaring, a police car went ahead to clear a way through the throng of parents who were already creating their very own traffic hazard.

From the angle of the bus and the mound of soft earth and grass it had gouged up, they expected things to be worse, but apart from bruising and mild shock, the school party was largely unhurt. Ms Mullins had already accounted for everyone, checked them over and dealt firmly with two mild outbreaks of hysteria and gave what arm's length comfort she could to a boy who had vomited. The entire class sat in a line along the grass verge at the roadside, looking in dazed fashion at the ploughed in mess their bus had become. They stayed like that until one by one, they were sympathetically gathered by a parent or neighbour and taken home.

Adam and Catriona sat side by side on the grassy slope where Ms Mullins had put them. Adam's mind was full of the uncanny experience of hearing Tam Dubh's voice and of what he'd just done. They had waited without speaking for several minutes until Catriona broke the ice with her newspaper taunt.

'Anyway,' Adam tried to explain, 'when I found that bit about Margaret Colquhoun in the diary, I looked for you to tell you but you'd gone. I wanted you to be the first to know. Honest.'

'Well, you could have dropped in at my place on your way home.' Catriona was providing him with excuses for his behaviour. A sure sign she was weakening.

'I didn't like to.'

'What? Are you afraid of me or something? Are you afraid of girls?'

Adam was saved from answering by the arrival of his mother in the Rover.

'All in one piece?' she called from the car window.

'We're fine. Just a bit shaky,' Adam stood up and made for the car. Catriona remained sitting on the grass verge.

'Offer Catriona a lift, Adam.' His mother raised her eyebrows and shook her head as if sharing a long standing female joke with Catriona. 'Men! Honestly, sometimes you have to kick start them!'

'Yeah . . . um . . . sorry.' He was flustered and turned around. 'Can we give you a lift, Catriona?'

'It's not out of your way, is it?' She stood up and brushed bits of grass and twig from her skirt.

'No, I have to go back to the surgery anyway,' Adam's mother said. 'So hop in and I'll take you home.'

Adam waved to Ms Mullins who nodded and checked off their names on her clipboard. The front seat of the Rover was already occupied with pages of notes and a box of groceries from the supermarket so he opened the back door for Catriona then climbed in after her.

'Was it bad?' his mother said as she drove the car further uphill to find a place to turn. 'And how did it happen?'

'The brakes didn't work,' Adam explained. 'So the bus ploughed into the side of the road. That's all.'

'He's being too modest, Doctor Hardy,' Catriona said. 'He gave Laurie Sinclair mouth to mouth.'

'True?'

'Yes, Mum,' Adam sighed. 'Laurie had a heart attack or something, you know, when the brakes failed.' He was mystified. Hadn't Catriona *seen* him take the wheel and turn the bus into the side of the road?

Ms Mullins hadn't said anything either, yet they'd both watched him come along the aisle to the front of the bus so they must have seen him take control and pull the wheel to the left. At the time, he remembered hearing Ms Mullins say something as he passed: 'Excuse me,' she had said. 'Who are you and what are you doing on this bus?'

Then when it happened, he had actually heard her scream out: '*What are you doing, man?*' Didn't she recognise him?

He wasn't looking for praise for what he did; after all, that was Tam Dubh's intervention, but he was confused about hearing the voice and uneasy that no one apparently had seen him do anything.

'Catriona helped,' he said. 'With the mouth to mouth bit, I mean. She was there too. So it wasn't just me.'

'Well done.' Adam's mother concentrated on her driving. The road narrowed at a single lane bridge and she stopped to let another car come on. 'And you're both all right? No pain, no injuries, no bruises?'

'Just a bit sort of trembly,' Catriona said. 'We'll be fine.'

'All the same, you should both go home and get into bed for an hour or two.' Adam's mother leaned forward to concentrate on the delicate business of guiding the car between the walls of the narrow bridge then realised what she'd just said and turned away and smiled into her hand. 'Separately, I mean.'

'*Mum!*' Adam protested and looked out of the car window but when he sneaked a look back again, Catriona didn't catch his eye but she had a small secret smile on her face.

Saturday 8th May, 1886
It seems a young sailor is paying particular attention to the mysterious Miss Margaret Colquhoun and who can blame

*him for she is quite a beauty and I have observed more than
one of the bachelors cast a glance or two in her direction.
The fortunate sailor is named Ramsay and he is none other
than the one who carried out the mizzen mast rescue of his
shipmate of which I have already written.*

☆　　☆　　☆

'She's got a birthday coming up soon,' Adam's mother
said.

'How'd you know, Mum?' They were in the kitchen,
sitting together at the table sharing a pot of tea. Adam
remembered the dinner table conversation he'd overheard
the night they discovered the cave.

'Ah well, there are ways,' his mother answered lightly.
'She'll be seventeen. Hint, hint.'

'What do you mean, hint, hint?'

'Every girl likes to receive a present, that's all.'

'Oh.'

'And how are you two getting on anyway? You seemed
very chummy, sitting there together by the side of the road.'

'Oh, all right. Nothing special. I mean, I only see her at
school so it's no big deal.'

'It's just that recently, you seem to be spending a lot of
time with each other. What with sharing the discovery
of the cave, being in the papers together and doing all that
interesting work for the museum. You're not sort of—
getting a bit keen on her, are you?'

'Mum!' Adam almost made a three note musical cadence
of that single word. His mother smiled as if she'd hit a
target with an arrow.

'Well, mothers like to know these things,' she said. 'And
by the way, her birthday's on Wednesday.'

*To carry off her masquerade as a young lad, Miss Colqu-
houn had not shorn her hair but had put it up into her hat,
which is a mercy for her tresses are particularly long and*

rich and dark. Her young suitor has produced, from who knows where, a green silken ribbon for her locks which sets them off magnificently.

☆　　☆　　☆

'Hello, Adam,' Barbara said from behind the shop counter. 'Catriona's not here. She's down at the library.'

'Oh.' Adam let his disappointment show and tried to hide the present behind his back but it would have been hard to conceal. In an antique store, he'd found an old book of poems and then, on an impulse, bought a green ribbon and wrapped the book in birthday paper and tied it with the ribbon.

'She won't be long,' Barbara added and smiled as she leaned to one side to see what Adam held behind his back. 'A present?'

'Yes, just a book.' There was no point in denying it now.

'That's nice. Cat loves books.'

'It's poetry. Can I leave it for her?'

'Well, that seems a shame, Adam. Won't you wait and give it to her yourself?'

'Yes, all right.' Having come this far he decided to plunge on.

'Look, we're having a birthday cake,' Barbara said. 'It's nothing big and fancy, I mean, we're not having people in or anything, just the two of us, but why not stay and share it?'

'Yeah, I'd like to, but are you sure Catriona won't mind?'

'She won't mind,' Barbara laughed. 'Besides, it's my party too. Catriona says it's to be the last one, you know, end of childhood and that sort of thing.'

'Yes, well, thanks if that's all right.'

'Look, why not pop upstairs and wait for us? I'll close the shop and come up and join you. Cat'll be home any minute now.'

'Yes, all right.'

Cat. He liked the sound of that name and imagined using it himself one day.

They fancy their tender interest in each other has escaped all notice but the Misses Cameron observe everything, and I myself confess to paying the affair more attention than it deserves. Such are the ways of passing time on a long voyage, where little innocent trivialities become items of major importance. Fortunately, we are sworn to keep our intelligence from Captain Stewart for there is a strict rule against liaisons between passenger and crewman.

Adam went upstairs and along a narrow landing. At the right, he came to the open door of the living room where he paused. Inside the table was set with tea things and there was a cake with Happy Birthday spelled out in icing and candles ready to be lit. Behind him across the landing was another open door which revealed a bedroom.

Cautiously, he moved over to the bedroom doorway and looked in. From the books and the school things in the room, it could only have been Catriona's. The room was neat and he imagined her in it. There was an athletics pennant on the wall, a photo of Catriona in school uniform and a swimming certificate pinned up so that the edges curled. A dressing table faced the door and he saw himself standing there, reflected in the mirror and felt oddly clumsy, somehow like an interloper, intruding into such a private feminine place. On the bed, an ancient baleful teddy bear sat guarding the pillow. Pinned to its fur was a peace badge and one of its eyes was higher up on its face than the other.

End of childhood. Adam smiled and went reluctantly into the living room and sat down to wait for the final birthday party to begin.

Young Ramsay often contrives to work in the shady part of the deck where Miss Colquhoun happens to spend her day. He splices a rope, fixes an awning or attends to some pulley or item of equipment, scheming to make the work drag out as long as he can. At times, he ventures to speak with her and shyly, in a low voice, she murmurs a reply.

Downstairs in the shop, the telephone rang and Adam heard Barbara answer it.

'Tom!' he heard her laugh aloud with pleasure when she recognised the caller. 'How nice, yes, of course, I'd love to.' Then the street door opened with a ting of its bell and breathless, Catriona called out something to her mother and began to mount the stairs. She sang as she came.

Adam stood up hesitantly and went around the table to greet her but she hurried along the landing without knowing he was there and turned into her bedroom opposite and disappeared somewhere behind the door. He'd have preferred Barbara to have been there when they met so he stood tentatively at the doorway, waiting for her to come into the living room. When she did emerge from behind the bedroom door, her appearance took his breath away.

Catriona had taken off her street clothes and came back to the dressing table wearing only brief white bikini pants. In her hand she held a pair of white shorts and a dark red t-shirt which she heedlessly tossed on a chair beside the dressing table then leaned in towards the mirror to inspect a small blemish on her face.

Adam was entranced by her appearance yet anguished at his predicament. He stood, not knowing whether to say anything or whether to duck back out of sight behind the door. To do either would make a noise and advertise his presence then he'd be caught like some sort of Peeping Tom. The question was resolved for him when Catriona, at her mirror, suddenly realised he was standing in the doorway opposite.

'Having a good look, are you?' She was calm and unhurried as she backed away from the dressing table. She picked up the white shorts and stepped into them and fastened the buttons at her waist.

'I'm sorry,' Adam said. 'I didn't mean . . . I'm sorry.'

Catriona turned to face him and took up the dark red t-shirt and searched for the neck then slipped the garment over her head and arms and let it slide down her body.

'Sorry?' she said calmly. 'What for? You were having a good look.'

She is one of those fortunate women who can take any old item of clothing and give to it an elegance which enhances her own beauty. She wears about her shoulders an ordinary cotton shawl, which on her looks as if it were fresh out of Paris; she has a bonnet which, on its original owner looked dowdy and commonplace but on this young miss, somehow turns all heads.

Were I not a fusty old bachelor farmer, I would instantly declare my own love for her but I find myself secretly cheering on young Ramsay's faltering attempts to woo this maiden.

'What are you sorry for?' Catriona said again.

'For not saying something. You know, for not warning you I was here.' Adam's heart was beating fast and he bit his lip. In the two days since the accident, he'd felt things had been getting better between them. She'd spoken to him at school a couple of times and even reminded him of her invitation to inspect the family Bible. And now he'd spoiled it all again, with this! Such a lowdown, stupid, childish, immature action on his part. To be caught *perving* on her!

In bare feet, she squeezed past him into the living room and turned the cups over and took up the teapot.

'You've got tears in your eyes,' she said. 'Have you been crying?'

'No.'

'Then why the tears? There has to be a reason for tears.'

Adam looked away then on a sudden impulse turned back to face her.

'It wasn't my fault,' he said. 'I didn't know you'd . . . you'd . . .'

'Do a strip-tease?' She was playing with him now.

'I didn't know. Honest. And I got a shock—seeing you like that.'

What he really wanted to say was the shock came from seeing how beautiful she was. He knew she was beautiful; he'd already made up his mind about that but seeing her the way she'd just been, it was almost painful. He wanted to say she'd taken his breath away and made his heart race because he'd never seen a girl like that before, apart from ones in magazines. He wanted to say a lot more about what he was feeling for her and how wretched he was because this latest blunder would make things worse between them but he was afraid to speak because he knew the words would come out in a clumsy, embarrassing jumble and they'd all be the wrong ones anyway. He blinked. 'I got a shock, if you must know.'

'Oh, dear,' she said.

'I'll go now.' He made for the door.

'But why'd you come?' She stopped him. 'Okay, so it wasn't to watch me in the nuddy, but why?' Catriona saw the green ribboned parcel on the table. 'And what's that?'

'For you,' he mumbled. 'Um—a birthday present.'

'For me? How'd you know it's my birthday. I never told anyone.'

'I just knew.'

'Your mother?'

'Yes.'

'They do have their uses.' She took up the parcel and tugged at the end of the green ribbon and it came away. She

held it to her hair briefly. 'I could use a ribbon,' she said.
The paper fell away and Catriona looked at the book of
poems he had bought for her.

*At one stage, Young Ramsay breaks off from splicing a rope
and tentatively slips to her a piece of folded paper, a poem
perhaps or a declaration of his love? Maybe he is shy
because he is unsure of his place in her heart, but whatever
the reason, Margaret opens the folded paper and reads its
contents then rewards him with a sweet smile.*

*O, to be young Ramsay and have that tender smile
bestowed upon me!*

The book was *Ballads of Ships & the Sea & Other Things*.
Catriona leafed through the pages.

'It's dated about 1900,' Adam said. 'I saw it and thought
you'd like it. Couldn't think of anything better.'

'It's really lovely.' She smiled at him then laughed
outright. 'Look, don't be so hang-dog, Adam. It's okay,
I didn't know you were there and you didn't expect me to—
you know.' She smiled again. 'Okay, so you *saw* me! It's
no big deal, you see even more on the beach anyway.' She
turned again to the book.

*Margaret carefully folds his note and slips it into the sleeve
of her dress and Young Ramsay takes up his work again.
Such a small token between them and yet so much.*

*O, to be so young, so tentative and shy, one with the
other!*

'It's really lovely,' Catriona said. 'The book. Stay,
Adam, please.'

The telephone extension in the living room gave a loud
ting and a few seconds later Barbara came upstairs.

'Tea made?' she said and saw that it wasn't and went to

the electric jug and switched it on. Catriona got out an extra cup and saucer and they sat around the table. Barbara examined the book of ballads and ran through a few of the titles she remembered from school.

They made the tea and cut the cake and talked of general things. They talked of the accident in the bus and of what Adam had transcribed from the diary. The conversation seemed to falter and Adam wondered if he should mention Tam Dubh's weird and unsettling intervention, but then he thought better of it. It was so way-out and fanciful it could sound like bragging on his part and he didn't want to be accused of that. Besides, Catriona hadn't mentioned him taking the wheel. Nor had Ms Mullins.

The accident had been written up in the local paper but thankfully, the reporter, who was not Ailsa Robertson, had only referred to two students who'd given mouth to mouth resuscitation to the driver after he'd suffered an apparent heart attack at the wheel. It hadn't been quite an accurate report but Adam was thankful to let it go.

'Has Catriona showed you her other present?' Barbara asked.

'No,' Adam said. Her *other* present? Had she only received two? His own birthdays were much more lavish affairs, involving gifts from multiple aunts and uncles from both sides of the family.

'Cat, go and fetch it,' Barbara said.

'Oh, Barbara!' Catriona got up and went into her bedroom. 'You're making me such a show off.'

'Her grandmother, old Mrs Chisholm, left it in her will,' Barbara explained.

Catriona came back with a flat wooden box and clicked it open and turned it so Adam could see what it contained. It was a golden heart locket on a long chain.

Adam stared at it and remembered a dream.

'It was Margaret Colquhoun's,' Barbara said. 'To be

given to Catriona when she turned seventeen.'

'Why seventeen?' Adam said.

'That's how old she was when she landed in Australia,' Catriona said. 'Amazing, isn't it? She went through all that and she was only seventeen, my age.'

Adam thought about Margaret Colquhoun being loved at that age and obviously returning it.

'Put it on and show Adam,' Barbara said. Catriona lifted the locket from its box and held it against her dark red t-shirt and he remembered the dream again.

'Do it up for me, Barbara,' she said. 'It's got a funny catch.'

'Haven't got my glasses,' Barbara said. 'Come on, Adam, make yourself useful.'

Catriona stretched out her hand and let the locket fall into his palm then went to her dressing table, sat down and lifted the hair from the back of her neck. Adam followed and carefully put the locket around her and dealt with the catch. Catriona dropped her hair and smoothed it back and Adam looked at her reflection and, vivid this time, there was the dream.

In the mirror, he saw Barbara looking at them but beyond her, there was a dark dressed figure standing in the shadowy background. The face was indistinct but then for a brief flash, it became clear—it was Richard Vernon, gazing at them with an angry look on his face and his jaw working savagely. As quickly as it had appeared, the face was indistinct again but further in the background, there was another dark figure, too far away to make out. Alarmed, Adam turned sharply away from the images in the mirror and looked at the room again but only Barbara was there. She saw the look on his face and misunderstood it.

'It's all right, Adam,' she laughed. 'You're *allowed* to be in there.'

'No,' he said. 'It's not that, it was something else.

I thought I saw something, that's all.' Catriona looked up at him in the mirror then turned to show herself wearing the locket around her neck with the heart nestling between her breasts. She too was caught by his sudden expression of fear.

'What's wrong, Adam?'

'Nothing.' He gulped and made an unconvincing lie of it.

Catriona looked at Barbara and shrugged. He saw the concern in their eyes.

'Look, I've got to go.'

'Are you sure, Adam?' Barbara said.

'Yes, I think I'd better go home. The party was great, I really enjoyed it.'

Catriona went downstairs with him and opened the shop door.

'Something's bothering you,' she said quietly. 'I saw the look on your face in the mirror. Something's wrong, isn't it?'

'No, I just remembered I've got things to do.' Tell her, tell her everything, an inner voice urged him. Go on, you need someone to share all this stuff. All the dreams, the visions, the voices and the faces. But he unchained his bike and made his own voice sound casual. 'Thanks for the tea and for the birthday cake.'

'And for the present,' she said. 'I really like it, Adam. Honest.'

She waited until he pedalled away and when he looked back briefly, she was still at the door, watching until he was out of sight.

☆　　☆　　☆

His father had gone to a meeting of the Railway Historical Society and Adam and his mother had dinner on their own.

'He is just a touch miffed, Adam,' she said. 'He wanted you to go with him.'

'Mum, it's so boring,' he said. 'I don't mind the times we go to work on the loco or even the working days in the station, but the meetings are dullsville. They show slides and get worked up about rusty old dog spikes and train couplings and old uniforms and tickets.'

'You get worked up about your old diary.'

'That's different,' he said. 'The diary's history.'

'So is the steam loco and all the old bits and pieces your father works on,' his mother said. 'Come on, he just wants you to pitch in and help.'

'But I'm too busy.'

'Oh well, it's just an idea—it would really be good if you and your father could get together a bit more. You don't exactly hit it off, man and boy. How did Catriona's birthday go?'

☆   ☆   ☆

They were standing outside David Riccio's coffee shop. Catriona had suggested it as they cycled home from school together. Adam hesitated briefly because he only had five dollars.

'Oh, Adam,' Catriona said in a mocking manner. 'I understand. You don't want to take me here because it's got such special memories. After all, didn't you come here with . . .' She lowered her voice to a husky whisper and breathed the name in a seductive way, '*Ailsa!*'

'Oh, come on, Cat,' he said. 'Give me a break!'

She smiled at his embarrassment and they parked their bikes and went inside. They ordered milk shakes and sat at a window seat watching the traffic in the street outside.

'Cat,' he said again, 'when we were on the bus, you know, just before we piled in, what did you see?'

'I don't know,' she said. 'It was all so fast—but I keep having this feeling I saw a man. I only got a glimpse of him. He was tall.'

'What did he do?'

'I saw him come along to the front of the bus.'

'And what then?'

'I only saw him for a second or two then we were in the ditch.' Her voice went down to a whisper. 'I think he tried to kill us.'

'No he didn't,' Adam said. 'He saved us. The brakes failed and Laurie had a heart attack and that guy steered the bus into the side of the road.'

Catriona looked past him to the street outside.

'There was something else about him,' she said. 'In the museum there's a model of an old fashioned sailor, you know, dressed in the style of the late 1800s.'

'Yes,' Adam said. 'I know the one.'

'That's how this man looked. Dressed as an old fashioned sailor. Isn't that crazy?'

☆　　☆　　☆

Adam's mother answered the telephone.

'Oh, it's you Catriona,' he heard her say, 'and you want to talk with my boy?' Adam went to take the receiver but his mother refused to part with it. 'Look, Catriona, while I've got you on the phone,' she went on, 'Adam's offered to help his father do some work down at the railway station, you know, polishing, painting, that sort of thing. Would you like to help out?' She paused. 'Saturday morning, nine till noon.'

Adam tried to wrest the telephone from his mother and shook his head violently to signal no. His mother smiled and held him off with her free hand.

'Oh, good,' she said. 'We'll pick you up about quarter to, that's great. Now here's Adam.' She smiled sweetly and passing the handset over she whispered, 'Too late, it's all arranged.'

'Thank you, mother,' he said with a frown and then to

Catriona: 'Talk about parents organising your life!'

'I don't mind helping,' Catriona said. 'Might even be fun.'

'Yes,' Adam said. 'My father's heaps of fun.'

'Look, I rang because I've found something in this Bible. You said you wanted to see it, do you want to come over now?'

'I've got . . . um,' he hesitated but Catriona cut him off.

'Oh, darling,' she quoted in a breathless voice. 'I'd swim the deepest ocean for you as long as it's not raining.'

'Okay, I'm on my way.' He replaced the handset and turned to his mother. 'You dropped me right in it, Mum.'

She said, 'Are you going out?'

'Yes,' he said.

'Proper little gadabout.'

Wednesday 19th May, 1886

Mr Colquhoun now keeps very much to himself and frequently leaves his daughter alone for all of the afternoon hours. She seems to prefer it this way for on those rare occasions he appears at her side she has little to say to him.

Young Ramsay 'doth make hay while the sun shines' as the saying goes, for I doubt if Margaret's father would permit such a liaison if he but knew of it.

The Bible was old and water-stained. Catriona had it out on the table in the living room along with the pile of old letters, postcards and newspaper clippings she'd been transcribing.

'There's some handwriting in the flyleaf,' she said and carefully opened the Bible. 'It belonged to Adam Colquhoun.' She invited him to read the smudged and stained handwritten words.

Adam Colquhoun, Born in Glasgow, 18th April, 1851.

And then, underneath in the same handwriting he read:

Adam Colquhoun married Marie Catherine DeLairgo,
        Grove Street, Glasgow, 15th June, 1883.

'Well?' Catriona said.

'Well, what?'

She picked up Adam's printout of the diary and showed him the date of the first entry. *Saturday 6th March, 1886.*

'Colquhoun was thirty-five when he left Scotland,' she said. 'With a seventeen-year-old daughter?'

'It means when Margaret was born, he must only have been seventeen himself,' Adam said.

'That's fair enough,' Catriona said. 'Some seventeen-year-olds do make love and they've got all the urges and the physical equipment to be fathers and mothers.'

'I know all that.' Adam brushed her suggestion aside. 'But he didn't get married until three years before he left Scotland, so maybe Margaret was his illegitimate daughter.'

'Huh!' Catriona said. 'Fat chance of that! I couldn't see any *man* of that time being lumbered with looking after a bastard. That was always the woman's problem.'

'Well, maybe he was married before and this Marie Catherine DeLairgo woman was his second wife.' Adam felt he was losing this particular debate.

'Maybe,' Catriona said. 'But if he was married before, or if Margaret was really his daughter, you'd think there'd be some mention of her in the front of the Bible, even if she was illegitimate.'

'We'll have to ask Hamish Leckie about that,' Adam said. 'He'd know about Scottish customs.'

'Look closely at his wife's name,' Catriona said. Adam leaned down to the page. The marks were faint but still visible; someone had taken a pencil and put three strokes through the name Marie Catherine DeLairgo.

'It's as if he wanted to—delete her,' Adam said.

'Or maybe she did it,' Catriona said. 'A sort of divorce.'

Saturday 22nd May, 1886
The Misses Cameron, who are the very fount of knowledge itself, inform me that Mr Colquhoun, robbed of the com-

*pany of his daughter, now spends much time in solitary
contemplation of his Bible.*

☆   ☆   ☆

'Hi, Adam,' Catriona said. 'What have you got for lunch?'

'Sandwiches,' he said moving along the bench to make
room for her. 'Salami.'

'Oh, exotic,' she said and almost as if it was hers by right
she took one of his sandwiches. Adam was pleased. They
sat side by side without speaking while a little way off the
inseparable M and M shared the grassy shade and exchanged
glances, their unspoken method of remarking on what they
were observing.

'I've got your book of poems in my bag,' Catriona said.
'Ballads.'

'Yes, ballads. I love them. Stirring Scottish stuff, Sir
Patrick Spens, the Three Ravens, the Twa Corbies.'

'Is there one about a character called Tam Dubh?' Adam
asked.

'No, but there's one about Tam Lin, he was Janet's elfin
lover.' Catriona sighed and stretched. 'Oh, it's romantic
stuff. I read them in bed last night.' She crossed her legs.

'That's good. I'm glad you like them.'

'But you didn't write anything in the flyleaf,' she said.

'I didn't think of doing that.'

'It's what people usually do with presents, you know,
Happy Birthday from Auntie Flo, that sort of stuff.'

'Would you like me to write something?'

'Oh, that's a nice idea.' Catriona made it sound as if he'd
thought of it and delved into her bag and brought out the
book.

'It seems a shame to write on an antique,' Adam said.

'Well, it's nearly an antique.'

'But I'll never sell it or give it away.' She opened the
book at the flyleaf. 'I'll probably keep it till I die. So write
something.'

'What'll I say?' Adam said.

'Oh, something like, *To Catriona, with love from Adam*.' She held out her ball pen.

'Is that what you want?'

'I think so,' she said.

Adam took the book and Catriona's pen and carefully wrote the words she had proposed.

He took a lot of time over it and made sure he didn't scribble as he sometimes did. M and M, sitting with their lunch sandwiches untasted, exchanged even more deeply meaningful glances which indicated that, before the end of the day, news of the incident would be all over school.

Adam didn't care.

Chapter Six

Sunday 23rd May, 1886

Our water supply has begun to exhibit a peculiar foulness of taste. I first noticed it in my morning tea and remarked upon it to Mr McWalter who sampled some of the contents of the pot for himself.

"Indeed it does taste foul, sir," said he and asked me not to drink any more of the tea until he could investigate the situation. I needed no further persuasion for the taste was particularly rank and bitter on the tongue.

When Mr McWalter went on deck, he found many of the passengers already ill and vomiting. All had taken the water in the last few hours.

The captain ordered an inspection of the tank from which our drinking water was drawn, whereupon the sailors quickly found the source of the contamination. A large wooden cask of arsenic, part of our cargo, had been broached and transferred into the tank where the movement of the ship swirled it around and mixed it with the water we were to drink.

"This was no accident," Captain Stewart said and his face was black and wrathful as a heavy rain cloud.

Fortunately, the ship has other fresh water tanks and

their contents were tested and proved to be fit for drinking. The contaminated tank was pumped out until it was quite dry.

The captain and his officers did not let the matter rest there but began questioning the sailors straightaway. Attention soon fell upon one particular individual, a Gaelic speaking seaman from the Western Islands. His shipmates reported that his behaviour had undergone a sudden change in that he had recently started acting in a suspicious manner. Normally of a cheerful and talkative disposition, of late he had become moody, withdrawn and kept to himself.

'This is getting to be an epic,' Adam said aloud as he read over the words he had transcribed. Catriona was busy at another computer nearby; she stopped typing and leaned back in her chair to listen to him.

'What have you got?' she said. M and M were working near-at-hand and they also stopped typing and made a great show of pretending not to be paying any attention.

'Poison in the water supply this time,' Adam said. 'Some crewman on the ship did it. Arsenic.'

'Not our Jamie Ramsay?' Catriona said.

'No, he's cool.'

She got up and went along the row to Adam's desk. Without moving their heads, M and M let their eyes swivel after her as Catriona took up a position beside Adam and began to read the screen over his left shoulder.

When they searched his possessions, which the captain was obliged to do, they found some of the man's clothing had been stained and Mr McWalter confirmed that it had been caused by the arsenic. Indeed, so liberally and heedlessly was it applied to the garments the man's skin was also found to be blackened by the substance, yet the poor wretch had not complained nor had he sought treatment of it.

He was transferred to the male hospital and put under the charge of two of his shipmates who took it in turn to watch over him for fear he would do further mischief either to himself or to the ship.

Adam eased his chair to the right to make room for her and she moved into the space he had vacated, gently and naturally resting her hand on his shoulder.

'Come on, scroll up,' she said after a few seconds. Adam pressed page up and together they read of the foulness in the water supply and of the Gaelic speaking sailor who'd deliberately done this strange thing without any obvious malice in his heart and with such reckless abandon that in the process he'd even stained his own flesh.

It is a sad case and no one has been able to account for such irrational behaviour. For a man to poison the very water supply which he himself must drink is strange indeed.

'The guy must have been nuts,' Adam observed.

'Or possessed,' Catriona said. 'Sounds like he didn't know what he was doing.' She was standing so near Adam could almost feel the heat of her body.

The diary was lying open on the computer table at the left of the disc drive and she took her hand away from his shoulder to turn a page. Adam's hand rested on the edge of the table a few centimetres from hers; it would take only the smallest movement on his part to let his fingers touch her hand. It could even be made to look like an accident, and what then? What would she say?

A bolder movement from him and he could rest his hand completely on hers and she wouldn't see that as an accident, she'd know he meant it, and what would she do? Would she snatch her hand away and make a big deal of it? That was the risk; with M and M making mental notes in the background.

He dithered. Come on, make a move, he urged himself but Catriona lifted her hand to point out the next entry in the diary and he lost his chance.

Sunday 24th May, 1886
A baby girl has died from the contamination of the water.
The child was one of twins, recently born on the ship and
her parents are utterly inconsolable and stand outside of the
hospital by the hour, keening and lamenting in their Irish
Gaelic for the bairn they have lost. They call on the man
inside to come forth and explain his actions, but there is no
movement from that quarter.

'This is heavy stuff, Adam,' she said.

'Yeah, first a fire, then a storm with all that damage and suicides and now this guy goes off his brain.'

'Not to mention Margaret starting out dressed as a boy then having a secret love affair,' she added. 'Why didn't I get the diary to transcribe?'

'I'm sharing it with you, aren't I?'

'Well, that's something, but are you sure you can handle all this excitement, passion and emotion? I mean, you're only a boy.'

'I can handle it,' he said and his face burned. 'Mind you, I've had a couple of—' He didn't finish the sentence.

'A couple of what?'

Adam looked around the computer room. Other people were working in adjacent computers and M and M were not far away with their ears oscillating like radar scanners at an airport. He tapped at the keyboard.

Dreams appeared on the screen. Catriona hit return and tapped with her left hand.

what sort of dreams?

confused, disturbing, Adam typed.

what happens?

this weird guy called tam dubh talks to me. tells me things. warns me.

what about?

don't know. some kind of threat. he warned me about the bus crash. that guy you saw turning the wheel—that was me. tam dubh told me to go forward because there was some kind of danger to come.

heavy!!!!!

i also saw you in one of the dreams.

what was i doing? Catriona typed.

wearing that locket you got for your birthday.

Adam was on the point of saying he'd seen it before Barbara gave it to her but that chance was lost too.

'Well, this is togetherness,' said a voice. It was Ms Mullins. 'Why are you two working on the same computer? Playing space invaders?'

'No, Miss,' Catriona said. 'Just looking at Adam's diary. We're cross referencing.' Adam deleted the words they had typed.

'Well, if you've finished *cross referencing*,' Ms Mullins laid heavy emphasis on those two words, 'you can get back to your own computer, Miss Chisholm, and keep it company for a while. It's probably missing you.'

M and M kept their heads down but allowed their eyes to have a final meaningful swivel as Catriona returned to her own keyboard.

'Now, Hardy.' Ms Mullins spoke in her forthright way and drew up a spare chair and sat down. 'When we had that accident on the bus, what did *you* see?'

'Nothing, Miss.'

'I've asked the others who tell me they saw this real old fashioned guy walking along towards the front,' she went on. 'Did you see him?'

'No, miss.'

'Laurie Sinclair swears he saw such a man in the rear

vision mirror. I saw something like that too and so did the others, but you didn't?'

'No miss.'

'Then how is it you got along to the front so soon after the crash?' Ms Mullins said. 'One second the man was there and the next, there you were, helping Laurie Sinclair.'

'Don't know, miss,' Adam said. 'I just went along after we piled in.'

'It's making things very difficult for Sergeant Balfour's report,' Ms Mullins said. 'Everyone says the man was dressed in nineteenth century sailor's gear. Some say he crashed the bus, others say he saved our lives by driving it into the roadside.' Ms Mullins sighed and stood up.

'Don't know anything about it, miss.'

'Very strange,' Ms Mullins said and went away.

☆   ☆   ☆

On Friday after school, Hamish Leckie waited until the museum closed for the night then asked Adam and Catriona to stay back and look at the new display.

'Since you're the ones who discovered the mandrake dolls,' he told them, 'it seems only right and proper you should be the first to see what I've done with them.'

In a corner of the main room of the museum, Hamish had used a grey painted canvas backdrop to create a small version of the cave. On the floor was a triangular mound of sand with the two surviving mandrake dolls on show. Tam Dubh was at the top of the mound standing alongside his empty coffin. To the side and a little way down the mound lay the figure of Swith, the doll Richard Vernon had kept. It was in its coffin with the lid lying alongside and again Adam marvelled at the contrast between the two figures. Swith appeared to be burned out and pale, yet in the cave he had almost glowed with a kind of intense energy; here the figure was a listless, pallid imitation of Tam Dubh.

'Is he the one you dream about?' Catriona said.

'Yeah, that's Tam Dubh,' Adam sighed. They were leaning together over the softly lit display.

'Who's having dreams?' Hamish asked sharply.

'Adam is,' Catriona said. 'It's all because of that diary. I think it's beginning to have an effect on him.'

'It's not,' Adam protested.

'Well, they're exciting discoveries,' Hamish said. 'But if it's disturbing you, Adam, or interfering with your school work—'

'It's not,' Adam cut him off. 'Cat's only jealous because her stuff's so boring.'

'Oh, you liar!' Catriona exploded and gave Adam a half playful dig in the ribs. 'I was only thinking of you!'

'Excuse me!' Hamish said sternly. 'A museum's not the place for horseplay.'

'Sorry, Hamish,' Catriona said. She gave Adam a 'you'll keep' look and turned her attention to the description Hamish had placed on a stand at the front of the display.

MANDRAGORA

These tiny figures were fashioned out of mandrake roots (*Mandragora Juss*) and were almost certainly brought to Australia aboard the ill fated immigrant ship *Dunarling* which was shipwrecked off the coast in the storm of Monday 14th June, 1886.

Their exact purpose is unclear but it is thought they were used by sailors as talismen or good luck charms. In other cases, they were bought and sold for evil motives, probably to exact revenge for a real or imagined grievance. The plant itself was also used to concoct love potions or to make women fertile.

The mandrake has been mentioned in the Bible and has appeared in the works of Shakespeare and John

Donne. Throughout the years, many superstitious beliefs grew up about the mandragora plant. Some people thought it was certain death to pull a mandrake root from the ground so a rope was tied to a dog and the unfortunate animal, on being chased, pulled out the root and died. Mandrakes were also supposed to utter a shriek when they were uprooted from the earth.

These present examples were found in the recently discovered cave in which Jamie Ramsay and Margaret Colquhoun, the *Dunarling* survivors, sheltered after the drama of the shipwreck.

'Well, what do you think of the display?' Hamish said.

'Great,' Catriona said. 'Pity about the other doll figures, the ones that got away.'

'Ah well, since they were said to have been chucked into the sea, you might even find them yourself, Catriona,' Hamish said. 'When you go on your beachcombing expeditions.'

'Haven't been beachcombing for a while,' she murmured. 'I'm sort of busy—pursuing other interests.'

Before they left the museum Adam took a last look at Tam Dubh and it may have been the light or his imagination but he almost felt the small figure's eyes flashed at him as if in recognition.

'Goodnight mate,' he whispered. 'And thanks.'

☆   ☆   ☆

'I forgot to tell you, Gordon dear,' Adam's mother said. 'We're picking up Catriona Chisholm.'

'Jean, whatever for?' Adam's father was already testy with the Saturday morning traffic.

'Because she kindly volunteered to help with the working bee.'

In the back seat of the Rover, Adam marvelled at the

way his mother organised events so that everything fell into place.

'Oh, very well,' said his father and tried to edge into the right turn lane at the traffic lights although there was a truck behind them whose driver was in an unyielding mood. The lights changed to green and his father sent the Rover surging forward into a screaming right turn.

'I set a spratt to catch a mackerel,' Adam's mother smiled. 'Many hands make light work and I killed three birds with one stone.'

'Your mother speaks in riddles,' his father observed. 'She always did. The chemist is forever sending her prescriptions back to be deciphered.' Adam was used to the medical jokes that flew back and forth between his parents.

They drove along the main street in silence until they drew up outside the souvenir shop. Catriona was waiting for them, dressed in old jeans and a t-shirt and ready for work. She took her place beside Adam and gently closed the car door with hardly a sound.

'In this car, Catriona, gentle door closing wins Brownie points,' Adam's mother smiled her approval.

'Good morning, Doctor Hardy, and good morning Doctor Hardy,' Catriona said with a wink at Adam.

'Mmm,' said his father as he waited to do a U turn. 'My wife is the doctor, I'm a surgeon so I'm just plain Mister.'

'Don't you mind not being called doctor?' Catriona said and Adam inwardly shook his head in wonder at her relaxed and easy way of talking with his father. 'I mean, after being called it now you're not called it.'

'No,' Adam's father answered stiffly. 'I don't mind in the least.'

'I would,' Catriona went on. 'If I studied to become a doctor, I'd make sure everyone knew about it.' Adam saw his mother hide a smile.

'You're not allowed to advertise,' Adam's father pointed out with his usual logic.

'What's the advertisement in calling yourself doctor?' Catriona said.

'I'll take it up with the A.M.A.,' Mr Hardy said dryly.

'Look, Catriona, why not call us by our first names,' Adam's mother said. 'I mean, you call your mother Barbara so I'm Jean and this is Gordon.'

'Hello, Jean and Gordon,' Catriona said and clicked her seat belt and settled back.

'Hello, Jean and Gordon,' Adam said and in the rear vision mirror, he saw his father give him a quick frosty glance then the eyes creased into a smile.

He looked at Catriona sitting alongside him but she was already absorbed in something that had taken her interest out of the side window of the car.

At Dunarling Station, other cheerful enthusiasts from the Railway Historical Society were already gathered with paint pots, brushes, polishing rags and tins of Brasso. There was much friendly banter and exuberant greeting as they set about the work they'd been allotted. Already the air was filled with the busy sound of sawing and hammering as people patched and repaired the fabric of the station.

'What do you want us to do, Dad?' Adam was still distinctly unenthusiastic about the idea of working on Saturday morning.

'There's some painting to be done,' his father said. 'Outside where the fire was. They've repaired the woodwork but it needs a coat of paint. Go and work with Charlie Boyd.'

'Okay, Gordon,' Catriona said. 'Painting it is.'

Adam saw his father react briefly at the familiarity, then a ghost of a smile flicked across his face.

They each had a brush but shared the same tin of green gloss enamel so they worked side by side for the first hour of the morning.

'Hey, go easy, Catriona!' Adam said at one stage. 'You're a bit slap happy with that brush!'

'And you're such a perfectionist,' she replied and began to imitate Adam's careful style of working. Then she started to ply her own brush with long exaggerated strokes, working vigorously like a demented artist, crossing into the area where Adam was painting, shoving him to one side with her body. Adam protested and pushed back and Catriona giggled and threatened to slap him with her brush.

'Hey, you lovebirds,' Charlie Boyd said. 'Knock it off. You'll end up with the paint on yourselves.' Charlie took his job as supervisor seriously and was in no mood for horseplay. He put his own brush down and stumped off to see about morning tea, leaving them alone.

'Ooooh, he called us lovebirds,' Catriona whispered.

'Yeah,' Adam said. He'd been quick to notice that too.

'I think I've got a spot of paint on my nose.' Catriona turned to face him, squinting at the tip of her nose with both eyes.

She gave him a rag which earlier she'd dampened with turpentine and turned her nose up to him to have the paint removed. He rested his left hand on her shoulder and gently rubbed at her nose until the spot was gone.

'How do I look?' she said.

'Beautiful.' He was looking into her face and he meant it.

'Thank you.' Catriona didn't back away but stayed close while Adam kept his hand on her shoulder. She looked at him.

'Hi, lovebird,' she whispered.

'Hi,' Adam said and his throat was dry. It was his move. His heart beat faster and he knew he should do something but it was Catriona who took the initiative and kissed him. He broke away and hugged her, burying his nose in her hair and breathing deeply.

'That's what lips were made for,' Catriona said and kissed him again and this time he vowed she'd have to be the one to break away.

'Oh, you two are getting on like a house on fire,' Adam

heard a familiar voice. Hastily, he drew away from Catriona and turned to meet his mother who came towards them with her eyes fixed firmly on the wall they'd just painted. 'What a beautiful sight.'

'Another ten minutes should do it,' he said and made a show of stirring the paint in the pot. Catriona smiled and took up her brush and began to work on the wall again.

'I've come to say we're having a tea-break soon,' Adam's mother said. 'So ten minutes will be fine.' She gave Adam a wink and went away.

'She saw us,' Adam said.

'So what?' Catriona said. 'Human beings do stuff like that.' She dipped her brush again and turned away from Adam. 'Haven't you ever kissed a girl before?'

Adam started to paint with small, careful, determined strokes.

'Well?' she said.

'You know, at parties. Games and stuff,' he said. 'Nothing serious.'

'I thought so.'

'What about you?'

'No,' she said seriously. 'I've never kissed a girl before.'

'I mean a boy!' Adam exploded but he enjoyed the banter.

'No,' she replied airily. 'Except at parties. I've never really wanted to.' She dipped her brush again and became serious. 'Until now.'

Adam looked away from her and concentrated on his own brushwork.

'What about last summer?' he said. 'Those university students?' As soon as he spoke, he wished he could snatch the words back. Catriona took so long to answer he thought she hadn't heard the question but when he turned he found her regarding him coldly.

'What about them?' Her voice had taken on an icy edge.

'Well, there was—' His voice tailed off. 'You know, a lot of talk going around.'

Catriona stabbed her brush into the pot of paint and slashed a vertical stroke down the wall.

'That's when you and I started,' she said. She stabbed into the pot again and flicked a long horizontal stoke away to the right. 'That's us together.' She made a third stab at the pot and slashed a line away to the left. 'And that's my life before.'

'Careful,' Adam said.

'Careful nothing,' she snapped. 'That bit of the line's our business, the bit on the left is mine. Okay? Got that?' She threw the brush into the pot and walked away.

'Catriona!' he called after her. 'Wait for me.'

'I'm going to the toilet,' she said over her shoulder. 'Don't follow me or you'll look even more of a nong than you are!'

Adam fixed up the mess she'd made and finished off the painting then went inside to see if he could find her and repair this new damage he'd done.

The interior of Dunarling Station was looking its splendid best. The volunteers had done their utmost to restore the building to its late nineteenth century grandeur and now with teacups in hand, they milled around admiring their work. They had steamed up the loco and brought it out of its shed for the occasion and it sat hissing gently in the morning air, resplendent in fresh paint, polished brass and steel side rods.

Adam saw his mother and father over by the refreshment buffet pouring themselves cups of tea from a huge pot.

'Adam, where's Catriona?' his father said.

'I don't know,' Adam answered.

'Gone to clean up,' his mother said. 'Got some paint on her hands, I think.'

Catriona emerged later, sat on a station seat and accepted

a cup of tea and a biscuit from Adam's father.

'I'm sorry,' Adam whispered and she nodded briefly but said nothing. Gingerly, he sat a little way along the seat from her and drank his own tea in silence.

Adam's father came over and took the space between them.

'Are you taking part in the re-enactment, Catriona?' he said. 'We need everyone we can get to fill the train.'

'I think Barbara felt we should do something,' she answered. 'Don't know if we'll manage to dress up though.'

'But that's half the fun of it,' Adam's father said. 'If we all dress in authentic costume it'll look really fantastic. Just imagine the station looking as it did a hundred years ago, military uniforms, ladies in crinolines and parasols, labourers and all sorts. Then we all get on the train and steam off for a round trip.'

'What are you going as, Gordon?' Catriona said.

'Well, my costume's easy,' he answered. 'I'm assistant on the loco, so I'll be wearing fireman's gear. I might even get to shovel in the coal.'

Catriona chatted lightly and naturally with his father and Adam began to feel excluded. Not only that; she hadn't asked what *he* was wearing to the re-enactment.

He stared miserably at his empty tea cup while Catriona and his father talked on and on about where the train would go and how many carriages there would be.

'For the occasion, the Railway Department's going to let the train cross Dunarling viaduct,' his father said. 'We don't use it these days, not since the new steel bridge was put in.'

'Yes, Gordon, I knew that,' Catriona said.

'But did you know the old viaduct contains some timber from the *Dunarling*?' his father went on. 'When they built it, they actually used timber from the wreck. Some of the planking and some of the deck supports came from the ship.'

'I didn't know that,' Catriona said.

'There you are then.'

His father was eating out of her hand, Adam thought.

☆   ☆   ☆

'Well, what do you think?' Jean Hardy asked.

'What do I think of what?' Gordon Hardy could be maddening at times. They had dropped Catriona off at the souvenir shop and were heading home in the Rover. [Bye, Gordon, bye, Jean she had said.]

'You know.'

'She's very intelligent,' Adam's father said. 'Very natural.'

'Who are we talking about?' Adam asked from the back seat.

'Catriona, of course,' said his mother from the front.

'Great little worker,' his father said. 'And we got two for the price of one. Never seen Adam do so much work.'

'I've got to hand it to you, darling,' Jean Hardy said to her husband. 'Brilliant strategy.'

Adam was still hurt about being left out of the conversation and angry at the way she'd reacted but it was really anger directed at himself for blowing it the way he'd done. They'd both gone back to clean up the paint brushes and pots and she'd hardly spoken a word to him and soon after that, she'd gone off with a group of people who were choosing patterns for their re-enactment costumes.

When they'd dropped Catriona off, she said 'See you, Adam,' as if there was nothing wrong between them.

'There was all that talk about her,' Adam said.

'What talk?' his mother said.

'About her and those university students,' Adam answered.

'Oh yes, the infamous hi-jinks,' his father said with feigned outrage. He was certainly on Catriona's side now.

'It was nothing,' his mother said. 'A bit of harmless, teenage fun. A few old fuddy duddies got upset about it and phoned the police and Sergeant Balfour caught them in the act.'

'But what were they doing?' Adam said.

'Why don't you ask Catriona?' his mother turned around to look at him.

'I did but she cracked or something.' He let his unhappiness show.

'Oh, did she?' his mother laughed. 'Well, if you must know, they climbed the swimming pool fence and had a moonlight dip.' She drew in her breath. 'In the *nude*, of course.'

'Naughty,' said his father with mock severity. 'Can't have bare bottoms in Dunarling. I hope Sergeant Balfour gave them a *stern* lecture.'

'Oh, he did,' Adam's mother said. 'It seems they went to a movie and on the way home the other two girls talked Catriona into having a swim.'

'The other *girls*?' Adam said. 'But I thought they were blokes.'

'No dear,' his mother was patient with him. 'They were girls.'

☆   ☆   ☆

The dream was vivid now and more disturbing than usual. He could taste Catriona's lips and feel the clean sweet smell of her hair. What was wrong with him? He should have kissed her but she had to make the first move.

At the computer she'd put her hand on his shoulder and he couldn't even put out a finger towards her. He tossed and turned with his head full of confused thoughts. Then he imagined her under the moonlight, swimming naked and remembered the day of her birthday how he'd seen her standing at the mirror, not hurrying to put her shirt on.

'Seventeen-year-olds do make love,' she had said. 'They've got all the urges and the physical equipment.' His own equipment reminded him very firmly of that.

She'd asked him to write *To Catriona, with Love from Adam* in the book he'd given her.

'Is that what you want?' he had said.

'I think so,' she had replied and he knew that she meant it to be more than just writing in the flyleaf.

Catriona had taken his book to her bed and read of Tam Lin, the elfin lover and his earthly Janet. Even the lucky, wall-eyed teddy bear with the peace badge was where he wanted to be. There were so many other things she had said and done, so many messages she'd sent him, yet he was afraid to act on them.

The dream changed and he saw his mother in the station drinking a cup of tea but suddenly, the brown liquid began to dribble from the sides of her mouth and run down her white blouse and her expression changed to one of violent revulsion. Adam stood helplessly watching then he saw other people in the station drink from their cups and become ill.

He turned around and there was Catriona, unsmiling, with a cup which she lifted to her lips.

'No!' Adam said and reached out a hand to take it from her but she dismissed him curtly and drank.

'It's poisoned! The water's poisoned!' His agitation grew. 'Don't you know about the foulness?'

'*Adam*,' said a deep yet familiar voice. '*Dae ye no' ken this is the work o' Smeddum?*'

'Tam Dubh?' Adam recognised the voice and turned to find him but there was only the ring of slumped bodies of those who had already drunk the poisoned tea.

'*It is thou must stop him*,' Tam Dubh's voice said.

'Who am I to stop?'

'*Smeddum is at the place of the water, making mischief. Thou must gang there and put a stop to it. There was none to stop the foulness before but thou art here so get thee to the place of the water.*'

'The place of the water?'

'*This very instant. Smeddum is there to make mischief,*' Tam Dubh's voice said and faded, leaving Adam standing in the station. A darkly dressed woman with gaunt, weeping face came slowly forward, picking her way around and over the bodies. She held out her dead baby to him so that its head and pallid face hung down.

'Who?' she said. 'Who?'

'*Tam Dubh.*' Another voice came to him, a familiar voice, spiteful and filled with hate. '*Dae ye no' ken thy man is curset? He is curset wi' fire, he is curset wi' mischance and now he is curset wi' foulness.*'

The dream changed and Adam found himself outside his own house in the night and he was astride his bike and pedalling. He did not use the light on the machine yet in the darkness he picked his way with ease for he already knew the way; the whole class had been there just two days ago and on the way back downhill, the bus had crashed.

It was the place of the water and it was there he went in his dream.

Adam dropped the bike in some long grass and made his way towards the pump room while above him in the background, the white bulk of the overhead tank glowed in the pale moonlight. As he approached, he heard a metallic clang as somebody carried out some self-absorbed mission inside. It was when he pulled open the door he realised the lock had been forced; at the same instant, he knew this was no longer a dream.

The interior of the pump room was lit only by pale moonlight from the windows and somebody, a dark figure, bent over the pump worked with grim determination. There came another dull clang as a metal lid came off and the figure picked up a heavy metal drum and began pouring its contents into the suction end of the silent pump. Adam heard the viscous gloop, gloop of an oily liquid blurting out of the drum.

'*Smeddum—thou art making mischief.*' Adam was surprised at the voice that came from his own mouth.

The dark figure turned and screamed in fear. He dropped the drum of liquid which splashed a great gulp of its contents over the floor. Whoever it was grabbed up something heavy, a crowbar, and flung it across the room. Adam ducked and the crowbar clattered harmlessly against the wall somewhere behind him. The figure dashed away and blundered out of the door. A sharp chemical smell came to Adam's nostrils.

In the pump room, he searched for the light switch and flicked it on and blinked in the sudden fluorescent brilliance of the white painted interior of the place. He saw a silvery drum lying on its side with its dark liquid contents slowly surging out on the concrete floor and trailing away into a corner. The drum bore the words *Railway Works Department* stencilled on it.

Adam went over to the neat, blue painted pump and saw that whoever it was had swung the metal cover plate aside to reveal the filters at the suction end. Inside the space which should have been covered by the lid he saw the water had already turned a milky coffee colour from the dark liquid that had been poured inside.

Then Adam remembered something.

On the day of the senior class visit, Andy Gibson, the man from the council had shown them how the pump worked.

'It's automatic,' he had explained. 'Turns itself on four times a day. Six am, noon, six pm and midnight.' Adam looked sharply at the digital clock on the wall. It stood at a minute to midnight.

He went to the switchboard as he had seen Andy Gibson do it and cancelled the automatic switching gear. Then he set the drum upright and stood looking at the dark liquid which had now spread far across the floor. It was at that point he heard the car labouring up the hill.

'Tam Dubh!' he whispered. 'Help me.' But there was no help.

The door of the pump room opened and two policemen came in, followed by a man in overalls.

'Red handed,' said the senior policeman.

'I reckon,' said the other one. 'Vandalism, eh?'

'No, it's nothing like that.' Adam made a feeble protest.

'He's only poured white ant killer into the suction end,' said the man in overalls. 'Drink that, who knows how you'd end up.'

'It wasn't me,' Adam said. 'I came in here and found somebody pouring that stuff into the pump.'

'And you just happened to be passing?' the senior policeman said.

'You're the doctor's son.' The other policeman made it sound like an accusation. 'You bored rich kids, you oughta stick to glue sniffing or something. Didn't you know this place has a silent alarm?'

Adam lapsed into a sullen silence.

They took him down to the police station and telephoned for his father to come and collect him.

'There could be charges laid,' the duty sergeant said. 'Trespassing, interfering with council property, maybe more serious stuff once we check where the white ant killer came from, although I've got a pretty fair idea.'

'Enough to be going on with,' Adam's father said shortly. 'Come on, let's go home.'

His father walked ahead of him out to the Rover and they drove away from the police station in silence.

Chapter Seven

The queue for the dot matrix printer moved slowly and it was already late in the afternoon before Adam could begin a printout of his own work. By that time there was only one other person in the computer room, and she gathered her things and walked out with barely a word, leaving him on his own. To make matters worse, the ribbon on the machine was worn almost beyond its useful life so the printing was faint.

As it slowly issued in neat folds from the printer, Adam read the latest transcription of the diary of Ewart McColl.

Wednesday 26th May, 1886
Writing is difficult because our little ship is in such a tumult, yet I wish to record the truly awful majesty of the waves that hurl us this way and that. Poor old Dunarling *is at times plunged to the floor of the deepest valley, with walls of dark water so steep and sheer, the very wind is stolen from her sails. Moments later, the ship is hoisted upon high where her empty, wind robbed sails fill again with the sharpest of cracks.*

Then as far as the eye can see, there is nothing but peak upon peak of freezing iron grey waves with their caps whipped off to a whiteness and all of this accompanied by the banshee howling of the gale and hideous groans of protest from the ship's timbers. Down below, unless one has been sufficiently prudent as to make everything secure, any loose items hurl themselves about the cabin. Sleep is well nigh impossible and food, for those with the stomach for it, is always cold because it is difficult if not dangerous to kindle a fire in the galley stove.

Passengers, for their own safety, are confined below deck and bidden to keep out of the path of the sailors who are hard enough put to it to man the ship. Everything is damp, cold and sodden and the place reeks of sea water, mould and vomit.

The cause of our torment lies in a certain geographical feature: to maintain a fast passage, sailing ships are required to go where the wind blows. The shortest distance between our departure point from the Atlantic ocean and the South Australian coast is a straight line—which takes us down into southern latitudes where growling icebergs abound and the only creature who would savour such hellish conditions is either an albatross or a madman!

We are deep in the roaring forties.

☆   ☆   ☆

The session with *The Diary of Ewart MacColl, Esq.* only served to depress Adam even more. The account of the *Dunarling*, tossed on stormy waters seemed to match the tumult in his own life and as he read the printout he felt even more dejected. He was nagged by the worry of the police investigation into Saturday night's affair in the pump room. To make things worse, Sunday at home with his parents had been distinctly frosty with frequent bouts of questioning from his father and reproachful sighs and glances from his mother.

'What the devil were you doing there?' his father asked for the tenth time.

'I don't know,' Adam answered but all the same he wondered how he could explain what couldn't be explained.

'What do you mean you don't know? How could you not know? The police caught you red handed with twenty litres of white ant killer, pouring it into the water pump for God's sake!'

'Adam, dear,' his mother said. 'If you're sick or under strain with your school work you should tell us.'

'And it was stolen from the railway store,' his father went on. 'So how did you come by it?'

'No, Mum, it's nothing like that.' He tried to answer one parent at a time but the questions kept piling up until it became difficult to keep track of what answer to give to which parent.

'Well, what then?' It was his father again.

'What was the question?' Adam said.

'Don't be flippant!' his mother said.

He was on the point of telling her about his dreams and about Tam Dubh and the warnings or visions or whatever they were, but with his logical father there, glowering at him, he couldn't bring himself to do it. He shook his head and looked away.

There must be many an honest, God fearing Scots man and woman, sheltering below deck, fearing the worst and attending this day to their Bible and to all their neglected prayers! Who among them would not wish to be safely home in the arms of Auld Scotia instead of pitching and roiling in this God abandoned madhouse?

'There'll be charges, Jean,' Adam's father said. 'I can't see how we can avoid them. I might go over and see a solicitor.'

'The Vernons are away in Melbourne,' Adam's mother said.

'I wouldn't use Vernon anyway,' he said. The suggestion

had only seemed to anger Adam's father more. 'I can't stand the man.'

Adam packed up the diary and ejected his disk from the drive and went out to the bike shed.

As he came upon a group of people from his class, they unravelled from their tight little gossiping knot so he knew he'd been under discussion. Any thoughts of keeping Saturday night's business quiet had been dispelled during the Monday morning assembly—at least two of the boys in class had policemen fathers and the council worker had a daughter in a lower form.

He could have counted on some support from Catriona but she'd been away from school all day, which made him even more despondent for he'd wanted to mend things between them, if only he could think of the right words.

The single bright note was the absence of Richard Vernon and his red sports car. It was all over school he'd gone with his parents to Melbourne on Friday night to take in a couple of stage shows over the weekend. Big deal for Vernon but at least he wasn't around to sneer at Adam's brush with the law.

On the way home, Adam stopped at the museum to give Hamish Leckie the latest printout of the diary. Inside the main room, there were one or two late visitors, slowly walking around the exhibits, their feet ringing woodenly on the polished floor and their voices turned down to hushed whispers, as if talking aloud was forbidden in such an establishment.

Adam paused in front of Tam Dubh's display and leaned on the rail, staring at the tiny figure; he was surprised to see how pale the doll had become. There was no sparkle from the eye, just a listless, downcast face. A little lower in the mound of sand the other doll, Swith, lay in its coffin and by contrast it seemed to have become healthier in general appearance. Perhaps he imagined it but about its face there seemed to be a sparkle—a look of gleeful triumph. Adam shivered.

'Hello then.' Hamish Leckie came up behind him. 'You're admiring my work again?'

'Yeah, Hamish, it's great.' The ominous feeling passed and he handed over the printout.

Hamish thanked him and put the sheaf of papers under his arm then moved past Adam to the outer door of the museum where he briefly looked out into the street before closing one half of the double doors and sliding the top and bottom bolts into place with loud authoritative clicks. The visitors took his action as a signal and quickened their pace around the remaining exhibits then passed out through the other half of the door.

'Come again soon,' Hamish farewelled them pleasantly. 'Och yes, it needs more than half a day to see it properly. A lot of people are surprised at the things we have here. Yes, cheerio.' He closed the doors behind them, set the lock and snapped out the lights in the main room. He turned in the semi-darkness to face Adam.

'I'll read your transcript later, Adam,' he said. 'You must be almost finished with the whole diary, eh?'

'Yeah, nearly finished, Hamish, but I'd better be going home too,' Adam started to say.

'No, stay a wee while,' Hamish said. 'Surely there's time for a chat.' He walked in the direction of the office and collected Adam by the arm. 'I've been hearing things. You're in a bit of trouble, I gather.'

'Yeah, you could say that.'

'Anything I can do to help?'

'No, not really,' Adam said.

'Here, come in and tell me all about it.' They found chairs in Hamish's cluttered little office and Adam gave a rough outline of what had happened in the pump room; the dark figure who had run out and the arrival of the police with the man from the council.

'This dark figure,' Hamish said. 'Did you get a good look at him?'

'Not really. The light was pretty feeble and he was dressed in dark coloured gear, maybe jeans and a windcheater with a hood, something like that.'

'And you went in and saw him pouring the chemical into the pump?'

'Well, I didn't see him. I heard the noises and recognised them for what they were. It was only when I put the light on I could see what he'd been up to.'

'Now, this is the question that's been nagging me.' Hamish said. 'What prompted you to go there in the first place?'

'I can't really explain,' Adam said. 'It sounds sort of unreal. The fact is, I had this dream about poison in the water supply.'

'Was it like what happened on the ship?' Hamish asked. 'I've read your transcript of that part of the diary, by the way.'

'It was sort of like that,' Adam said. 'Only in the dream, people from town were drinking from tea cups.' He hesitated, not wanting to mention dreaming about Catriona. That part was strictly private. 'Then a voice told me to go to the place of the water.'

'The place of the water?' Hamish broke in. 'They're the words?'

'Yes. The voice said I would find Smeddum at the place of the water, making mischief.'

'Smeddum?'

'Yeah, that's what the voice said. Smeddum. I'm sure of it.'

Hamish leaned back in his chair and put his hands behind his head and in a faraway voice, began to quote a line of poetry.

'*O for some rank mercurial rozet, Or fell, red smeddum, I'd gie ye sic a hearty dose o't, Wad dress yer droddum!*'

He looked at Adam keenly and waited.

'I don't know that one,' Adam said.

'It's Burns, Robert Burns, from the poem *To a Louse*. Y'see, Burns was in church one Sunday morning and he saw a louse on a lady's bonnet. He was so amused by the impudence of the little pest he wrote a poem, *To a Louse*.'

'Yeah,' Adam said. He didn't see where all this was leading.

'So in his poem, Burns said if he had some *rank mercurial rozet or fell red smeddum*,' he paused at that word, 'he'd give the louse such a hearty dose of it, it would dress its droddum. In other words, it would settle its hash for good!'

'You said the word "smeddum"?' Adam said.

'It's the old Scots dialect word for insecticide, Adam. A kind of poison. Smeddum.'

'Yeah. That makes sense.'

'Do you not see a connection then?'

'What with?'

'Between the poisoned water supply on the ship and what happened at the pump room on Saturday night.'

'Two poisoned water supplies,' Adam said. 'Yes— I noticed that myself. It's been sort of bugging me.'

'And an attempted poisoning happens straight after we learn about the one on the *Dunarling*.' Hamish Leckie paused. 'Where a baby died because of it.'

'Yeah,' Adam said and remembered the woman in his dream, showing him the limp corpse of her infant.

'Bit of a coincidence,' Hamish said. 'Do you not think so?'

'What are you saying, Hamish?'

'I'm saying, you've been having all these dreams, Adam. Catriona told me. You've been working hard with the diary and perhaps you've become too much involved with it, you know, caught up with it, maybe even become a bit emotionally affected by it.'

'No!' Adam rose to his feet, almost shouting. 'I'm not

affected by it! I'm doing it in my spare time.'

'I think you should give it up, Adam. Don't do any more of the diary. Not for a while anyway.'

'No. What are you saying? Are you saying *I* poisoned the water supply? You think I got the idea from the diary and did a crazy thing like that?'

'I don't know what to think, Adam, but I don't want to be responsible for you getting into any more trouble.'

'I didn't do it!' Adam said. 'There was someone else there. He did it, not me!'

'It's too far fetched, Adam. All this talk of a dark figure and voices telling you to go to the pump.'

Adam almost ran to the outer door of the museum and undid the lock.

'I don't want to hear any more of this,' he said. 'Surely you can believe me? There was someone else in the pump room.'

'Was he dressed as a sailor?' Hamish Leckie gently followed Adam to the door. He turned and pointed to a shadowy corner of the room where a tailor's dummy stood, wearing the dark gear of a nineteenth century sailor. 'Was he dressed like him?'

Adam stopped with his hand on the door.

'How do you know about that?'

'I heard about the sailor who appeared on the bus,' Hamish said. 'A lot of your friends saw him take over and crash into the side of the road.'

'He didn't crash the bus!' Adam almost screamed in his frustration. 'He saved everyone's life!'

'Come on, Adam, how do you know that?'

'There wasn't any sailor, it was me! I did it. The voice told me to do it so I took over the steering wheel and turned the bus into the roadside!'

'That's what I thought, Adam,' Hamish Leckie said gently. 'First the bus and now the water. Why not give me the diary? I see you've got it there.' He held out his hand.

'No!' Adam slammed the door and ran outside to his bike.

☆   ☆   ☆

In his own room, he lay face down on the bed and fought back tears. He'd always regarded Hamish Leckie as an ally, now here he was accusing him of being mad or criminally insane or something.

He'd arrived home and gone straight upstairs. His father was attending a meeting of the Railway Historical Society and had phoned to say he'd be late home. Adam made an excuse and left his mother eating alone in the dining-room.

Lying on his bed, he punched the ends of his pillow and buried his face deep in the soft valley he'd created and thought of Catriona. She had hurt him too; she'd dobbed him in, that was plain. She'd told Leckie about his dreams. Anyway, sod her! She could get stuffed with all the rest of them. She was just the same as the others and not worth the effort. In a way he was glad he'd said that about the university students because it brought her down a peg or two.

And Leckie—what a friend he turned out to be! How long had he been thinking that stuff about him?

The diary was in his school bag so he pulled it out and opened it where he had marked his place with a slip of paper. He turned over on the bed and began to read the familiar handwriting that was calm and rational and some-how well ordered, even soothing.

Monday 7th June, 1886
We have had yet another distraction aboard our small, sea borne community! The weather remains rough and windy but there is turbulence of another kind. Mr Colquhoun has gone completely insane!

He came upon deck this morning screaming and ranting

that his Bible said the ship was cursed by four demons and he begged the captain to turn back to Scotland before we all perish.

Poor fellow, he even set about untying one of the ropes that held a sail, as if this puny act by itself would bring about his wishes. Then he rushed about in a frenzy, clutching at whoever was in his path, begging them to turn the ship around.

Some sailors tried to reason with him but this only made things worse and eventually the surgeon was sent for and ordered Mr Colquhoun to be confined in a special room of the hospital where he was tied with soft ropes lest he injure himself.

Oh, it was piteous! For the rest of the day, we could hear him calling out while his daughter sat by the window of his Bedlam and tried to pacify him but the sight of her sweet, concerned face only made him more distracted than ever until at last, some kindly women friends coaxed her away.

I noticed the young sailor, Ramsay, was dawdling nearby, obviously wanting to comfort the girl but he was still not assured of his position with her. As the women took the distressed girl to their quarters, Ramsay caught my eye and the look on his face told me everything of his feelings for her.

'Adam, dear.' It was his mother, bearing a tray with warm milk and some toasted sandwiches.

'Oh, hello, Mum.' He rolled to one side to let his mother sit on the edge of the bed.

'Now, what's your beef, big boy?' she set the tray down on the desk and offered him a sandwich from the plate.

'Things are just getting on top of me,' he said. 'The business with the police on Saturday and the way Dad went on.'

'You can't really blame him, Adam. He's worried and

upset about what's going to happen if the police press charges.'

'But Mum, I'm innocent!' he said.

'Innocent? It's not a word I imagined my son would ever need to use,' she said. 'Here, eat and drink. Doctor's orders.' She put the glass of warm milk on the edge of the desk. Adam sighed and started eating.

'Even Catriona's let me down,' he said between mouthfuls. 'Told Hamish Leckie I've become emotionally affected by the diary.' His mother moved the glass of warm milk closer.

'Very thoughtful of her,' she said. 'It must be some diary.' She took it from him and read the next entry aloud.

Tuesday 8th June, 1886
The weather is still snell and windy and the seas are rough.

I'm afraid that poor fellow, Mr Colquhoun's, condition has not improved but he is just one of many who have suffered some kind of injury during this voyage.

Crewmen and passengers alike have endured broken limbs and so cold has it become, some of the sailors even suffer from frostbitten fingers after they have been aloft attending to the sails!

At dinner in the evening, the captain explained that madness at sea, such as afflicted Mr Colquhoun, was not a rare occurrence and the poor fellow would be well looked after once we landed. The surgeon stated that it was often a temporary disorder, sometimes brought about by the stress of turbulent weather and his condition would probably ease once we made a landfall.

Mr Colquhoun apparently has demanded all his boxes be brought up out of the baggage hold because he is certain there are demons contained therein of which he is anxious to rid himself. To pacify the man, the captain bid some sailors fetch the boxes as requested.

'It's very dramatic stuff, Adam,' his mother said and passed the glass of warm milk to him. He drank as his mother continued to read.

In the evening, the surgeon administered laudanum. Mr Colquhoun's frenzy gradually lessened until sleep brought a merciful release.

'It's nearly finished now,' Adam said. 'Then I'll let you see the whole transcript. There's all sorts of stuff we didn't know.'

'And you've been having weird dreams about it?'

'Well, yes.'

'Sleep's what you need. So drink the rest of your milk while it's hot then get into bed properly.' As his mother left the bedroom she turned out the main light. Adam got up unsteadily and undressed then got into bed. His eyes were heavy but he took up the diary and read the final entry on the page.

Wednesday 9th June, 1886
Weather as before. Gale, high seas running.

Miss Colquhoun lingers daily by the hospital window, keen to be with her father but the surgeon will not let her remain in the room with him. She sits by the hour under the shelter of a piece of canvas, her face bleak and drawn.

There is talk that young Ramsay plans to desert the ship to be with Miss Colquhoun and they are now meeting more openly, heedless of the comments of others.

Young Ramsay's love and concern shines from his eyes.

Someone was bending over him and he looked up into her face which swam in and out of focus.

'Catriona,' he said. 'I'm sorry I said all that. I really love you.'

'Shh, darling,' said his mother and kissed his forehead. She took the diary away from him and turned off the bedside light.

☆ ☆ ☆

The school secretary came into the classroom and tapped her way on high heel shoes across the parquet floor, conscious of the youthful male eyes that swivelled after her. She whispered briefly to Ms Mullins then turned and swayed out of the room again.

'Cor!' said a voice and another boy suppressed a titter. Ms Mullins frowned.

'You're like a row of those mechanical clowns at the Easter Show,' she said and demonstrated by opening her mouth and moving her head from side to side with a vacant look in her eyes. A couple of girls laughed outright. 'Anyway, Hardy. To the principal's office. Right away!'

There was a general stir of interest as Adam rose in front of the entire class and made for the door.

'And enough of the conjecture,' Ms Mullins said to the others. 'It's none of your business so get on with what you're doing.'

Catriona was one who took longer than most to turn her eyes down to her work. She was still looking as Adam closed the classroom door after him.

Sergeant Balfour was in the office with a woman police constable.

'Adam Hardy,' the sergeant said. 'I'd like a word if you don't mind.'

'If it's about Saturday night,' Adam began. 'I think maybe my father should be here.'

'No, no, no, it's not about Saturday night,' Sergeant Balfour assured him. 'It's a routine enquiry into the bus accident. We've spoken with most of the others but not with you.'

'Oh,' Adam said. Mr Grant the Deputy Principal hovered nearby, viewing the proceedings with some disfavour. Adam imagined it was because he was forced to stay out of it.

'You're the one who gave Laurie Sinclair mouth to mouth resuscitation,' the sergeant began.

'Catriona Chisholm did it too,' Adam said. 'I mean, we took turns but Laurie didn't really need all that much.'

'Even so, it was a pretty smart thing to do,' Sergeant Balfour went on. 'So it doesn't figure, does it?'

'What doesn't?' Adam said.

'You don't give a stricken man mouth to mouth then five minutes later try to poison half the town!'

'I thought you weren't going to talk about Saturday night.'

'Sorry, it just slipped out,' the sergeant said easily and the woman police constable smiled and the tension slipped away. At that moment Adam felt better than he had for days. He took a great relieved lungful of free air.

'You might as well know it,' he said. 'I felt the bus was going out of control so I went along and took over and turned it into the ditch at the side of the road.'

'That's what I was coming to,' Sergeant Balfour said. 'According to Laurie, he pumped the brakes but they didn't work. That's what brought on his attack, he says. Nothing to do with smoking forty ciggies a day. So we checked out the front hydraulic brake lines on the bus and we found they'd been cut half way through with some sort of fine serrated instrument. By the time the bus got moving, most of the brake fluid had already dripped out. A couple of pumps from old Laurie and the brakes were useless.'

'I had nothing to do with that!' Adam flushed red.

'I know,' Sergeant Balfour said. 'Your girlfriend, Catriona Chisholm, says she had her eye on you constantly and you never left the pump room.'

Did she, Adam thought. He wished he'd known *that* at the time.

'One or two of your mates also verify that fact, as does Ms Mullins,' Sergeant Balfour went on. 'So I agree with you, young Hardy; you had nothing to do with setting up the bus crash.'

Adam stayed silent and waited.

'For what it's worth, I don't think you had anything to do with the business on Saturday night,' the sergeant went on. 'In fact, I'm sure of it.'

'How do you know that?'

'We've got our methods,' Sergeant Balfour tapped the side of his nose. 'Fingerprints. There were some nice clean prints on the drum of chemicals and they didn't match the ones we found on your bike which we checked before we brought it back to you on Sunday. We also found footprints outside the pump room with traces of chemical in them and both of your shoes were pretty clean. You didn't get a spot of the stuff on you so, as you said, there must have been someone else in there.'

'What about the idea that I was with whoever did it?' Adam said. 'You know, one of your policemen said we were working together.'

'So why did you put the lights on?' Sergeant Balfour said. 'And why did you turn off the pump at the switchboard? And why did your so-called "accomplice" chuck a crowbar at you? It made a mark on the wall just by the door.'

Adam bit his lip. An even greater surge of relief flooded through him.

'Is that all then?' he said.

'No, it's not,' Sergeant Balfour said. 'We've had two near disasters in this town and somehow, young Hardy, you've averted both of them. Had you not taken over the bus, it would have gone off the road on the other side and it would have rolled at least three times before dropping about seventeen metres into a gully. There would have been deaths for sure.'

The woman police constable shifted her weight from one foot to the other.

'Had that pump operated with the chemical inside it,' the sergeant continued. 'Well, there's no need to dwell on it. But the thing is, just how are you involved in both incidents?'

'I don't know,' Adam said.

'I'm Australian,' Sergeant Balfour said after a long pause. 'My mother was Scottish and so was my father. Immigrants, see, came out in the early fifties. Dad used to tell me tales about *his* mother, my old Scottish Granny. Never met her myself but Dad said she was what the Scots call "fey".' He paused again. 'She was able to see deaths of other people before they happened and she correctly forecast her own death when it was her turn to go. Is that what it is with you, young Hardy, a touch of feyness? Are you able to see things?'

'I just did it,' Adam said. 'That's all. I've no idea what made me do what I did.'

'And this old fashioned sailor on the bus,' Sergeant Balfour went on. 'What was that? Mass hallucination?'

'I don't know,' Adam said.

☆　　☆　　☆

After school, he cycled home with Catriona and when they passed the museum, she wanted to stop and deliver the latest transcripts of her work to Hamish Leckie.

'Come on in with me, Adam,' she said.

'No!' he resisted fiercely. 'And you shouldn't go in either.'

'Hey, come on, what's wrong?'

'Nothing,' he sounded lame and embarrassed and

dropped his voice to a mumble. 'Just can't be bothered, that's all.'

'Well, wait for me, then.'

She gave him her bike to hold upright and took the transcripts from her bag and went inside. In a few minutes she came back and smiled when she saw the anxious look on Adam's face.

'He didn't lay a finger on me,' she assured him. 'Honest.' Catriona mounted her bike and pushed off and Adam followed a few metres behind until she turned and slowed to let him catch up with her. 'You know, the thing I love about you, Adam Hardy, is you're so cheerful. You tell me you just got off the hook with the cops and now you're nearly tripping over your long face.'

'Yeah, it's been a rotten two or three days,' he said. 'Got me down a bit.'

'Come on then, let's celebrate,' she said. 'I'll take you to David Riccio's and cheer you up with a milkshake. Okay?'

He smiled at last and said okay.

They lingered over their milkshakes and Catriona told him a couple of jokes she had heard. She had to put her head close to his and keep her voice low because they weren't the kind of joke you told to just anybody. Adam laughed at the punch lines but didn't risk telling any of his own because the only ones he knew were a bit less sophisticated.

He wondered idly where you got good jokes to tell a girl.

David Riccio himself came to mop up their table and somehow let them know they had sat long enough for the price of a couple of milkshakes.

Adam went home with Catriona and waited until she'd gone safely inside the shop then turned and cycled off into the growing darkness.

The night air turned chilly so he cycled faster.

☆   ☆   ☆

Both of his parents had already heard the news from Sergeant Balfour. His mother hugged him but his father just nodded briefly.

'All the same, Adam,' he was still containing himself on the edge of anger, 'I still don't know why you went up to the pump room in the first place.'

'Yes, Gordon dear,' Adam's mother said. 'And right at this moment we're not going to enquire into it too deeply. I've had a bitch of a day and it would be nice to relax. Now, Adam, dinner'll be another half hour. We're having a sherry while we watch the news, then we eat.'

'I've got some notes to sort out,' Adam said. 'Might do that first then come down.'

He went up to his room with his ears burning. What was with the guy? Why couldn't he just say terrific or say he was pleased he was off the hook or something?

Adam briefly reflected that his father was the reason he'd given up active interest in sports as soon as he could. There always seemed to be some imperfection to take the shine off any of his achievements. All the time there was someone with a more spectacular goal or another player who'd made a more difficult catch.

It got so Adam didn't bother reporting his own results after a game and then he started missing practice sessions and the sports teacher soon dropped him from the teams. When his father found out he just said it was typical and left it at that.

With the half hour up, Adam padded softly down to the dining-room. The television was still on in the lounge so he wandered in to catch the promos for the evening shows. His parents were talking over the newsreader and Adam paused at the door and heard the end of their conversation.

'And why was your day such a bitch?' he heard his father say. The television news was over so it was time to talk.

'Oh, I was called out to an absolutely *wrenching* case,' his mother answered. 'Suicide attempt. A boy. Took about every single pill in the bathroom cabinet.'

'Successful?' his father asked.

'I think *I* was,' his mother said shortly. 'Managed to pump him out and get him to hospital where he's under twenty-four hour observation. Poor kid's an absolute wreck. A pathetic and frightful mess.'

'Is that a medical diagnosis?'

'No, it's how he is, how he looks. He's haggard, withdrawn and absolutely terrified. I think kids these days get into occult books or something, you know, demonology or witchcraft or whatever it is, anyway, there was this poor sod backed into the darkest corner of his bedroom with the bedsheet pulled up to his face, absolutely screaming that his master was coming for him, his master was *angry* with him.'

'*Who* was angry with him?'

'His master,' Adam's mother repeated and took a sip of her sherry. 'The boy said his master was out in the garage and had told him to destroy himself for he had failed and was of no further use.'

'Charming,' Adam's father said.

'It wasn't a charming sight, I can assure you. The boy's mother was almost demented and we both had to struggle to try to calm him down and he's a big lad.'

'I suppose he's on drugs. Hallucinogens at least.'

'No, nothing like that,' Adam's mother said. 'Doesn't even smoke. Clean living type I believe. Likes sport, mad keen on tennis, a bit stupid, a bit gullible, easily led and all of a sudden, this happens. It was actually quite frightening.'

'In what way?'

Adam heard his mother shiver briefly before replying.

'The way he kept pointing behind us to the open door of his bedroom, as if he could see something out there that we couldn't.'

'Mmm, nasty case,' Adam's father sympathised. 'And what's his name, this boy?'

'I think Adam knows him,' his mother said. 'It's Michael Carter.'

Adam left his parents and went silently up to his room. He had remembered an entry in the diary and wanted to read it again just to be sure.

'Do you not see a connection, Adam?' Hamish Leckie had said. A connection between the poisoned water on the ship and what took place on Saturday night. There was a connection, yes.

But Adam had found another one. He took the diary out and read the entry.

Thursday 10th June, 1886
We have just learned that another sailor has been swept overboard and lost in the tempest. He was the Gaelic speaking seaman who put poison in the water tank.

He had been watched around the clock but in the heavy weather his companions were somewhat less than vigilant and it seems the man escaped from hospital and took his own life.

Suddenly, Adam didn't feel like eating dinner.

Chapter Eight

Adam's mother finished stitching the second last button to her Railway Re-enactment costume then held it out at arm's length to consider the effect. It was a rich dress made of purple and mauve material.

'Adam, have you made up your mind what you're wearing?' she said. 'Time's getting on.'

'Haven't thought about it,' he said.

'You could always hire a costume.' She started on the last button.

'Yeah, only I don't know what to go as.'

'What's Catriona wearing?'

'Don't know,' he answered. 'She's going as a young lady with a straw hat, I think.'

The telephone rang in the lounge room and Adam's mother put down her sewing and picked up the handset.

'Hello, Catriona,' Adam heard her say. 'Speak of the devil, and have you recovered from last Saturday? Well, yes, Gordon would love you to come again. He's not home tonight or he'd tell you himself but he really appreciated the work you did.' Adam was already hovering by the side of her chair and raised an eyebrow but his mother fended him off with her free hand. 'Yes, fine. Next Saturday's the last work-bee before the big event, we'll pick you up. And I suppose you really want to speak with Adam. He's here.'

Adam took the handset and made a face as if to suggest the conversation could be private. His mother briefly pretended not to understand then went out to the kitchen.

'Hello, Catriona,' he said when he was alone.

'Hi,' she answered and was breathless. 'Look, can you come over, Adam?' There was an edge of concern in her voice. 'I mean, now?'

It was half-past-nine at night and Adam was about to raise a protest but he hesitated for the merest second, remembering that caustic remark she had once made on the telephone.

'Yes,' he made up his mind. 'I can be there. Fifteen minutes, okay?'

'Yes, it's really important, Adam, so hurry and bring the diary transcript. All of it. I've got something to show you.' Catriona hung up as his mother came back into the lounge room.

'I've put the kettle on for coffee, Adam dear, but it's your turn to make it.'

'Look Mum,' he said. 'I've got to go out—to see Catriona.'

'Oh yes?' she glanced briefly at the clock. 'Important is it?'

He nodded. His mother took up her sewing again.

'Well, be careful,' she bit a thread off with her teeth, 'on the road. Make sure there are lights on your bike.'

'The lights are okay, Mum. I'll be back in an hour.'

Catriona was waiting at the door of the souvenir shop and instead of allowing Adam to waste time fussing with chain and lock, she let him bring the bike inside then led the way upstairs to the living room.

'Barbara's out,' she said and paused before adding: 'With

a friend.' From the way she spoke, Adam sensed an air of disapproval over Barbara's choice of companion, but he let it go. This wasn't why she'd asked him to come. Catriona pulled out a chair for him and he sat and put the folder containing the diary transcript on the table.

'What have you got?' he said.

'Back in a second,' she whispered. 'Stay there.'

Catriona went across the hallway into her bedroom leaving him to wonder what she was up to. When she returned to the living room, she walked slowly and carried, like an offering in her outstretched hands, Adam Colquhoun's family Bible.

'Don't know why I was reading this, but I was.' She placed the Bible on the table in front of him and opened the pages so he could read it. 'It's in the Old Testament.' There was half a blank page at the end of the second chapter of *Kings* and in that area of whiteness she showed him a message, faintly pencilled.

The writing was crude and executed with almost childlike simplicity; the letters were uneven but the words were clear enough:

> *Four Demons I send wi' ye,*
> *Adam Colquhoun.*
> *Bleeze, Mischance and Foulness,*
> *then All Fa' Doon.*

Adam looked up at Catriona, who stood with hands on hips keenly watching him. All sorts of thoughts raced through his mind. She opened Adam's folder and searched the pages of the transcript and found the entry in *The Diary of Ewart MacColl, Esq*.

'Read this bit,' she pointed with her finger. 'It's about Adam Colquhoun.'

He came upon deck this morning screaming and ranting that his Bible said the ship was cursed by four demons and he begged the captain to turn back to Scotland before we all perish.

'So *this* must have been what he read in the Bible,' Adam said. 'It wasn't the *text*; it was this message.' He read the words again: *Four Demons I send wi' ye , Adam Colquhoun*. 'Finding that would be enough to make anyone go mad.'

'Just imagine him in all that wild weather,' Catriona shook her head in disbelief. 'Sheltering below decks, scared out of his wits, reading his Bible for comfort; then he finds that! I mean, look how he reacted.' She found the next entry:

. . . Poor fellow, he even set about untying one of the ropes that held a sail, as if this puny act by itself would bring about his wishes. Then he rushed about in a frenzy, clutching at whoever was in his path, begging them to turn the ship around.

'Four demons,' Adam said and marked the entry with a highlighter pen. 'Bleeze, Mischance and Foulness, but what does 'bleeze' mean?'

'It's in our book of ballads.' Catriona went to the bookshelf and pulled out the birthday present Adam had given her. She flicked the pages until she found the glossary and showed him the word simply meant blaze or flame.

'I should have guessed that,' Adam said. 'They had a fire on the *Dunarling*. In one of the holds, early in the voyage, a bleeze.'

'And they had mischance,' Catriona added. 'The business with the mizzen mast, and they had foulness—the poison in the water tank.' She stood looking down at him, counting off the events on her fingers. There were tears in her eyes and Adam felt he ought to hold her but he wasn't sure.

'They were all deliberate acts,' he said. 'A sailor cut the cables with a hacksaw and another one put poison in the water tank.'

'What about the fire?' she sniffed. 'Was that deliberate?' She turned to the part of the diary that described the aftermath of the blaze on the *Dunarling*. A tear fell on the page.

. . . One crewman, by name Buchanan, received severe burns on his forearms so he was given light duties and an extra ration of rum. This morning, I saw him on deck bandaged to the elbows, staring at the hold where the fire had been. On his face he had a strange, puzzled expression as if he were trying to make sense of what had happened in that place.

'All right, so why was he going on like that?' Catriona had recovered her composure. 'Did he have something to do with the fire? Was it guilty conscience, or had he just come out of a trance?'

'Or had he been possessed?' Already, another connection was forming in Adam's mind. He leafed through the transcript of the diary, searching for something he had read. At last, he marked another entry with the highlighter and together they leaned over the table and read the words:

. . . Mr Colquhoun apparently has demanded all his boxes be brought up out of the baggage hold because he is certain four demons are contained therein of which he is anxious to rid himself. To pacify the man, the captain bid some sailors fetch the boxes as requested.

Catriona's voice dropped almost to a whisper: 'Four demons. There's the proof written in the Bible and in the diary. And we found five little mandrake men in coffins and we know there's all that superstitious belief surrounding them, all that demonology and witchcraft; bought and sold for evil motives, to bring about revenge.' She paused and shivered. '*They* were Adam Colquhoun's four demons!'

Since he'd begun working on the diary, it had been staring Adam in the face. Bleeze, Mischance and Foulness had happened on the *Dunarling*; in the same order, similar events had occured in town. First a series of fires, deliberately lit then the incident on the school bus which had been no accident and most recently, the attempt to put poison in the water pump.

'It's like Adam Colquhoun's demons were at their business again,' he said. 'Only this time they're working on the town—the other Dunarling.'

'And at the end of that voyage,' Catriona said. 'The last thing: *All Fa' Doon*.'

'All fall down,' Adam repeated the words and his throat was dry. 'Four demons, four events. And the last one took the whole ship.'

'Adam, this is dynamite!' She shook her head. 'You know, it's weird, it's uncanny!'

'But the dolls couldn't have done all that stuff,' he said. 'It's crazy. I mean, they're only just bits of mandrake root.'

'No, the dolls don't do things for themselves,' she said. 'But what if they got other people to do their work? What if they were able to possess people—sailors on the ship, for example?'

'Yeah, that makes sense,' he agreed. 'I mean, three events happened on the ship and the diary gives three different descriptions of what sailors did—you know, how they behaved before and afterwards.'

Catriona flicked over the pages of the transcript and read an entry briefly.

'Look at this one,' she pointed. 'It's the bit about poisoning the water tank.' The ribbon in the dot matrix printer had been well worn and the printing on the transcript was faint. Adam bent over to read it with her.

. . . Attention soon fell upon one particular individual, a Gaelic speaking seaman from the Western Islands. His shipmates reported that his behaviour had undergone a sudden change in that he had recently started acting in a suspicious manner. Normally of a cheerful and talkative disposition, of late he had become moody, withdrawn and kept to himself.

'There's evidence,' Catriona said and read on.

. . . When they searched his possessions, which the captain was obliged to do, they found some of the man's clothing had been stained and Mr McWalter confirmed that it had been caused by the arsenic. Indeed, so liberally and heedlessly was it applied to the garments the man's skin was also found to be blackened by the substance, yet the poor wretch had not complained nor had he sought treatment of it.

He was transferred to the male hospital and put under the charge of two of his shipmates who took it in turn to watch over him for fear he would do further mischief either to himself or to the ship.

'It's as if he hadn't cared about being found out,' Adam highlighted the entries and straightened up and folded his arms as he looked down at the pages.

'Or about himself,' Catriona added. 'He was possessed, Adam. He wasn't in control of his own body or his own mind.' She pointed to the next entry:

. . . It is a sad case and no one has been able to account for such irrational behaviour. For a man to poison the very water supply which he himself must drink is strange indeed.

'There's another entry about this guy.' Now almost in a fever, Adam turned the pages and traced down each one with a finger then stopped. 'This happened much later in the voyage, Catriona. Read this bit.'

. . . We have just learned that another sailor has been swept overboard and lost in the tempest. He was the Gaelic speaking seaman who put poison in the water tank.

Catriona looked up and saw Adam was agitated.

. . . He had been watched around the clock but in the heavy weather his companions were somewhat less than vigilant and it seems the man escaped from hospital and took his own life.

'And the same thing happened to the other two,' Catriona said. 'The one who was suspected of cutting the cable and the one who got burned in the fire.' She took more than a minute to find the entry then she turned the pages around so Adam could read the words.

. . . The sailor McDermott was apparently lost by his own hands. Another who died in this way was Buchanan, the hero of the fire. One morning, he was not found to be in the hospital where he should have been, whereupon the ship was searched stem to stern, ending with the conclusion he had either fallen to his death in the night or he had jumped, there is no way of knowing.

'But we know,' Catriona said. 'We know.'

'All that stuff's been really bugging me,' Adam said and stood up and walked away from the table to stare at the bookshelf. 'I read the whole thing the other night and it's been getting to me. Ever since . . .' He paused. 'Ever since . . .'

'Ever since what, Adam?'

'Ever since. That's all.' He continued to stare at the books on the shelf.

'Come on, Adam.' She went to him and gently put her hand on his arm. 'Ever since what?' She waited patiently until he spoke again.

'At home,' he began. 'Mum and Dad sometimes talk about things, you know, about their work; medical cases. Sometimes they talk in front of me and other times, I just sort of overhear.'

'They talk about people's illnesses and things?'

'Yeah, injuries, operations and how patients respond to treatment, only they don't use names. I'm pretty used to it so it's no big deal. They even discuss gory bits at meal times.' He turned to her and made a wry face. 'Operations and stuff.'

'So what's bugging you?'

'There's a sort of rule,' Adam went on. 'Mum spoke to me once about it. The rule is, I don't talk about anything I hear—you know—outside the house, I don't talk about anything.'

'Fair enough.' Catriona was mystified.

'And I keep that rule,' Adam said doggedly. 'I keep it.'

'Yes, but what's it got to do with—'

'But I'm going to break it,' he went on seriously. 'With you, Catriona. I'm going to break that rule and tell you something I heard my parents talk about.' He turned away from her and looked at the bookshelf again.

'All right, Adam.' She went to the table and sat down with her back to him as if to make it easier for him to betray confidences. 'I won't pass it on if that's what you're thinking.'

Still gazing fixedly at the books, he quickly recounted the main facts of what he'd overheard about Mike Carter's suicide attempt. He spared Catriona none of the details.

'Mike's in hospital,' he said at last. 'They've got him

under twenty-four hour observation. A pathetic and frightful mess—that's how Mum described him.' He took a deep
breath before going on. 'He's like that sailor who poisoned
the water on the ship. His mates watched him around the
clock but he still managed to do it in the end, didn't he? So
did the other two. They were all *made* to do it—their
master *ordered* them. He took possession of them from start
to finish—poor sods, they didn't stand a chance. Do this
job for me, then destroy yourself. Simple as that.'

'Mike talked about his master,' Catriona said. 'Adam,
who is the master?'

'He's in Mike's garage. I'm sure of it.'

'The mandrake dolls,' Catriona said. 'He didn't throw
them into the sea after all.'

'No—the dolls had a job for him. Just as they did on
the ship.'

'And now it's done.' She turned to look at Adam.
'Bleeze, mischance and foulness.'

'Yeah,' Adam said. 'The first three. Then all fall down.'

Catriona's face slowly drained of colour.

They sat staring miserably at the pages of the transcript
then Catriona picked up the highlighter and went through,
marking off the passages they had read.

'Adam, don't go home yet,' she pleaded when she'd
finished. 'Stay with me.'

'Yeah, okay,' he answered. 'That's cool, I'll wait till
Barbara gets back.'

'She won't be long. I think they only went to a movie.'

They made coffee and sat drinking it. Catriona put on a
record but neither of them was in the mood for that so she
took it off again and they had more coffee.

'Adam, this is too much for us,' she said. 'I mean—it's
unreal, it's supernatural or something.'

'Yeah, but who do we tell? Who's going to believe us?
Who'd believe *me*? Especially after that business with

the water pump. I only got out of that with the skin of my teeth.'

'We've got the diary, and the message in the Bible,' she said. 'That's proof so we could tell Hamish Leckie. He'd help.'

'No, not him!' Adam spoke sharply. 'He already thinks I'm crazy or something. Thinks I've been emotionally affected by the diary. I don't want to talk to him, not yet anyway.'

'But he's studied these things. He knows about them.'

'But he turned on me,' Adam said. 'So not him, eh.'

'Okay, well who then?'

'I don't know.'

'We could go to Mike Carter's house,' Catriona said.

'What for?'

'Get the dolls and burn them—or something,' she said and shrugged helplessly. 'I mean, we saw Mike and Richard take the other four dolls from the cave and Hamish Leckie only got one of them back from Richard—so it stands to reason Mike's got all the others. If we got them back and destroyed them then that'd be the end of it.'

'How do we get inside Mike's house?' Adam said. 'And besides, if we go there and we're caught, what'll my parents say? I mean, they'll know I found out about Mike from them. I couldn't take that, not on top of all that other stuff last Saturday night. It'd be curtains!'

'I don't mean we break and enter,' she sounded scornful. 'Nothing criminal.'

'Well, what then?'

'We'll have to think of something intelligent,' she said. 'Leave that to me.'

'Oh, thanks,' Adam said and Catriona smiled for the first time.

Downstairs there was a click as the front door opened and they heard Barbara's sudden laughter.

'Oh, someone's here,' Adam heard her say. 'A visitor, with a bicycle no less.'

They heard a man's rumbling laugh then footsteps mounted the stairs.

'Only us, darling,' Barbara knocked lightly on the living room door. She came into the room followed by a man dressed in a tweed sports coat and slacks. It was Sergeant Balfour.

'Hello, you two,' he said easily. 'Homework, is it?'

Barbara went over and kissed Catriona lightly on the forehead and gave her a hug.

'How was the picture?' Catriona asked with a formal edge to her voice.

'Oh, pretty so-so,' Barbara said airily. 'But the *company* was nice.' She was playing with her daughter. 'You both know Sergeant Balfour?'

'Tom,' said Sergeant Balfour. 'Yep, we've all met, at one time or another.' He turned to the pages of the transcript spread out on the table. 'And what are you working on, Adam?'

'Transcribing an old diary,' Adam explained. 'Off the *Dunarling*. Incidents on the voyage and stuff like that.'

'I read a bit of it in the paper,' Sergeant Balfour said and took up a sheet of the transcript.

Adam turned to catch Catriona's eye. Was Tom Balfour the answer? Should they confide in him?

After all, Sergeant Balfour was the one who seemed closest to understanding; earlier, he himself had brought up the fey allusion so maybe he'd be receptive to the idea of demons and curses and all the dark, old unmeasurable powers. Maybe he'd know more about those glowering relics out of Scotland and he'd give Adam and Catriona a patient hearing and even have an answer for them. If anyone knew anything about it, he'd be the one.

Barbara shook the electric jug to make sure it had water

in it then switched it on and got out two coffee mugs while
Tom Balfour picked up another sheet of the transcript and
began to read some of the diary entries. Behind his back,
Adam caught Catriona's eye and nodded slightly in Tom's
direction and raised one eyebrow. He tried to read an
answer in her eyes but at the far end of the table, she
gathered the family Bible to her and closed it firmly,
slightly shaking her head. So that decided the matter.

She yawned aloud and touched the back of her hand to
her mouth.

'Oh dear,' Barbara looked up from the coffee mugs and
caught her daughter's movement and laughed. 'There's
body language for you, Adam.'

'Yeah,' he smiled. 'I must go home anyway. School
tomorrow.'

Sergeant Balfour was still intent upon the diary and he
raised his head.

'Can I hang on to this for a while?' he said. 'Looks like
good reading.'

'Yes, why not?' Barbara said. 'I'd like to read it too, if
that's all right, Adam?'

'Oh, yeah,' he said. 'I'll pick it up later. It's all on
disc anyway.'

Without a word, Catriona gathered the Bible into her
arms and stood up and went to her bedroom. Moments later,
she reappeared at the door of the living room and beckoned
to Adam with her eyes.

'I'll see you out,' she said.

Downstairs at the open front door he hesitated, tinkering
with his bike to eke out the moment.

'I think Tom Balfour would be all right,' he decided.
'I mean, he'd understand, wouldn't he?'

'Oh, it's "Tom" now.' The cool edge was back. 'Very
matey all of a sudden.'

'Don't you like him?'

'Depends on how you see the situation,' she answered. 'As a cop I suppose he's very efficient.'

'You're a bit cool all of a sudden.'

'Am I?'

'Yeah, what's Balfour ever done to you?' Then the penny dropped. 'Oh, I get it; he's the one who caught you!'

'What do you mean?'

'In the swimming pool.'

'Oh, really! Goodnight!' Catriona dismissed him and started to close the door. Adam smiled and mounted his bike and pushed off from the kerb. He switched on his headlight.

'Goodnight,' he called back to her over his shoulder.

'Adam, come back!' she cried suddenly and stepped out into the street but he only turned and waved and was gone and she stood watching the frail beam of his light dance away into the darkness.

☆   ☆   ☆

'Leave the talking to me,' Catriona said and rang the front door bell. They stood on the doorstep of Mike Carter's house.

'We shouldn't be here at all,' Adam answered. 'I don't even play tennis.'

Catriona was dressed in a tennis skirt and wore an eye shade and carried a racquet. To better fit the part, she had her hair in a pony tail. Adam rang the bell again and they heard it sound somewhere deep in the house.

'Maybe she's not in,' Adam said. 'Let's go.'

'No, shh. Somebody's coming.'

The door opened slowly. A crack at first then wider and they saw Mrs Carter looking out at them. She wore a housecoat and her eyes were red and puffy.

'What do you want?' she sniffed.

'Um, Mrs Carter,' Catriona began. 'Is Mike in?'

'No,' Mrs Carter said warily. 'No, he's—' she hesitated. 'He's—gone away.'

'Yeah, we missed him at school and we wondered,' Catriona said.

'Are you his friends?'

'Yes.'

'He hasn't got any friends—except that Vernon.' There was contempt in her voice.

'Look, I'm Catriona Chisholm and this is Adam Hardy. Mike's got a tennis racket of mine,' she said. 'He borrowed it a couple of weeks ago and I need it back. We've got a court booked and everything.'

'What kind was it?' Mrs Carter said.

'A Slazenger,' Adam suggested. He felt he should have some input into this deception.

'Yes, Slazenger,' Catriona confirmed the brand name.

'Wait here and I'll look.' Mrs Carter said. 'The doctor says I should rest. I'm under sedation.' She closed the door on them.

'That's not going to help,' Adam said. 'We're supposed to go in and look.'

'It's a start,' Catriona said.

Mrs Carter opened the door again and showed them an old, brown tennis racquet. It had broken strings and a twisted frame.

'Is this it?'

'No,' Catriona shook her head. 'Mine was a bit newer than that.'

'Well, that's all there is in his bedroom. Sorry.'

'Oh, well,' Catriona said. 'We'll just have to borrow one. How is Mike anyway?'

'What do you mean, how is he?' Mrs Carter spoke sharply. 'There's nothing wrong with him. He's well enough, he's just gone away.' She opened the door a little wider and looked more closely at Adam. 'Here, you're

Doctor Hardy's son? Adam is it?'

'Yes,' Adam said it as if he were confessing to a crime.

'I thought so,' she said with scorn. 'In this town, word sure gets around quickly, doesn't it?' Then she almost slammed the door and Adam stood there for full ten seconds until Catriona pulled him away.

'Sorry, Adam,' she said. 'My fault. I think I said too much or something.'

'Or something,' he agreed bitterly. 'And we didn't get very far, did we?'

They crunched down the short gravel driveway and Adam risked a look back at the house but behind the white net curtains, there was nothing to see. Catriona also looked back but she saw something else.

'The garage,' she said. 'What did your mother say about the garage?'

'Nothing,' Adam said quickly but his look betrayed him.

'She did,' Catriona insisted. 'She said something about Mike and the garage. You told me last night, Adam. What was it?'

Adam heard again his mother's voice recounting Mike's words: *The boy said his master was in the garage and had told him to destroy himself for he had failed and was of no further use.*

The roll-a-door was wide open. There was a vacant space where Mr Carter's car usually rested and in the other bay stood his wife's tired old Morris Minor with bald tires and bruised paintwork.

'We could take a look,' Catriona said. 'Maybe he keeps things in there—who knows.'

'No, come on, Catriona,' Adam pleaded but she had already turned back and scrunched her way up the driveway towards the garage so he was forced to tiptoe after her.

'If she's under sedation,' Catriona whispered when Adam caught up with her, 'she'll be out like a light.' Still he dithered but Catriona dismissed him and started to look around.

In a half-hearted way, he began the search too, looking under a workbench, opening a toolbox and all the while, feeling guilty and apprehensive. Catriona was having no luck either and only managed to get a couple of grease spots on her white tennis skirt. With her fingers she pulled the pleats apart to show him and made a wry face.

Serves you right, he thought and then he saw what they'd come for. In a corner of the garage, a piece of wall panelling had a large crack in it. A triangular shaped section had been broken out and the piece had been put back and held in place with a house brick. Adam slid the brick away and the loose piece of panelling fell forward on the cement floor with a crack.

'Shh!' Catriona said and came to join him. From the deep recess behind the wall panelling, Adam pulled out a pair of white sneakers that had been stained brown with something. He sniffed them and there again was the familiar smell of the white ant killer from last Saturday night. There was also a pair of black overalls, again smelling strongly of the chemical. Suddenly, with the smell in his nostrils, he was back in the pump room.

'This is it,' he said.

Lying on the floor where the overalls had been he found a mini hacksaw with a yellow price tag still fluttering from it—Dunarling Hardware, it read and the price was $8.95. He showed it to Catriona.

'Dunarling Hardware was burned down,' she said. 'Remember?'

He nodded and recalled something else. The brake lines on Laurie Sinclair's bus had been cut by a fine, thin blade with a serrated edge. Sergeant Balfour had told him that.

'Is that all?' Catriona said.

'I think so,' Adam answered. He knelt and looked inside

the deep space behind the panelling. 'It's dark, I can't see.'

Catriona went to the workbench and came back with a long silver torch and gave it to him. He flashed it inside and then recoiled for there in the darkest corner of that space, the beam of the torch picked out two small coffins with their lids off—and staring back at him he saw twin faces of evil.

In his fright, he dropped the torch and its light went out. He almost threw himself back from the hole in the wall but his ears were suddenly assailed by taunting voices.

'*Tam Dubh, dae ye no' ken thy man is curset?*' the first voice rang inside his head. '*Thou canst dae nothing against the four o' us!*'

'*Swith, Agley, Smeddum and Snell.*' A second voice spoke in ugly triumph. '*Wi' agramie and ancient, honeyed words thy man's gudewife has given us oor grim charge tae make a' kinds o' mischief upon him.*'

'*Tak ye heed, Tam Dubh!*'

'They're in there!' Adam almost screamed and kicked with his feet against the wall to push himself further back from the hole. He brushed feverishly at the front of his shirt with both hands as if to rid himself of a staining foulness. 'Didn't you hear what they said, Catriona?'

'Adam!' Catriona was desperately trying to keep calm. She knelt and put her arms around him. 'I didn't hear anything. Oh, please, don't freak out on me!'

'The masters are there!' he shouted. 'Two of them, they're alive!' He tried to get to his feet to run away from the wall and from what he'd seen but Catriona struggled to hold him, fearful of the noise he was making. He turned his head to look away from the horrors of the place.

From the garden outside clean wholesome sunlight flooded through the open door but then silhouetted in it he saw another shape, larger and looming indistinct so that he had to screw up his eyes to make sense of it. Mrs Carter came into the garage and looked down at them on the floor together.

'Oh, this is cosy,' she said. 'A love-in?'

'Sorry, Mrs Carter,' Catriona said and disengaged herself from Adam and stood up.

'Sorry, for what?'

'For this,' Catriona helplessly waved her hands around at the disturbance they had created in the garage. Mrs Carter took in Mike's stained sneakers, the overalls and the gaping hole in the wall. Adam got to his feet and stood in dazed fashion, still not fully comprehending all that he had witnessed.

'We didn't think you'd mind,' Catriona said. 'If we had a look around—for the racquet.'

'Oh, I mind,' Mrs Carter's voice trembled. 'I mind very much. I mind so much I made a couple of phone calls. Soon as I saw you two come in here, I started ringing.'

'Oh,' Catriona's shoulders slumped.

'Look, Mrs Carter,' Adam began. 'Mike's been—' He searched for the right phrase. 'He's been getting mixed up in a couple of heavy things. It wasn't his fault.'

'Oh, and you'd know all about it,' Mrs Carter's bitterness spilled out. 'Coming from a medical family. What is it with you? Inside information? Is that what gives you the nerve to come around people's houses and do what you like?'

'No, it's not like that,' Adam started to say but in the street outside, a car drew up and the motor cut. In the garage, all three of them turned to watch two policemen come up the gravel driveway out of the sunlight. They were in no particular hurry and they seemed to grow bigger as they walked until their bulk almost filled the doorway.

'Well, well, well,' one of them said and Adam recognised him. 'You're making a habit of this, Mister Hardy. Saturday night, now here we are again!'

'Acting in concert,' the other one said. 'Who's your accomplice this time?'

'I want them both charged,' Mrs Carter said harshly. 'They've broken in here.'

'We didn't,' Catriona said. 'We just walked in. The door was open.'

'They broke that wall panel,' Mrs Carter went on and then she turned sharply and looked to the street. A Holden Kingswood swung into the driveway and stopped a few metres from the open door. Mr Carter got out heavily and came into the shade of the garage, hitching up his large belt.

'What's going on, Jan?' he said.

'Caught them red handed,' his wife said. 'As if I haven't got enough. And they know all about Mike.'

'Yeah, bloody liberty,' Mr Carter said. 'What did they steal?'

'Haven't worked that out yet,' the first policeman said and stepped past Adam and Catriona and inspected the broken wall panel. 'You do this?'

'It was already like that,' Adam said. 'We found those overalls and the sneakers. That's all.'

The policeman looked at the sodden overalls and sniffed at them. He took in the mini hacksaw with its price tag lying flat on the floor revealing the name on it.

'Are these your property, Mr Carter?' he said.

'Never seen them before.'

'Yeah, look, we're not going to get anything sorted out here,' the policeman said. 'So I say we all go down to the station and see what's what. Come on you two.' He put a hand, not unkindly, on Adam and Catriona's shoulder and steered them towards the driveway.

'I want them charged,' Mrs Carter's voice trembled.

'We'll see about that,' the second policeman said and turned to leave but then he paused.

Someone else was walking up the driveway carrying a small suitcase.

'Hello, Adam. Hello, Catriona,' the new arrival greeted them cheerfully. It was Hamish Leckie.

Chapter Nine

'The two dolls, Adam?' Hamish Leckie all but ignored Mr and Mrs Carter and the policemen. 'Have you found them? That is the most important thing, the two mandrake dolls.'

'Dolls?' said the first policeman. 'What are you on about?'

'I've reason to believe there are two important historical artefacts concealed on these premises,' Hamish said formally. 'As Curator of Dunarling Museum, I'm empowered under *The Historic Shipwrecks Act of 1976* to take possession of them for the Commonwealth.'

'They're in the hole in the wall,' Adam said quietly and stepped away to let Hamish see the triangular shaped opening.

'Here, what is all this?' Mr Carter said.

'We're the ones who discovered Jamie Ramsay's cave,' Adam explained. 'Catriona and I did, but Mike was with us and when we explored we found five little dolls.'

'Mandrake men,' Catriona added.

'And instead of giving them up as he should have,' Hamish went on, 'I'm afraid your son Michael kept them for himself.'

'You've been here before.' Mrs Carter remembered his face. 'Looking for these dolls.'

'Yes,' Hamish confirmed. 'And it would've saved a lot of bother if Mike had given them up there and then. In the wall, you say?'

Adam nodded.

'Er, maybe we ought to take them,' the first policeman made a move. 'If there's any allegation of a crime being committed here—'

'They're historical artefacts, man!' Hamish almost exploded. 'They're old and perhaps already damaged. They need expert care and preservation, not mishandling and throwing in some old plastic bag marked evidence.' He walked towards the hole in the wall and knelt down. 'If you need to have a look at them any time you'll find they'll be safe and sound in the museum, with me.'

From his case, Hamish produced a long silver torch and flashed it inside the hole in the wall. His face lit up when he saw the dolls.

'Are they all right?' Mrs Carter was anxious now.

'They appear to be all right.' Hamish said as he stuck his head and shoulders inside the triangular opening. 'Och, come to me, my little darlings,' they heard his muffled voice croon. 'Have I been looking forward to meeting you.' One of the policemen looked at the other and raised an eyebrow. It takes all types, his expression seemed to say.

Smiling, Hamish Leckie emerged from the hole in the wall and the others crowded around to see what he held protectively in his hands. Nestling in their coffins, the dolls wore twin faces of bland innocence, giving no hint of the evil and malign appearance Adam had seen earlier.

☆ ☆ ☆

Just as Gordon Hardy returned home from his day of surgical duties at the hospital, the two constables delivered Adam to the front gate in a police car. They didn't use the siren or the flashing blue light but even so, their timing could not have been more excruciating.

'What's this?' Adam's father demanded of the senior constable. 'Is he in more trouble?'

'Haven't quite got to the bottom of this one yet, sir,' the policeman said. 'Enquiries are still going on but at this stage, it looks as if young Adam here's been doing some detective work on his own behalf.' Then bit by bit, by directing curt and probing questions firstly to Adam and then the policeman, his father found out about the visit to Mike Carter's house.

'Well, thank you for bringing my son home,' Adam's father said. 'It's getting to be a regular event.' The policemen went back to their car leaving Adam and his father to enter the house in silence.

Once the front door closed behind them it was a different matter. Adam's father let loose a torrent of bitter questions and recriminations. He was incensed that a son of his would make use of information he had overheard about one of his mother's patients. What on earth was he thinking of?

Adam warded off the questions as best he could. It would have been easier if they had some common ground to start from but there was none and there was no easy explanation for what had happened in these last hours. His father was certainly in no mood to accept anything but a totally rational explanation and there was little chance of finding one of those!

Adam's mother returned from late surgery to find the ruins of the confrontation still smouldering. Instead of hosing things down, her intervention only served to fan the flames and Adam finally raged out and left them. He went upstairs and slammed his own bedroom door to shut out the bitter noises from below.

He lay face down on his bed and listened until their warring voices muted to a stiff and uneasy peace. He knew they'd be sitting in different rooms and each would have poured their own drink which they'd consume in glacial silence without enjoyment. At the appointed time, his father would turn on the television news and his mother would want to watch it but wouldn't deign to share the same room as her husband. She'd read a magazine instead, although if Adam were to ask her in the morning what she had taken in she wouldn't be able to remember a single detail.

He rolled over on the bed and lay gazing at the ceiling with his hands behind his head. His mother would eventually knock at the door and come in to have a calmer and more considered argument with him. He could almost write the script.

'Look Adam,' she would say reproachfully. 'What on earth possessed you?'

Possessed? Me? That's rich! Don't you know Mike's the one who was possessed? That's what's wrong with him. He was taken over by mandrake dolls, evil presences with the power to cause damage, destruction and death and they're working their way through our town. That's what this is about! But the script didn't go as planned.

Downstairs the doorbell rang and Adam heard his father answer it. There was a brief conversation at the front door then Gordon Hardy called out from the foot of the stairs.

'Adam,' he raised his voice slightly. 'It's the police again. For you.' His tone was calm, but Adam reasoned that was only because he was holding himself in check on account of the cops being there.

Downstairs in the lounge, Tom Balfour was already seated and comfortable in a chair by the fireplace. His father stood facing the door and Sergeant Balfour smiled when Adam entered the room.

'Hi, Tom,' Adam said and at this familiarity, his father gave a frown.

Adam's mother came into the room and Tom Balfour stood up quickly and said hello. She took the chair at the other side of the fireplace.

'Well,' Tom Balfour began. 'Some interesting stuff you found this afternoon, Adam. Hamish Leckie's got his mandrake dolls and he's gone off like a little pig with two tails but the other things are interesting too.'

'Yeah,' Adam said. 'I was sort of relieved when I found them.'

'Fair enough. We've given them a quick once over at our end,' Tom Balfour went on. 'The dark garment, a boiler suit, is reeking of white ant killer, almost certainly stolen from the railway works department store. We're having forensic in Melbourne take a look at the mini hacksaw, looking for traces of metal, rubber and brake fluid on it. In other words, finding out what it's most recently been used to cut.'

'What is all this?' Adam's father demanded.

'It's the stuff I found at Mike Carter's place, Dad,' Adam said. 'Evidence.'

'Yes, evidence,' Tom Balfour agreed. 'Tends to confirm that young Adam here had nothing to do with the business at the pump room on Saturday night. Also might show the source of the interference with the brakes on the school bus last week. We should be able to gather some decent fingerprints and do a bit of matching.'

'It wasn't Mike's fault,' Adam said quickly and his parents exchanged glances.

'Yes, we're on tricky ground there,' Tom Balfour said. 'Mike Carter being the way he is right now he's not in a fit state to be interviewed.'

'Not in a fit state for anything,' Adam's mother said defensively.

'Yes, it puts a different complexion on things,' Tom Balfour conceded. 'Still, we'll press on with our enquiry as best we can but I doubt if we'll get all the answers we need.' He paused and clearly had something else on his mind. 'Interesting diary, Adam.'

'Yes,' Adam agreed. 'Have you read it right through?'

'Oh yes. Waiting for the next chapter.'

'There's not a lot more,' Adam said. 'I'll finish it soon.'

'Yes,' Tom Balfour scratched his chin thoughtfully. 'Very interesting revelations and very intriguing parallels in that diary. Especially the bits you marked with the high-lighter. We might have a talk about them sometime.'

'That'll be good,' Adam said. His father turned and looked at the clock on the mantlepiece. *The 7.30 Report* would be on. Suffer, Adam thought. Tom Balfour rose to go.

'I'll show you out, Sergeant,' Adam's mother said.

At least, Adam mused, *somebody* was showing an interest in the welfare of the community.

☆　　☆　　☆

The following morning, Catriona waited for Adam at the place where their two roads met and they cycled to school together.

'I'm sorry,' she said simply.

'What for?'

'For getting you into all that stuff,' she answered. 'It was my idea to go to the Carters' place.'

'I could have refused to go,' Adam said. 'Besides, it was worth it. What did Barbara say when the cops brought you home?'

'She cracked. What do you think she did?'

'Can't imagine Barbara cracking.'

'I'm in her bad books anyway because I'm so cool towards lover boy.'

'Tom Balfour? He's all right.'

'He's a—' A truck rolled past on the main road and the rest of her words were lost to him.

☆　　☆　　☆

Richard Vernon was missing. That was the latest sensation to sweep the school. The true circumstances surrounding Mike's absence had not been made public but Richard's sudden departure attracted wide and immediate interest. From the first day his parents advertised the disappearance extensively and provided details for the local papers and television to fill their quota of news.

Richard had not gone off on his own accord, they said. He had taken nothing but the clothes he wore to school that morning. His red sports car had been found abandoned in the railway station car park with the keys still in it. As his mother tearfully explained, he had no money worth taking, his bank book and cash card were still in his room, he had not been under any strain and he had no obvious worries in his life. Although there were no signs of a struggle his parents suspected he had been kidnapped and the police began to treat it that way too.

On the third day, Richard had still not been seen and the local news outlets continued to make headlines of the case and the story had already appeared in the Melbourne papers. Richard's father went to the expense of having missing person posters printed and distributed through the district. When she saw one of them at school, Catriona suggested it should be a wanted poster.

'Oh, come on, Cat,' Adam said. 'Be charitable.'

'Charitable nothing,' she said. 'He'll turn up soon enough and he'll have some swanky, way-out reason for going off. You'll see.'

But another day passed and the case had already turned from one of suspected kidnapping to a murder hunt. Police cadets came from Melbourne to comb waste ground while divers searched the river for Richard's body.

☆ ☆ ☆

'Gordon, don't forget we're picking up Catriona in the morning,' Adam's mother said. 'She's promised to help out with the work-bee.'

'Oh yes,' Adam's father said absently. 'That's good. There's still a lot of last minute things to do.'

'Adam, you're coming, aren't you?' his mother said. They sat in the lounge after dinner on Friday night. The movies on television hadn't been worth the effort so Adam's mother had worked on her costume for the railway re-enactment while his father read a novel.

'Yes, I'll be there,' Adam tried to make his voice carry enthusiasm.

'Have you thought any more about what you're going to wear to the re-enactment, Adam?' his mother said.

'I wasn't going to dress up,' he answered, knowing that decision would annoy his father, who merely sniffed and turned a page of his novel.

'Your turn to make the coffee, Gordon,' his wife reminded him during the small break in his concentration.

'Right,' Adam's father said shortly. He put his book and his reading glasses aside and went out to the kitchen.

'Make an effort, Adam,' his mother whispered.

'What, tell him I've decided to go as Ned Kelly?' Adam said.

'You know what I mean,' his mother hissed. 'Make conversation or something.'

'He hates anybody talking to him while he's reading.'

'I don't mean just now, I mean generally. Try to see things his way.'

'Well, I'm going to the work-bee tomorrow,' Adam said. 'That's seeing things his way.' His mother sighed deeply.

'Men!' she said.

'I think I'll skip coffee, Mum,' he said.

'Well, be sure to tell your father,' she reminded him. 'At least that would be some sort of communication.'

Adam went to the door of the lounge room and told his father he didn't want coffee.

'Okay.' He put Adam's cup back on the shelf.

'There you are, Mum,' Adam reported. 'We communicated.'

'Men!' his mother said with even deeper feeling.

Adam went up to his bedroom and got out his old portable typewriter and opened Ewart McColl's diary. There were only a dozen or so lines to transcribe and then the whole thing would be finished, apart from some entries that had been too badly waterstained or where the pages had stuck together. He was pleased with the work he'd done with the diary and felt it gave a pretty good account of the highlights of the voyage of the *Dunarling* and had revealed many secrets.

He rolled a sheet of paper into the portable and began to type, and was briefly amused at the stiffness of the keys and the slowness of the response of a typewriter after using the computer.

Friday 11th June, 1886
Since we are within days of our first landfall, Captain Stewart begged us to excuse him if, from now on, he spent little time in the saloon sharing our company. He is worried and distracted about something and, after the captain's departure, Mr McWalter explained that because of the loss of the three sails at the upper part of the mizzen mast, the ship is not steering as well as is desirable in the heavy weather we must encounter as we near the South Australian coastline. In addition, there has been no proper sighting of the sun these several days past, in consequence of which no one is entirely confident of our position.

It seems as we rapidly approach the coast, all eyes are needed to look for the sight of a welcoming lighthouse and all ears to listen for the sound of breaking waves.

☆   ☆   ☆

On the day of the final work-bee before the re-enactment, the weather broke. For the best part of a week, the skies had been clear and everyone crossed their fingers and hoped the big day would be just as balmy but as soon as Adam opened his eyes on Saturday morning, he saw long raindrops streaking down his bedroom window. The skies were heavy with the promise of more to come.

'Will the work-bee still be on?' he said generally at the breakfast table. 'I mean, with all this rain.'

'Of course it'll be on,' his father answered sharply then moderated his tone for his next utterance. 'Lots of little jobs to do inside the station, last minute clearing up, polishing brass and things.' He buried himself in the morning paper again and Adam's mother winked at him and smiled as she poured herself more tea.

'The Vernon boy's still missing,' Adam's father said.

'It's been nearly a week,' Adam offered and looked to his mother to see if she approved of the conversational gambits he was making. She nodded enthusiastically and made a circling motion with her forefinger as if to suggest Adam keep up the good work. Gordon Hardy caught his wife's movement and looked around the edge of the newspaper and she turned the motion with her fingers into one of indecision as to which piece of toast she should take from the rack.

'I'd say he's gone off somewhere,' she observed with a straight face.

'Well, that's obvious,' her husband said. 'I mean, he's not home, is he?'

'The work-bee starts at nine,' Adam reminded his parents and got up from the table and took his breakfast dishes to the sink.

☆   ☆   ☆

Catriona was sheltering in the doorway of the souvenir shop waiting for them to pick her up. She dashed across the wet pavement for the open door of the Rover and crowded in beside Adam with raindrops glistening on her hair.

'Good morning, Jean, good morning, Gordon, good

morning, Adam,' she was out of breath and clicked her seat belt.

Barbara was at the door of the shop to wave them off.

'Sorry I can't come to the work-bee,' she said, ducking low to look in the car window.

'Another time, Barbara,' Adam's mother called back. 'Are you coming on the re-enactment run?'

'Oh yes, wouldn't miss it, but I hope it's not like this! Bye.'

Gordon Hardy waved and did a U turn and they were off.

'Barbara's solved your costume problem, Adam,' Catriona said.

'Oh yes, what is it?' he was wary.

'Wait and see,' she answered. 'But she's made one for you. It's a beauty. Hope it fits.'

'A nineteenth century bludger's outfit,' his father said from the front seat and smiled in the rear vision mirror to make a joke of it.

'Wrong, Gordon!' Catriona said. 'You'll just have to wait and see.'

The Rover splashed along the length of the main street, past the burnt out shell of Dunarling Hardware, past the Fire Station and the Museum then finally into the car-park at the station. The four of them dashed inside as the rain increased.

Charlie Boyd was in charge of issuing jobs and gave them out on a first come, first served basis. Adam stayed close to Catriona, hoping to be assigned to work with her but Charlie had other ideas. Catriona went off with some other women to polish the brass door handles of the three restored carriages which were standing under cover in a siding. Adam had the job of sorting out plastic bunting which would adorn the interior of the station on the big day.

They came together over morning tea and Catriona sat on a bench beside him.

'Hi,' she said and showed him her hands, stained dark from the metal polish.

'Hi,' he answered.

'One of the women on our team's got to go home.' She delicately took a biscuit with thumb and forefinger to avoid the Brasso stains. 'What say you come and work with us?'

Adam nodded. His father and mother arrived with their mugs of tea and joined them on the bench. His father sat next to Catriona and Adam's mother took the empty space at the other end.

'This is cosy,' she said.

'It's going to be a wonderful day,' Adam's father said. 'Next Saturday this place will be like a hundred years ago. Just imagine it—a sea of colour.'

'It's a sea of colour now,' Adam observed reasonably and his mother raised her eyes to the high roof of the station.

'Everyone'll have a video camera or something,' Catriona pointed out. 'That'll spoil the authenticity.'

'Good point, Catriona,' Adam's father said. 'I'll raise it at the next committee meeting.' He was eating out of her hand again.

Charlie Boyd fussed along at that moment and demanded Gordon Hardy's immediate attention.

'We're having a run through with some safety procedures on the loco,' Charlie said. 'Guy from the railway department's here so we all have to go and watch.'

His father drained his tea and left with Charlie while Adam's mother sang 'Hi-ho, hi-ho' and went back to work.

'How do you do it?' Adam said.

'What do you mean, how do I do it?'

'The way you've got my father eating out of your hand,' he said. 'I wish it was like that with me.'

'You've got to work on it,' Catriona said.

'I do,' Adam answered. 'At least, I think I do.'

The rest of the morning passed quickly. Adam worked

with Catriona at one end of the line of carriages and the two remaining women kept themselves busy at the other.

'We've got to talk with somebody,' Adam said. 'About the curses. I reckon we should talk with Tom Balfour.'

'No!' Catriona said suddenly and Adam saw one of the women look in their direction and raise an eyebrow and say something to the other. 'Besides, Hamish Leckie got the dolls back, so everything's all right now, isn't it?'

'But there's still a doll missing,' Adam persisted.

'Didn't Richard toss it into the sea?'

'And you believed that?' He was scornful. 'What's the betting he's still got the doll?'

Adam shivered as a thought came to his mind: *Or it's got him.*

☆   ☆   ☆

Saturday 12th June, 1886
The sea stays rough and the Dunarling *carries all the canvas she dares to spread in such a gale. We are still not sure of our position but we continue to sail at a brisk pace, for Captain Stewart is anxious to complete the voyage within a hundred days.*

Adam turned the page but there were no more entries for him to transcribe. It was Saturday night and the chronicle was finished but for Ewart McColl at that moment in his life, there had been little else in store; two more nights in a pitching bunk, a handful of exchanged pleasantries with his fellow voyagers, six cold meals and then the end. The date on the final entry said it all; every boy and girl who'd been to school in the district knew what happened to the *Dunarling* a scant two days after that Saturday the 12th day of June in 1886.

Adam felt sad when he thought of the people he'd met in the pages of the diary and how they had come to their end.

He thought of the gossiping Misses Cameron and their brother in the militia who would wait in vain for them in Sydney. He remembered the bluff Captain Stewart and Mr McWalter and all the bairns on the ship, the Highland men and their wives and the Liverpool Irish woman who'd given birth to twins then lost one to the poison in the water tank and at the end, he spared a thought for the gentle Ewart McColl, whose diligent writing had brought them all to him.

The more he thought about the ship and the people in their final tragedy, the more Adam became preoccupied with the missing doll and the last of the four curses: *All Fa' Doon*. He got up from the desk and paced the floor.

Tom Balfour was the answer. He'd read the diary and said it had very interesting revelations and intriguing parallels, so he'd been putting things together too. We might have a talk about them sometime, he had said. That was the answer; Catriona would have to get over her objections and show Tom Balfour the Bible with its message and they'd have to share with him all the things they'd found out, even the information he'd overheard about Mike Carter and what had caused him to end up the way he was.

Relieved that he'd made a wise decision, Adam lay on his bed and looked upwards into the familiar circle of light and thought about how he'd tackle the situation. It was too late to do anything tonight and besides, the wind and rain still lashed at his bedroom window. Tomorrow was Sunday; in the morning he'd go to Catriona and tell her it had to be Tom Balfour. No ifs, no buts, Catriona, he'd say and looked upwards, trying to picture the way she'd react to *that* edict. Instead, in the circle of light he saw Richard Vernon's face.

This was not the Richard he'd ever seen before; this face held no expression of triumph but a look of pain, mixed with sheer exhaustion and abject terror.

Richard was cowering fearfully against an iron railing,

still wearing the remnants of his school uniform. He was being lashed by wind whipped rain so his hair was plastered over his face. The background was too indistinct to reveal anything about the place. As Adam looked at the scene, Richard held out a hand in his direction. It was dark with blood.

'Tam Dubh,' Adam said. 'Tell me where he is. Tell me, Tam Dubh. Tell me.' Richard cast a haggard glance over his shoulder into the darkness beyond then turned back and looked wildly at Adam.

'*Go ye tae the boy's side*,' Tam Dubh's voice came at last. '*He is in peril and but a bairn against the one who has him in thrall.*'

'Who's got him? And where am I to go?'

'*Snell has him—at the place of my old ship timbers.*'

'Old ship timbers?' Adam repeated. 'What, you mean spars and planks, you mean the museum?'

'*The place where the timbers still do service.*'

This was crazy, Adam thought. In the vision, Richard was outside somewhere with rain soaking him and a high wind blowing. So where was he?

Then he heard his father's words on that first work-bee. He was speaking with Catriona: 'Did you know the old railway viaduct contains some timber from the *Dunarling*?' She'd been almost dutiful in her interest. 'I didn't know that, Gordon.' 'Yes, they actually used timber from the wreck—the planking and some of the deck supports came from the ship.'

Dunarling Viaduct.

It was late at night when Adam set out on his bicycle. At times the wind drove the rain in horizontal sheets and he had trouble pushing into it. His eyes stung and he averted his face. When at last he changed direction, the wind, like a vast icy hand, began to hurl him along so he barely had to touch the pedals. He concentrated his energies on guiding the machine while his single headlight did it's best to brighten the way for him.

The road from town ran beside the railway line for a kilometre then veered off to the left to go around the end of Dunarling Gorge. The railway line kept going along a high embankment that led to the viaduct. At the bend in the road, Adam got off and hid his bicycle in the long grass behind a low wall. He took the headlight and pulled his way up the grassy slope of the embankment until his light picked out the railway lines.

He was suddenly exposed to the sharpness of the driving rain while on his lips, he tasted salt in the wind from the sea. He ducked low and began to step out along the sleepers.

Dunarling Viaduct was rarely used for rail traffic but it was still a tourist attraction because of the breathtaking audacity of its construction. It curved across the gorge in a wide semi-circle while far below, the sea sucked and surged against its three massive support columns. To pass over it in a storm was an ordeal few rail travellers ever forgot.

And out there was Richard Vernon. *And who else?*

'*Snell has him in thrall—at the place of my old ship timbers.*'

As Adam drew nearer, faintly from somewhere on the viaduct he heard a long, wailing scream which chilled him. He paused, straining his ears to catch the sound if it came again. But there was nothing. Only the wind moaned at him and whipped his face with spray. He went on.

Before he reached the centre of the viaduct, his flashing headlight picked out something white. It was by the railing and he witnessed it only for a second. Adam was about to dismiss it when he saw the white again—then it vanished.

His heart pounded as he quickened his pace. By now, he had reached the edge of the viaduct and his feet sounded on the wooden planking under him. Far below, he heard the waves roll up the gorge in a white roiling foam, battering into the wooden supports as they went. With every impact the viaduct trembled and the timbers creaked. Then above it all, Adam heard another sound and his blood chilled once more.

The white object he had earlier picked out was a face. It was Richard's face, sometimes raised as if seeking salvation and at times drooping hopelessly on his chest. Adam shone the light and saw him only five metres ahead. He was huddled against the steel railing at the edge of the viaduct but made no sign he'd seen Adam. Richard was absorbed in something of far greater urgency.

He seemed to be locked in a fierce and bitter argument, for Adam could hear raised voices. One was shrill with fear and terror while a quieter one reasoned with cold and steely indifference.

Adam held his spot, afraid to venture forward because he realised with horrible fascination that Richard's dispute was *with himself*. The two voices in the encounter came from the same person. Heedless of the rain Richard turned his face upwards.

'No!' Adam heard him scream. 'I've done all I can for you.' Just as suddenly, his head lolled forward on his chest.

'*But thou art useless tae me now,*' the calmer tones also came from Richard. '*Staun up man, and hurl yerself intae the foam.*'

It was said in a reasonable tone of voice and in answer, Richard lifted his head once more.

'No, master,' he screamed and gripped the handrail fiercely with both hands. 'I can't do what you ask, I don't know how to. I've helped you all I can so leave me alone!'

'*Oh, but thou hast failed and thou must destroy thyself for there's nae salvation for ye.*'

The wind picked up in a fierce gust and drowned the rest

of the debate and Adam rallied and took a step forward.

'*Now*,' Tam Dubh's voice growled in his ear and Adam nodded and kept walking along the planks until he came to Richard. He shone his light on him and Richard looked up and held out a blood encrusted hand and croaked something and sobbed briefly. Then all at once, his expression changed to one of deep loathing.

'*Tam Dubh*,' Richard said in a mocking voice. '*Have ye come tae see me at my duty?*'

Adam spoke and was surprised once more at the sound that came from his own throat.

'*Snell, thou hast nae business wi' this man. Leave him be!*'

Richard's expression didn't change but he held up one hand and leaned back against the railing.

'*So I shall gie thee best for noo*,' he said in a crooning, sing-song voice. '*But mind, there are four o' us and jist the wan o' thee. Until the curses be laid tae rest, we'll fight ye ower and ower again. Till the end o' time if need be.*'

Richard slumped suddenly and his eyes closed. Then his body arched and he seemed to go into a convulsion. He vomited and his hands which had become bloodied from the tightness of the grip on the rusty iron handrail, relaxed and he sprawled on the footboards, sobbing in relief.

Adam went to his side and crouched and shook him and called his name.

'Hey, mate,' he said gently. 'It's me. Adam Hardy.'

'Hardy!' Richard almost snarled the name as he turned with a wild stare. 'It was you! You gave me the dolls and look what's happened.'

'Easy, mate,' Adam said. 'It's over now. Let's get you home, eh.'

Richard was half a head taller and suddenly he began to lash out, knocking the light from Adam's hand, sending it spinning down into the gorge with its beam circling through the slanting rain. He heard a crack and glass broke as it struck a rock and the light was gone.

Richard lashed out in a frenzy and threw punch after punch in the darkness, connecting painfully with the side of Adam's head. Adam fell heavily against the handrail and Richard jumped on him and began to lift him over the edge.

'You! You! You!' he snarled and beat at Adam with one fist while trying to lift him with his free hand. 'The dolls, the girl, everything.'

In the corner of his eye, Adam saw a light cutting through the rain. It glanced off the wet railway lines, probing the darkness, like a lance. Its bearer came towards him. He heard footsteps. Running.

'Hurry!' Adam shouted as another of Richard's blows made contact. He gasped in pain. 'This way!'

The newcomer wore a glistening dark oilskin which reflected light from his torch. It was Hamish Leckie.

'Adam,' he shouted. 'You need a hand!' Richard flung another furious punch and Adam jerked backwards to avoid it. In a swift move Hamish had Richard down on his face on the footboards. He gasped once and slumped and there was no more fight in him.

'Old army training.' Hamish stood up cheerfully. 'Never leave home without it, that's my motto. Are you all right, Adam?'

'Give me a minute.' He felt tears on his face and turned away.

'Take your time, son,' Hamish answered gently and turned to kneel beside Richard.

It took a full three minutes for Adam to recover. He had bruises and there was a searing pain in his ribs which were tender to touch. His back ached from where he'd made heavy contact with the railing. He found a handkerchief and wiped his face then he was ready to turn around and face Hamish.

'Great timing,' he said. 'But why'd you come?'

'Never look a gift horse in the mouth, young Hardy,' Hamish said briskly. 'Come on, let's get this chap back to his ain fireside where he belongs. He's frozen stiff.'

'But why'd *you* come?' Adam repeated.

Hamish picked up his torch so that Adam could see the smile on his face.

'I've been reading the diary transcript,' he said. 'So I decided you needed some help. Okay? We'll talk about it in the morning, but right now, it's first things first. The wee doll that Richard took, where do you reckon it is, Adam?'

They searched around until they found the fifth coffin standing propped up against the railway line. The lid was off and the doll was wet but it looked at ease, almost friendly and peaceful—the sort of toy you'd happily give to a child as a plaything. In the light of the torch, Hamish inspected it.

'Take more than a bit of foul weather to do mischief to him,' he said and put the lid on and slipped the coffin into the pocket of his oilskin. He knelt beside Richard. 'Now, I reckon it'll have to be a fireman's lift for this fella. You carry the torch Adam, and lead the way back to my car.'

With a slight grunt, Hamish hefted Richard on to his shoulder and staggered behind Adam along the narrow, wet footboards. The rain and sea spray beat at their faces, the freezing wind plucked at them and howled its anger into the night but they were safe and they were going home and Adam had an ally.

Chapter Ten

When they reached the town end of the viaduct, Adam took
a hand and they carried Richard between them down the
slippery grass of the embankment and across the road where
Hamish had left his utility. Richard was still unconscious,
but beginning to mumble and they had a brief problem
getting him into the passenger's seat but finally managed it.

'Nip over and fetch your bike, Adam,' Hamish said.
'Sling it in the back of the ute and we'll be home in five
minutes.' Painfully, Adam crossed the deserted main road
and stepped over the low wall where he groped around in
the long grass until he finally located his bike. Seconds
later, he wheeled it back through the pelting rain and placed
it on top of a pile of sodden cardboard boxes and other junk
in the back of the utility.

He crammed into the front seat next to Richard as Hamish
let in the clutch. They moved off and Adam shivered as
he did his best to keep Richard from slumping forward on
the dashboard.

'They'll be pleased to see him back,' Hamish commented.

'Yeah,' Adam said and was silent. All sorts of thoughts
were coursing through his mind and they drove for a few
kilometres until finally he asked Hamish to pull over.

'What's up, Adam?'

'I don't want to face this,' he said and his lip was swollen from where Richard had punched him. The left side of his rib cage hurt profoundly. 'I mean, finding Richard. All the fuss, the reporters and worst of all the questions that I can't answer.'

'I know what you mean.' Hamish let the motor tick over. 'You've had a fair bit of that, eh?'

'A fair bit, yeah. Cops, parents, you name it.'

'So you don't want the honour and the glory?'

'No. Just let me be one of the great unknown.'

Hamish engaged first gear and rolled off again and instead of turning at the lights which would take them to the upper part of town where Richard's parents lived, he executed a U turn and drove back along the main street.

'I've got an idea,' he said. 'Richard needs urgent medical help and he needs to be reunited with his folks. So, let's be anonymous. Watch this, Adam.'

The plan was simple; Hamish drove a little way along the main street and did another U turn then slid gently to a stop in front of Dunarling Fire Station and switched off the headlights. He left the engine running then stepped out into the rain.

'Give me a hand with him,' he said. Together, they lifted Richard and took him into the shelter of the fire station door. Hamish pushed the fire alarm button and they sprinted the few metres to the utility and raced off into the night. Until they were well away, Hamish kept his headlights off and drove by the street lights.

'They'll be out there in a few seconds,' he said and laughed. 'Job done, eh?'

'Yeah, fantastic,' Adam said. 'But could you turn on the heater? I'm freezing.'

'Haven't got one in this car.' Hamish switched on the headlights instead. 'Sorry.'

'Not half as sorry as I'm going to be.'

☆   ☆   ☆

Dunarling Museum was empty of people when Adam arrived stiff, sore and breathless. It was still raining outside so there were no Sunday morning tourists moving dutifully past the exhibits and no local residents come to see the new acquisitions since the discovery of Jamie Ramsay's cave, there wasn't even a caretaker. A note pinned to the door informed the world that Mrs Parry would return to her post in five minutes. [She was a Museum in the Community volunteer, doing her few hours on this rainy morning.]

'Not very security conscious is Mrs Parry,' Adam muttered. 'But that's fine by me.'

Following the events of the night, he had slept badly and woke early with a throbbing head and tender rib cage. He had collected the Sunday papers from the front garden but found no mention of Richard. The local radio said nothing either so he would have to wait till the television news in the evening. If Richard remembered anything about last night's encounter on the viaduct, Adam would have some penetrating questions to answer but they'd come later. Right now, he had a burning question of his own to ask.

He leaned into the display of dolls that Hamish had set up and took out the figure of Tam Dubh.

'Come on, you've got to show me some things. I need to *know!*'

The other three dolls were on display and gazed at him with frigid expressions of evil.

Adam remembered the visions he'd witnessed in the circle of light on his bedroom ceiling. Tam Dubh had caused those visions; he did it once, he could do it again.

'We've stopped the fourth curse from happening but I need to know who laid the curses, Tam Dubh,' Adam pleaded, looking into the smiling face of the doll. 'I *want* to know why.'

He stood in the silent museum and then, for some reason, experienced an urge to go into Hamish Leckie's office. Like a hand guiding him, he let the impulse take over and he felt himself moving in past the door marked private. There was a cupboard against the wall and although he'd never seen inside it, he already knew what it contained. The double doors opened easily and Adam took out a large silver torch and switched it on to check the state of the batteries. Light flooded a dark corner of the office.

'This is what I need to make a vision,' he cried. 'Eh, Tam Dubh? But I can't watch it here. Mrs Parry'll be back, so where do I go?'

Within minutes, the same impetus hurried him through the driving rain along the cliff path in the direction of Jamie Ramsay's cave.

Heedless of the sand in his shoes and his rain soaked clothes, he walked painfully then crawled the length of the tunnel leading to the inner cave. As he elbowed his way along, the beam of the torch flashed eerily overhead, glancing long shadows off the roughnesses in the ceiling. He found the inner cave and stood up.

Adam planted the torch in the soft cave floor and heaped sand around in a triangle to keep it vertical so that a rough circle of light shone on the cave roof. Next to the torch, he stood Tam Dubh, as if he too should have a view of whatever was to appear.

Satisfied, he lay on his back in the sandy floor with his hands behind his head and stared up at the light on the ceiling. He had no idea how long he stayed in his rain-soaked clothes looking upwards but he held his gaze until the edges of the ring became fuzzy and indistinct. All else in the cave was black and silent and then, quietly at first, voices began to come. In this tranquil state, his pain began to ebb away. The voices were but vague snatches of talk that seemed to be at a distance but then they were closer and he began to understand them.

'It's all right, Margaret,' a man's voice said. He spoke quietly, with a wheedling, fatherly quality to his words as if making an appeal to a child. 'We'll be together, that's all that matters, lass.'

'Aye, but what about your wife? What will she make of it?' a young girl's voice said. 'She looked a right French, Gypsy sort of woman, Marie Catherine or whatever she calls herself.'

'Marie Catherine DeLairgo,' Adam breathed the name aloud as he pictured the words in Catriona's Bible:

Adam Colquhoun married Marie Catherine DeLairgo,
Grove Street, Glasgow, 15th June, 1883.

'Och, Marie was never my wife, not my true wedded wife,' the man's voice explained. 'She never was, Margaret. She was only a woman I knew for a wee while. You know, we just kept company, that's all. I want you to be my proper wife, my only wife.'

'Show me, Tam Dubh!' Adam whispered. 'Who are they, *where* are they?' The voices continued as if they hadn't heard Adam's plea.

'But, Adam, I'll not be your wife till we get where we're going,' the girl said and Adam started at the sound of his own name and thought for a second she was talking to him. Then, in the circle of light, he began to see the speakers. They were faint at first, then he saw them with a firmer, clear-edged vision. It was day-time and they were in a dark, brown painted room and Adam was there with them, so close he marvelled that they didn't see him.

The man was folding clothes into wooden boxes. He was dressed in thin black trousers with braces to keep them up and wore a badly pressed linen shirt without a collar.

In the background, the girl sat at a table near the smoky fireplace, watching him pack. She wore a long, grey dress that reached to the floor so that only the toes of her shoes peeped from under the hem; her dark hair hung in ringlets.

She had a shawl draped over her shoulders.

It was Catriona!

Adam started and called her name and reached out to her but she ignored him and kept looking at the man who knelt beside the boxes on the floor.

'Ay, that's right, Margaret lass,' the man went on. 'We'll not be wed till we get tae oor destination. I'm a patient man, I can bide my time.' He continued to pack his clothes away, then put a few items into the smaller box and shut the lid. Smiling, he stood up and came to her almost shyly.

'There's a wee thing I've got for ye, lass,' he said and produced a flat wooden box and clicked it open and turned it so she could see what it contained. It was a golden heart locket on a long chain.

'Oh, it's pretty, Adam,' she said and took it from the box and held it by the chain. 'Can I put it on?'

'Oh, aye,' the man laughed. 'That's what it's for. The heart opens up, y'see, and later we can get oor likenesses taken and put them inside; me and you together, then I'll always be near yer heart.'

The girl called Margaret put the chain over her head and settled the locket at her breast then stood up and went to admire the effect in a small mirror.

'It looks grand,' she said. 'Like a lady.'

With the girl still busy looking at herself in the mirror, the man picked up a brown paper wrapped parcel and held it awkwardly by his side.

'And there's one wee thing I'd like ye tae dae for me,' he said. 'When we're on the ship, would ye call me—faither?'

'Faither?' She turned to face him. 'Why am I to do that?'

'Och well, it's just to stop folks asking questions about us travelling together while we're not wed.'

'Oh, well, I'll try tae remember—faither.' The girl tested the unfamiliar word. 'Mind you, I've never known a faither, or a mother come to that, so ye'll forgive me if I'm ill-used tae the notion.'

'Another thing, Margaret,' the man said. 'I've bought ye these new clothes—they'll fit ye fine but they're for a lad.' He placed the parcel on the table in front of her.

'Why am I to wear a boy's clothes?'

'Och, it's like I said. It's best we don't let too many people know oor business. If everybody thinks ye're a lad and I'm yer faither, we'll not be bothered, and besides, that way I can protect ye better. There's lots of rogues sail on these ships, single men on the look-out for pretty girls like yersell, wild sailors and a good deal worse, so if we travel as man and boy, I can keep a better eye on ye if we're in the same cabin, side by side.'

'Aye, side by side is all right, faither,' she said, still hesitant with that word. 'But remember, we'll not be man and wife.'

'Oh, I'll respect that, Margaret lass, right enough,' the man said. 'It'll only be for a wee while.'

'Just how long does it take tae get to Australia?' Margaret asked.

'Och, two, maybe three weeks,' he answered. 'Just a wee while. So I'll get oot o' the room and let ye try on the boy's clothes, then we'll awa doon tae the Broomielaw tae get on the wee steam boat that'll take us down the Tail o' the Bank tae the ship. The carter's coming in tae lift oor boxes at three o'clock.'

The man put on a jacket and went over to the right side of the room and opened a door, which had a strange old fashioned handle on it. The door closed and Adam heard him clumping downstairs then his sound was gone. Margaret looked at the clothes in the parcel and turned them over in distaste, then she sighed and took off her new locket and began one by one to undo the cloth buttons at the neck of her dress.

Adam turned away.

When he looked again, there was nothing in the circle of light for several minutes then he was in the room again but now it was empty, so there was time to take in details.

There was a bed on the left of the room, but not a free standing one such as he had at home. This bed was in an alcove set into the wall, with a red patched coverlet on it. On the back wall was the fireplace with iron bars and a glowing red fire from which a wisp of blue-grey smoke arose. A dark heavy kettle simmered at the side and a black metal box of coal lay open nearby with a small shovel sticking out. Above the fire was a mantelpiece with a square tin box on it.

The table had a few books and papers scattered around, there was a newspaper and an ink stand and pen. Adam strained to read the name or even the date on the newspaper but that was impossible from where he was.

In the background, there were vague noises—street sounds, he could tell; an occasional voice raised, calling something Adam couldn't make out. A street hawker of some sort, he imagined. From somewhere deep inside the building, there came a snatch of shrill argument; a door slammed violently, a child cried then from above came the thin scrape of a violin, rasping out a Scottish air. He heard the clop of slow horses hooves passing in the street outside and a rumble as of heavy iron-rimmed wagon wheels rolling over cobbles. A whip cracked but there was no sound of anything more modern.

From amongst the noises, there came the familiar click of the door latch but it was no more than the noise. He stared at the door for a long time until at last, he saw it open slightly. Not a wide, authorised opening, but a furtive sliver of a one, with someone behind it, testing the room to see if it was ripe to be entered. Adam waited and the crack opened just wide enough to allow a woman to slip in silently and close the door behind her.

She wore a shawl over her head from which a strand of untidy red hair escaped. Her face was white and her eyes flashed grim determination and Adam knew he had seen her before, not in a picture, but in words. The look on her face confirmed it; a compound of hate and triumph mixed in one. She was the woman of the diary; the Gypsy woman on the dockside at the Broomielaw.

Quickly and without a sound she crossed the room and knelt by the wooden cases. The smaller one was closed and secured but the larger one opened when she tried the lid. The woman had a small cloth bag with her which she put on the floor by her side and took from it a small coffin which she held in her hand with something akin to motherly affection. She prised off the lid.

'I shall gie thee a name,' she crooned. 'In return, ye're tae find a servant tae dae my bidding. I shall name thee Swith.' She put the lid on the coffin and thrust it into the wooden case and hid it amongst the clothes.

From her bag, the woman produced a second coffin and in the same way, named its occupant Agley. The third she called Smeddum and the fourth, Snell. When all the coffins were hidden in the luggage to her satisfaction, she tenderly smoothed out the clothing as if she'd done such a thing before then put the lid back on the wooden box and crossed to the table.

One of the books was a Bible which she opened and leafed through until she came to half a blank page at the end of a chapter. Amongst the writing instruments she found a stump of pencil and began to write slowly, speaking the words aloud as she did so.

Adam had seen that Bible and he already knew what she would write so he whispered aloud with her.

'*Four Demons I send wi' ye, Adam Colquhoun. Bleeze, Mischance and Foulness, and All Fall Doon.*' She closed the Bible then opened it again at the flyleaf and read the inscription there and made a bitter exclamation of disgust. She made three rapid strokes through her name and closed the Bible and tossed the pencil on the table.

Fascinated, Adam watched her take a last look around the room then go to the door, open it this time with a bold, satisfied click, step through and let it fall shut behind her.

The vision of the empty room stayed on the cave roof for some time then it appeared to grow darker as the fire settled in the grate and night fell. The scene faded but Adam continued to stare upwards at the circle of light on the ceiling of the cave.

Again, he heard sounds before he saw an image; it was the noise of heavy ship's timbers creaking and the sound of someone being sick. Adam peered at the circle of light and for a long time he could see nothing and then he saw the reason why. It was dawn and a cold grey light gradually filtered in to reveal the scene.

It was a cabin, which was no more than a space for two bunks, one on top of the other with a small floor space and a curtain instead of a door. The cabin seemed to move as if it had a life of its own then Adam realised he was seeing the ship in a heavy seaway. In the lower bunk, a pale hand moved and someone climbed painfully out into the light. It was Margaret, but she was dressed in trousers and shirt, the clothes of a young man. Her face was pallid and the shirt was streaked and her long hair hung down her back.

In the upper bunk, the man named Adam Colquhoun lay watching her.

'Hullo, lass,' he said. 'Were you sick again?'

'Ay, sick, always sick,' she said. 'And I've found out that it's not two or three weeks to Australia, it's more like four months. Like this! A hundred days!' She took up a comb and began running it through her hair.

'Who's been telling ye that?'

'I heard one of the sailors talking to a passenger.'

'Here, ye're not tae go talking wi' sailors. They're rantin' tykes and ever ready wi' a lie tae tell, especially tae a defenceless woman.'

Adam Colquhoun climbed out of the bed and tried to put his arm around Margaret's shoulders but she shrugged him off.

'I didn't talk to him,' she said. 'But I've a good mind to. At least he was talking the honest truth, not like you. You lied tae me, Adam Colquhoun. And how many more lies have ye tellt?'

'Wheesht! Keep yer voice doon!' Adam Colquhoun went to the curtained door and looked out apprehensively. 'We dinna want people tae ken oor private business.'

'I want tae get off this ship.' Margaret began putting her hair up into a cap. 'I want tae go hame.'

'Oh, ye canna dae that, lass,' Adam Colquhoun said. 'We're in the Atlantic Ocean.'

'Then I want tae dress as a woman,' she said. 'It's awful like this. How am I tae do my toilet, how am I tae wash my skin?'

'Oh lass, ye canna change now,' Adam Colquhoun said. 'It would go bad wi' me. The days'll pass quickly, then we'll be taegither in Australia. You and me in oor new life.' Once again he tried to put his arms around her but she pushed him away.

'I don't want tae know about oor new life,' she said coldly. 'If it's had such a bad beginning, then it's sure tae have a bad end. Now let me be. I'm going on deck for some of God's good air.'

'Then be sure not tae talk wi' any o' thae sailors,' Adam Colquhoun warned her. 'Dae ye hear what I'm tellin' ye?'

'I'm not listening,' she answered. 'I'll talk with who I care to.'

With that, she shrugged into a jacket and did up the buttons then passed out of the cabin, leaving Adam Colquhoun standing there rocking back and forth with the movement of the deck under his feet.

The scene faded but the noise continued. Then it grew louder until Adam heard the sound of wind howling and the groan of the ship now labouring in massive seas. He heard shuddering timber straining as wave after wave broke on it. Then he saw them, two men standing one each side of the ship's wheel, straining to keep the vessel on course against the thrust of wind and waves. The deck bucketed and heaved under them as they laboured at the wheel.

A figure emerged from the roil of foam and spray, dragging himself hand over hand along a lifeline rigged across the deck of the ship.

'You, Ramsay!' the newcomer shouted. 'Go you below tae my cabin and search in my small sea chest until you find a wee death's box. Fetch it here, and hurry man!'

'Ye mean a coffin, captain?'

'Aye, the same. Now fetch it back tae me for I have need of it right noo. Go, man, I'll tak the wheel in your stead. And you, Gibson,' he said to the other man. 'If ye ken a church prayer, then now's the time tae spout it!'

'I'm saying one already!' Gibson shouted back as the captain joined him at the wheel.

The man Ramsay painfully clasped his way along the lifeline, pausing to time his movements to the roll of the ship and the crash of waves that washed aboard. Adam watched him make a short dash then brace himself as another bigger wave washed over him. When it cleared, he saw the girl Margaret's pinched white face looking outwards from the shelter of a doorway. Ramsay clawed past her and another wave washed over and hid the scene and the vision disappeared.

Adam blinked his eyes furiously until tears came to wash away the dryness. He'd been staring so fixedly at the ceiling he'd forgotten the necessity of that simple action. His throat was burning and he felt chilled and raw but he couldn't leave the scene. Not yet.

In the cave, somebody sparked a big old lucifer match and lit a candle from its smoky flame and he saw it was the sailor, Ramsay. There was a noise from the tunnel entrance and Margaret crawled in and stood up and tried to shake the sand from her wet dress. She had a cloth bag with her which she threw heedlessly on the floor.

This was no image on the ceiling—they were with him in the cave, they were presences, living, breathing, making noises and footprints in the sandy floor. He could even see their clothes were wet and Margaret's long, dark hair was plastered and bedraggled. Ramsay had blood on his forehead as he calmly put his matches back into a waterproof pouch and stuck it in his belt.

'Oh, James,' Margaret had tears in her voice. 'It's terrible out there. There's bodies and . . . worse . . . wee bairns too, and the storm's blowing that cruel like it never wants tae stop.'

'Aye, but ye're safe here, Margaret,' James Ramsay said. 'It's dry and the sea and storm cannot touch us. When it blaws itself oot, we can go and find a hoose or a village.'

'But there could be wild men waiting for us, and fierce animals.'

'Och no. We'll fine—and here, I've got the captain's wee coffin with his mandrake man in it,' Ramsay produced the coffin from his pocket. 'Didna do the captain any good at the end, or the ship either, alas, but it must have served us right enough.'

Margaret shuddered at the sight of the coffin.

'Oh no,' she recoiled. 'Not another one of them!'

James Ramsay was all concern. He went over and took her by the hands.

'What is it, Margaret?'

'I've got *four* of them,' she said. 'They're what caused his madness—Adam Colquhoun. He kept going on about the demons that had come with him on the ship. Found news of it in his Bible, he said. I thought he was dighted mad and havering but he bid the sailors fetch up his box from the hold and he searched inside and sure enough, he found four of them. Said they'd already caused the fire, the poisoned water and the mischance that broke the mast. Said the last one would destroy the ship. And look what happened. He was right!'

'Here, Margaret, where are these demons?' James Ramsay's concern showed.

'They're in that bag there by that wee hole we came in,' she said. 'Adam bid me throw them over the side of the ship but I was too afraid to leave the hospital door and the sea was so rough I was in mortal fear of dying, so I forgot about them 'til now.'

James Ramsay walked across to the bag and picked it up and took out four small coffins which he placed one by one on the sandy floor.

'Demons, ye say?'

'Ay. Cursing demons. It was written in his Bible.'

'What, printed like scripture?'

'No, written by hand, someone had put it in for him tae find,' she said. 'I've a notion he had a wife before he met up wi' me. A wild Gypsy looking woman she was, it might have been her doing.'

James Ramsay looked at the four coffins and shook his head.

'Well, if demons they are, they've done their work,' he said. 'Help me bury them, Margaret. The captain's wee man's done his share too, for us, so we'll gie him charge ower these bad ones.'

Solemnly, Margaret and James Ramsay crouched on the floor and by the light of the candle, heaped a pyramid of sand over the five small coffins. As they worked at this simple almost childlike task, Margaret's anxiety eased and their hands touched over the sand and when they'd finished the burial, they kept holding hands and looked at each other in the soft light.

'Oh, Jamie.'

'Och, Margaret,' he said. 'Tae be able tae hold your hands at last and not tae be feart o' what others might say.' He kissed the back of her left hand then her right and pulled her to him and kissed her lips.

'Oh, Jamie,' Adam heard her sigh and he looked away.

He dozed and woke with a start. Only a single stump of candle lit the cave and in its wan glow, he saw Catriona sitting alone, staring at a small grey fire on the sandy floor. In her hands, she held a tiny doll-like figure made of yellow rope which she gently hugged to her breast as she rocked to and fro. Then she sang softly:

> *'Now in her green mantle, blythe nature arrays,*
> *And listens the lambkins that bleat o'er the braes,*
> *While birds warble welcome in every green shaw,*
> *But tae me it's delightless—my Jamie's awa'.*

She smiled when she said his name and bowed her head to kiss the doll, her long hair hung down, framing her face.

'Catriona,' Adam said gently but she made no sign she'd heard him so he was able to watch her for a full minute. He called her name again then realised he was looking not at Catriona, but at Margaret's image.

There came a shuffling from the entrance and she turned sharply and peered into the gloom at the same time, hiding the rope doll in the folds of her dress.

'It's me, Margaret,' James Ramsay said. 'Dinna tak' fright, lass. The night's come and out there the wind's still howling along the shore like a banshee houlet.'

'When can we go from this place, Jamie? We've been held fast here two days.'

'When the storm dies,' he said. 'Go out in this weather, and you'll catch a chill, and having found ye, Margaret, I'm not about tae lose ye tae some common malady.'

'Oh, ye're beautiful, Jamie.' Margaret smiled at him gently.

'Well, I wouldna say beautiful,' he said. 'That's no' a word for a man. I'd say lucky tae have found such a lass as you.'

'Tae have found each other,' she corrected him and tried to hide the rope doll deeper in the folds of her dress but Jamie saw the movement and took hold of her hand and turned it over.

'Here, whatever's this?'

Margaret smiled shyly.

'I saw you make it for one of the bairns on the ship,' she confessed. 'So I gave a penny for it.'

'It's only an old bit of tow,' he said. 'Why'd you want that?'

'I just wanted one for myself,' she replied simply then shivered and changed the subject. 'Oh, it's so cold, Jamie. Can we not light another fire?'

'The kindling's still too wet,' he said. 'You've got a blanket and I have my sea jacket. We can wrap ourselves in them and maybe we can lie close to each other for warmth.'

'Mister Ramsay! Me and you, lying down together!' Margaret pretended to be shocked. 'Sir, what a notion! The very idea!'

'Well then, lie by yourself, if that's your wish.' James Ramsay turned his back on her and dropped to his knees and busied himself gathering fragments of unburned wood and trying to blow some life into the small fire. Margaret went to him and put her hand on his shoulder and pulled him up towards her.

'No, ye needna look so offtaken, Jamie,' she said. 'I was only teasing. If I had all the blanket, you'd freeze the whole night through and I couldna bear tae think of that. Come, we'll lie together and share our warmth.'

'All right then, well lie doon, lass, and curl up and I'll

cover ye,' Jamie said, bashful now for not having seen her gentle mockery for what it was. He spread the blanket on the cave floor and Margaret lay on it. Carefully he took off her shoes and rubbed her feet briefly then covered her with one side of the blanket. He lay beside her and stretched his arm out to make a pillow for her head and pulled the other edge of the blanket over himself.

'Oh, that's braw, Jamie,' she whispered in a voice so low Adam could hardly hear it. 'I'm near asleep already. You do look after me well—and I love you for it.'

'Aye. That's my pleasure, Margaret, my love. Now, just hold still, lass, till I reach and snuff the candle. There.'

In the sudden darkness, Adam heard their brief whispers and Margaret laughed gently then they were silent and he felt lonely and chilled for the first time and the tears came again. The light from the torch had long since gone and there was no covering blanket and no one to share her warmth with him. At last, he dozed.

He woke to find himself still sitting upright, cramped and stiff. There was a painful crick in his neck from his head having lolled forward as he slept and his ribs ached continually with a dull, penetrating throb. Everything was pitch black and he knew there was nothing more to see. He rolled over on his uninjured side and dozed again.

Someone was holding him and there was a light nearby while a voice kept saying his name, over and over. Adam opened his eyes and saw Margaret nursing his head on her lap and rocking him. Her long hair hung down on either side of her face and she smiled in sudden relief, glad to see him awake.

'Oh, Margaret,' he recognised her. 'My love.'

'Adam, come on.' She shook him gently. 'We've got to go now. The storm's getting worse.'

'Then stay with me till it's over, lass,' he said. His eyes

swam in and out of focus and his head throbbed. 'We can't light a fire. The kindling's too wet.' He tried to pull her down to him. 'Lie with me in my blanket and we'll keep each other warm; my arm for a pillow, Margaret, my love.'

'Shh, Adam! Come on. Don't be silly. It's Catriona!' Gently, she freed herself from his embrace and shook him again.

'I know all about the demons, Margaret,' he said. 'I was looking in the room, see. While you and that man were out, the Gypsy woman came in and hid the coffins in his luggage. I saw her. She gave them names, Swith, Smeddum, Agley and Snell and she asked them to find servants to do her bidding.'

'Adam, please make an effort,' Catriona pleaded with him. A tear splashed down on to his face. 'You're lucky I found you.'

'We're lucky to have found each other,' Adam said then he focussed on her face and he saw the light reflected from the tears in her eyes.

'Catriona?'

'Adam, it's me.'

He tried to get up but an agonising wave of nausea and pain took hold of him and he settled back again. Suddenly, he felt the chill in his bones and shivered.

'You can't move, can you?' she said. 'I'll have to go for help.'

'How'd you ever find me out here, Cat?' His words were slurred.

'I don't know,' she answered. 'I was writing and suddenly my pen just wrote the words *cave—light—Adam—* like that. It wasn't my doing.'

'Then it must have been old Tam Dubh,' he said with a laugh. 'Up to his tricks; *he* brought you to me.' His head rolled to one side and a surge of pain flashed behind his eyes.

'Yes, sure Adam. Whatever you say.' She tried to sound normal in the face of Adam's delirious utterances. 'I'm going for help to get you out of here.'

'Get my father,' he said in a matter of fact voice. 'My old man, who will know exactly what to do for my welfare.'

'I'll leave you the lantern,' Catriona said. 'And my windcheater.' She gently disengaged his head from her lap and took off her windcheater and tucked it around his shoulders.

'You look after me well, Catriona, and I love you for it.' His voice was slurred and his eyes closed as he sank into a semi dream state, half dozing, half conscious.

'Thank you, Adam,' he heard her say. 'I just wish they were your words and not the fever's.' She went to the entrance and ducked low and was gone.

The lantern cast a pool of light on the sandy floor. Adam's eyes opened again and he rolled to the side and he saw the silvery gleam of the torch, lifeless now with its batteries long exhausted. Beside it stood Tam Dubh.

The doll's face, once so filled with expression and comfort, was now dead and spiritless. Adam closed his eyes and imagined Catriona looking down at him again. He felt her warm tear on his cheek and he heard her voice.

'*I just wish they were your words and not the fever's.*'

'They *were* my words!' he said aloud, half sitting up although his head was ringing with pain, his ribs seared with agony and every joint ached. 'Catriona! That *was* me talking, and when I see you, I'll say them again!'

Chapter Eleven

Adam lay in a fevered state, sometimes drowsing half awake and at other times held fast in a deep sleep. He wasn't cold any more and vaguely knew this was what people felt when they were freezing to death; a kind of numb warmness that made the passing easier. As long as he didn't try to put up a fight he'd be fine; he'd just go, which would be a shame in lots of ways, what with finding out so many things and getting closer to Margaret and Catriona the way he'd done, but there it was.

In one of his other ventures into wakefulness, Adam received a fleeting impression of there being a light in the cave by which he was able to see Tam Dubh, still standing upright and level with his eye; but it was not the Tam Dubh of the bright and cheerful face. In that brief flash of wakefulness he realised the doll was now pale and burned out.

'What's up, Tam Dubh?' he asked and his own words were an effort. 'Been going it a bit have you? Too much, eh?'

Somebody close at hand said his name in an enquiring way but he swam away from them and began to sink into yet another cosy dream.

Catriona was there, or was it Margaret, trying to lift him and showing concern for his welfare.

'Careful!' he heard her say and there were others too and they wrapped him in a blanket.

'Come and lie with me, Catriona,' Adam mumbled and reached out for her. 'Use my arm for your pillow, share our warmth together.'

'Shh, Adam,' her voice came quickly and her fingers stopped his lips.

'I didn't hear a word of that,' another voice said and in reply somebody else laughed softly. A man's voice.

They worked around him for a while, making medical smells then harsh light and rain momentarily touched his face until he was rocked gently in a vehicle which bumped and Catriona, or was it Margaret, held him steady against the motion.

☆   ☆   ☆

When he opened his eyes, Tam Dubh was there again, still at the edge of his vision, standing as if on sentry duty but looking sad and withered and clearly unfit for such a task.

There was someone else there, sitting by his bedside with head bowed. It was an effort to change focus so he could identify who it was and then he recognised Catriona. For a while he watched her and thought how much she looked like Margaret the way he'd seen her sitting in the cave waiting for Jamie to return. Catriona was reading and lifted her head when she turned a page of her book and saw him with his eyes open, looking at her.

'Oh, there you are,' she smiled and stood up and came to him.

'Hi.' He kept his eyes on her face.

'You've been out of things for a while,' she said.

'Yes.'

'Your mother's at the surgery and I volunteered to stay with you,' Catriona kneeled by the bedside. 'She'll be pleased you're awake. I'll telephone in a minute.'

'What's been happening?'

'You, mainly.' She touched his hand. 'Whatever happened was weird. Unreal. Everyone's been worried.'

'Yes,' he said and thought about it.

'Something made me go to the cave,' she said. 'I had no say in it at all. I was doing an assignment when these three words just appeared on the page. I mean, I wrote them and everything but—'

'I've got it all now, Catriona,' he butted in. 'The whole story, I saw it all. She's very like you.'

'Who is?'

'Margaret Colquhoun.'

'She's dead,' Catriona said. 'She's been dead for years. Her grave's in the cemetery.'

'Well, she *was* just like you.' He changed tense. 'Hair the same, face like yours, same build and everything. She was really beautiful.'

'There's no picture of her, Adam, so how do you know?'

'Only her voice was different,' he ignored her objection and went on. 'She had an accent, well you'd expect that, wouldn't you?'

'Adam,' Catriona tried to soothe him.

'I saw her and I heard her speak,' he became agitated and in an effort to convince her he tried to rise from the bed. There came a sudden sharp pain at his ribs and he winced deeply and held his side.

'Hey, wait a minute,' Catriona became uneasy. She held his shoulders to keep him from getting up. 'Just hang on and I'll ring your mother.'

'It wasn't a dream,' he said. 'I saw everything. Jamie Ramsay was there with her and I saw Adam Colquhoun who wanted her to call him father. Tam Dubh showed me.' The pain from his exertion was becoming acute and he lay back on the pillow and she looked at him in concern.

'Look, don't move, Adam,' she stood up. 'I'm going to the telephone.'

'No,' he spoke sharply. 'It's hard to believe but just listen and I'll tell you.' But she had already gone and he was left with the pain.

'Well, talk about the long sleep,' his mother said. 'It's Tuesday afternoon and you've been out since Sunday.' Catriona hovered in the background while his mother sat by the side of his bed. 'We were worried.'

'Sorry,' he answered. 'What was wrong with me?'

'Not was, *is*. You're suffering from chronic fatigue, emotional exhaustion, chilled to the bone, bruised all over and you've got a couple of dodgy ribs for good measure.'

'Is that a medical diagnosis?' He quoted a line his father used when his mother applied lay expressions like that.

'Never mind the surgical one-upmanship,' she said. 'What have you been up to to get in such a state? I gave you a bed bath, dressed your wounds and bruises and got you into your pyjamas, so I know, big boy.'

'He says he's been finding things out,' Catriona said.

'Oh yes.' His mother nodded her head wisely. 'Such as how it feels to be on the wrong end of a serious fist fight?'

Adam put a hand on his rib cage and found it tightly bandaged and painful to the touch. He winced.

'And what a coincidence Richard Vernon should turn up early Sunday morning, just after you'd been out all night,' his mother went on.

'Oh,' Adam said.

'Yes, oh.' His mother turned around to Catriona as she spoke. 'I popped my head in here early Sunday morning to close his windows because of the rain, about two o' clock it must have been and lo and behold, there's not a sign of him in bed or in the house. Funny that. Next morning, I'm called out to check Richard Vernon over and he's mumbling and incoherent, gabbling on about Adam Hardy and how he's the cause of it all.'

'I'm sure there's an explanation, Jean,' Catriona said, but

Adam could see she was concerned at the news of Richard's condition.

'And I'm sure it will be wonderfully inventive,' Adam's mother went on. 'But all in good time.'

'How's Dad?' Adam said.

'Impatient for an explanation,' his mother answered. 'But that can wait too. It's good to see you on the mend, Adam dear.' She bent and kissed him on the forehead. 'You must be starving. I'll bring you something special.'

After Adam had eaten and Catriona had gone home, his father came to the bedroom and stood by the chest of drawers near the door, picking things up and examining them as he spoke.

'Your mother says you're feeling better,' he said and spun the wheels of a model 2-6-0 locomotive before settling it back on its short length of rail.

'Yes, a lot better, Dad. Thanks.'

'There's been a lot going on,' his father said. 'The business at the pump station, being caught in Mike Carter's garage and being away on Saturday night or Sunday morning, and now this latest episode. A lot going on.'

'Yes.' Adam decided to let his father do the talking.

'Any explanation?'

'I went to Mike Carter's place because I thought I recognised him at the pump station,' Adam said. It sounded implausible and even as he uttered the words, he could see half a dozen follow-up questions and objections that would arise. 'I went looking for evidence,' he added.

'Why not just tell the police and let them sort it out?'

'I didn't want to dob in a mate,' he said and even that feeble answer didn't work.

'Fair enough,' his father responded. In Adam's weakened and vulnerable state, his father was being gentle with him and Adam guessed his mother would have issued instructions to tread softly. 'So you didn't want to dob in your mate, but what were you going to do with this evidence when you got it?'

Touché, Dad. Adam decided to try a medical solution.

'I've been under a lot of pressure,' he said. 'You know, since the bus accident.' That was a brainwave. Bus accident creates emotional turmoil which accounts for son's irrational behaviour. Brilliant!

'Mmm,' his father said. 'So you went back to the scene of the accident, found somebody in the pump station and got caught by the police?'

'I suppose so.'

'Well, that takes care of the first Saturday night,' his father said. 'So what about last Saturday? From your injuries I'd say you'd been under a different kind of pressure, so what happened?'

Things were becoming tricky. To say he'd met Richard Vernon and come off second best could open up a whole new line of questioning. It was his mother who solved the problem.

She came into the bedroom and moved between her husband and Adam and sat on the edge of the bed.

'How's my patient?' She felt his forehead.

'I'm fine, Mum,' he said. 'Really, I'm fine, now.'

☆　☆　☆

Late on Wednesday night, Adam was alone. The bedroom was dark except for his bedside light. He had tried getting up and found it both a painful and unnerving experience where the floor seemed to rush up to meet him and his legs were unequal to the task of supporting his body weight. That brought on a bout of head-swimming nausea and his mother had to help him back to bed.

'It'll take time,' she assured him.

They had given Adam the small portable television set,

the one that kept changing from colour to black and white and made night time football games difficult to follow. He soon gave it up as a bad job and tried to read a novel but the memories of the cave experience were far more vivid and absorbing than any book could be.

Tam Dubh stood propped against the bedside light and Adam smiled. Someone must have picked the doll up from the cave floor and put it there; Catriona's doing, he imagined.

'Hello, Tam Dubh,' he whispered. But there was no flicker of interest from the doll's face. It was now a dead and lifeless thing. Adam looked up to the ring of light cast by the bedside lamp but only a moth circled there, its shadow moving in and out of the patch of brightness.

'I suppose any day now Hamish Leckie will be along to collect you,' he remarked aloud. He smiled to himself as he remembered the determined way Hamish had gone after the other four dolls and then he thought of the stern lecture he would receive for taking Tam Dubh from the museum display in the first place.

Never mind, one day soon he'd be able to tell Hamish what he'd seen and wouldn't he be interested in that? A visit to nineteenth century Glasgow and then on the ship and in the cave with Jamie Ramsay and Margaret Colquhoun, only he'd have to stop calling her that because she had only taken that surname as part of the deception.

The story was all complete now; the diary, the dolls, the curses, the possession of Mike and Richard and the aftermath. A plan was forming in his mind to tell it to his father, firstly, to explain what had been going on and secondly, so he'd know what a narrow escape they'd all had.

There was a cassette recorder in his bedside cabinet with a cassette already in it, so maybe that was the way; he'd speak his thoughts into it while they were fresh. He pressed the record button and a red light glowed and he heard the whirr as the tape began to roll.

'This is for you, Dad,' he said into the microphone, 'it's my way of explaining what's been going on, not just over the last couple of weeks, but in general. Let's face it, we didn't choose each other and I can't make you the kind of father I'd like any more than you can make me into the guy you want for a son.'

Adam pressed the pause button and lay for a long time with the machine waiting for him to go on. There was a lot he wanted to say but he needed the words to say it. What the hell, he could always erase the cassette if it didn't come out right. He'd begin with an explanation of what had been happening and that would be something done. He flicked the pause button again and the tape rolled once more and he spoke into the microphone.

'So I'm going to start with an account of a nineteenth century sailing ship that left Scotland full of migrants bound for Australia. Strange thing about this ship is it had four curses laid on it,' he paused. 'Now, what's this got to do with me, I hear you ask; well, over a hundred years later, in our own little town of Dunarling, three of those curses started acting again . . .'

'But mind, there are four o' us and jist the wan o' thee.' A mocking sing song voice came from somewhere in his memory. *Until the curses be laid tae rest, we'll fight ye ower and ower again. Till the end o' time if need be.'*

After that reminder, Adam pressed the pause button again and lay for a long time before picking up the thread of his story.

The cassette was finished. He decided not to listen to it or do it over again. He reflected briefly that it might have been a more mature thing to have sat his father down and just told him the story, but he could imagine the interruptions, the disbelief and cross questioning that would flow.

This was a better way. When he became fully mobile

again, he'd give it to his father. It was a start anyway. He thought about the next hurdle; Catriona.

It would be nice, he thought, to get the strapping off his ribs and be able to lie on his side again, but that would come.

It would be nice to be able to do a lot of things.

☆   ☆   ☆

On Thursday afternoon, on her way home Catriona dropped in to bring him up to date with local events and news from school. His mates were missing him and every day they asked Catriona how he was. Only that morning M and M had cornered her in the toilets and enquired very kindly after Adam while Ms Mullins had baled her up and asked in that forthright way of hers, what was wrong with Hardy and when was he was coming back.

Secretly, Adam was pleased that so many people had asked Catriona about him; it was almost as if they all knew they were *linked*. An item, going steady or whatever the words were. Nice words.

'Have you seen Hamish Leckie?' he asked her. 'I suppose he'll go off on another of his rampages when he sees me.' Briefly he imitated Hamish and the way he carried on when something upset him.

'I saw him Wednesday,' she said. 'Had to give him some letters I'd transcribed. Boring stuff about the sale of a house in 1879. No, he's cool.'

'I mean, did he ask about me?'

'Oh yes, he just asked how you were.'

Adam looked at Tam Dubh then at Catriona.

'Did he say anything about me taking the doll?'

'No, he didn't mention that,' she said. 'He's got the other four on display now, you know—all lit with a cold, blue light in that little grey cave he made for them; they look quite spooky.'

'Well, if everything's so cool I can relax,' Adam said. 'What else is news?'

Richard Vernon was now in hospital, Catriona went on to report, and he was still under sedation but the police didn't appear to be looking for anyone in connection with his disappearance. She had also heard, but wouldn't say from where, that they were treating Richard as a runaway and they were waiting to interview him to get his side of the story. They seemed to suspect a connection between Mike Carter's highly disturbed condition and Richard's mysterious disappearance.

There were similarities in the way the two boys looked and acted and very marked comparisons to be made between the things they were saying.

'Has Tom Balfour spoken with you yet?' he asked.

'Um . . .' she hedged.

'Well, what did he say?'

'He just asked me what prompted us to go to Mike Carter's place.'

'And you said?'

'I said we thought he was the one you saw at the pump station.'

'Oh yes,' Adam said. 'And he asked why we didn't go to the police if we suspected Mike.'

'Something like that,' she agreed. 'But I don't think he was altogether satisfied with my answers.'

'I wonder why,' Adam said with a sniff.

She picked up the novel he had been reading and made a show of being interested. Quite suddenly she lifted her head and caught him staring at her.

'Why are you looking at me like that?'

'Just thinking,' he said and paused. 'Catriona, when you came to the cave, you know, when you found me and put your windcheater around me.'

'Ye-es,' she was cautious.

'Well, I said something to you.'

'Did you?'

'Yes,' he was serious. 'Do you remember what I said?'

'Vaguely,' she looked up to the ceiling as if trying to remember then she spoke quickly. 'You were saying crazy things and I was scared stiff, what with crawling along that tunnel all by myself not knowing what I'd find or why I was even going there. So it's all a bit hazy, you know, blurred.'

'Oh well, never mind,' he dropped his eyes. 'It's not important.'

Catriona went back to the novel but she couldn't keep up the pretence for long. A slow smile broke out on her face and she dropped her head so her hair would hide it. Then she relented and looked up.

'Of course I remember what you said.' She smiled at him.

'I said, you look after me well,' Adam repeated his words. 'And I love you for it.'

Catriona nodded and went back to the novel as if it were vastly more interesting than anything he had to say. She turned another unread page and kept her eyes down.

'I suppose that was just the fever talking,' she observed. 'Made you say silly things; things you didn't mean.'

He looked at her bowed head.

'I meant it,' he said and steeled himself to say more. 'I've—loved you for a long time.' Then his words came out in a rush. 'I'm sure it's love only I don't really know, but I think about you and I'd rather be with you than with anyone and I've been trying to get you alone somewhere away from school, just to talk because I love talking with you, then maybe I could see what you thought.'

'That's nice,' she said simply.

'Is that all?' he said. 'It's nice?'

'Yes, it's very nice. Really, it's—very nice.'

They stayed for a long time without speaking until there

was a noise downstairs and they knew it was his mother home from surgery and starting to come upstairs.

'I love you too,' Catriona said to him quickly. 'Couldn't you tell?' Then his mother came into the bedroom, idly sorting through the personal mail that had come that day.

'Hello, Catriona,' she said. 'And how's our patient?'

'A lot better now,' Adam answered.

'Well, you've certainly got a lot more colour in your cheeks,' his mother said.

Late on Thursday night, after the television had stopped for the day, Adam's father popped his head into the bedroom.

'Hello,' he said. 'Just doing the rounds. Your mother reports good progress.'

'Yes, Dad, I feel a lot better.'

'Good. You'll soon be up and about. And what then, I ask myself.'

'It's okay, Dad,' Adam said. 'It's over, all that stuff.'

'Ah yes, but while it lasted, what stuff it was.'

'Fair enough.' Adam sighed deeply and caused a pain in his ribs. He reached for the cassette he had recorded. 'I'd like you to do something, Dad.'

'Yes?' His father waited.

'This is a cassette I did for you. It's all about—that stuff. Explanations and everything.'

His father took the cassette and looked at it. Adam had written 'For Dad' on it.

'I want you to listen to it right through,' Adam went on. 'It's the truth and it's about you and me.'

'Right through, you say?'

'Yes. Both sides. Then we'll talk, eh?'

'Okay, Adam. I'm off to Geelong in the morning so I'll listen to it in the car.'

'Good.' Adam sighed in relief and this time he stopped the intake of breath before the pain came.

☆   ☆   ☆

On Friday morning, Adam got out of bed and began to get around under his own power. His ribs still ached and he moved with difficulty. His mother had stayed home for the morning to oversee the event.

'Just make sure a certain person doesn't embrace you too vigorously,' was her comment.

'Mum!' He showed his embarrassment. 'As if a certain person would!'

'Oh, just good friends, are we?' She sat on the edge of his bed and looked at him over by the window. 'What's the matter with you both?'

Adam ignored her banter and concentrated on walking up and down the length of his bedroom.

His father hadn't gone to Geelong after all; something had come up at the hospital which took precedence so Adam imagined the cassette would have to wait for a hearing.

Later he went out to the garden and tried making a few more strenuous movements. His mother came to join him and they sat together under the shade of a tree.

'Mum,' he said, as if testing the water. 'Do you think I could go to the re-enactment tomorrow?'

'Well, you don't want to rush things,' she responded. 'There'll be a lot of people; I think the whole town's going to be on that train. We're leaving the station on buses then returning by the train in the afternoon so it'll be a full day with a lot of travel. On and off the bus, on and off the train and a lot of jostling in between. Are you sure you're ready?'

'I think so,' he said. 'I feel okay; bit of pain still but otherwise I'm fit. Besides, Barbara Chisholm's made me a costume so it would be sort of bad manners for me not to go.'

'Ah, the costume,' his mother said and nodded seriously. 'Oh yes, if Barbara's gone to all that trouble, you couldn't very well not go, could you? Of course it would be bad manners.'

'Yes, that's what I thought.'

'Any other reason?'

'Well, yes,' he admitted and looked at her. 'I'd like to go with Catriona.' His mother smiled.

'Then I think you should go, Adam.'

'Great,' he said. 'I'll give Catriona a ring and tell her.'

Catriona was delighted with Adam's news and they soon made plans for her to come over with Barbara later that night for a final dress rehearsal. Adam was to try on his costume so it could receive comments and last minute adjustments. His father, who planned to dress as a turn of the century locomotive fireman, complete with a bowler hat, was to attend another safety check and briefing given by the man from the railways department.

'Goodness,' Barbara said, coming into the lounge with two armfuls of flowing garment. 'What a lot women wore in those days. Must have taken hours to dress.' Catriona followed behind with her costume and a parcel for Adam.

'Ta-ra!' she said and held it out to him. 'The famous costume!'

'Well, let's try things on and see how we look,' Adam's mother said. 'The sewing machine's there if anything needs alteration.' They gathered their bundles of clothing and headed off in different directions to find places to change.

Adam's costume, when he undid the parcel, was that of a nineteenth century sailor. Barbara had copied it from the one in the Dunarling museum and had even gone to the trouble of providing a canvas bag on a rope so he could look like he was going home on leave or travelling to join a ship. He put the outfit on, smiling at his reflection in the bedroom mirror, then went downstairs to wait for the others to join him.

Barbara was first to come into the lounge wearing a green dress and carrying a parasol of some matching material.

'Barbara, you look fantastic,' Adam said. 'You've gone to a lot of trouble.'

'I hope the sun's out tomorrow so I can use my parasol,' she said.

'This is a great costume.' He held out his arms to let her see the effect. 'Thanks for doing it for me.'

'Ah well, I'm glad you like it, Adam. It looks good on you. You fill it well.'

His mother came next into the room wearing a deep lilac dress and matching bonnet.

'Make way for a nineteenth century lady of high fashion,' she said and went over and posed with Barbara by the fireplace.

'Come on, Catriona,' Barbara called. 'Show yourself, girl!'

'My zip's stuck,' Adam heard her call from upstairs. 'Damn!'

'A zip?' his mother called back. 'They didn't have zip fasteners in those days. Who's been skimping on the authenticity?'

'Coming, coming.' Adam eventually heard Catriona's voice on the stairs. She was flustered and came into the room still fussing with the zip fastener at her waist.

'There!' she said. 'What do you think?'

She wore a russet dress and a shawl. Dark hair framed her face in twin ringlets and at the sight of her, Adam was instantly back in that brown painted room in Glasgow. *She was Margaret*.

Everything else faded from his vision until in the centre of a vagueness, there was only Margaret. The colour drained from his face as he stared at her.

'Adam,' she looked at him with concern. 'What's wrong?'

'Margaret,' he said and at the edge of the greyness, there came sounds of disquiet. She turned to him and let him see what she was wearing around her neck, the gold heart shaped locket with the long chain and he remembered how she had received them.

'*Later we can get oor likenesses taken and put them inside; me and you together, then I'll always be near yer heart,*' he heard Adam Colquhoun say in his wheedling voice.

'Margaret, why do you wear his locket?' Adam said. 'After all Colquhoun did to you. He was a liar and a cheat so how can you bear to even *touch* anything of his?'

'Adam!' Margaret looked helplessly to some other people who were there and went to him to put her hand on his arm. 'What's wrong?'

'Margaret, I know everything,' he said in a rush. 'I was there all the time, watching and I saw the Gypsy woman come in and put the dolls in his baggage. She gave them names and charged them to do her bidding. Swith, Agley, Smeddum and Snell—I've met them all and they're evil.'

Someone was taking hold of him and trying to make him sit down while Margaret looked at him with her eyes full of concern. But now he had a chance to warn the girl and let her know what was to happen if she went on that voyage.

'She wrote in the Bible, I saw her and I saw her score her own name out. It was her, the Gypsy woman—she did it and I know what's going to happen to everybody. Bleeze, mischance and foulness and all fa' doon. You mustn't go, you mustn't go!'

The vagueness that encircled Margaret began to close in from all around until it appeared she was in a deep tunnel and receding but still reaching for him with outstretched hands. The vagueness closed in completely until there was nothing but black.

☆　　☆　　☆

It seemed to Adam the process was reversing itself. First, there was a moving, pink shape that appeared to hover in front of him. Gradually, it took form and he saw it was a face and it was nice looking so he decided to trust it.

'Hello,' his voice was thick.

'Hi,' said the face. 'You're awake?' Bright light filled the room and everything was white with it. 'They brought you in last night,' the pink face said and moved away out of range, humming and bustling.

'This is a hospital?' he said.

'Nursing home,' the voice with the pink face corrected him. 'Your Mum brought you in. For observation. You had a bit of a funny turn.'

'What day is it?'

'Saturday. Lovely morning for the re-enactment.' She came into view again. 'Feeling all right? You had an injection so you might be a bit woozy still. If you feel sick, there's a basin.'

'What time is it?'

'Oh, early,' the voice said from over by the door. 'We thought it was something straight out of the museum when you came in. Your sailor's outfit's on a hanger behind the door. It's really cute.' The face flitted around briefly. 'I'm off duty soon. Going on the re-enactment. I'm going as a nun. Cheerio.'

Adam lay on the stiff white bed, gradually adjusting to this new antiseptic reality and trying to recall what he'd done to warrant such treatment. The door opened and it was his mother with his father in the background.

'Hello, darling,' she said and bent to kiss him.

'Looks like I blew it,' Adam's voice showed his disappointment.

'Never mind, I think we tried too much too soon,' his mother said.

'There's another doctor coming from Melbourne to have a look at you,' his father spoke from the doorway.

'A head shrinker?' Adam said. 'You think I'm going the way Mike Carter did? And Richard Vernon?'

'Shh, darling, let's not talk about it now,' his mother said. 'I won't go on the re-enactment.'

'Wait a minute, Jean!' his father protested and they began a muted conference while Adam raised an eyebrow.

'Look, *go*, Mum.' He turned away from them. 'I'm in good hands here.' He put up with the pain in his side until they said their goodbyes and left.

Catriona and Barbara arrived bearing flowers cut from their own garden and wrapped in a cone of newspaper. Barbara went for a vase and water leaving Catriona alone with him.

'Last night was really scary,' she said. 'It was as if you thought I was her.'

'You could be sisters, or even twins,' he said.

'How can you know all this?' Catriona shook her head.

'I was there,' he said and Barbara came back with the vase and set it down on a table by the door.

'We can only stay a minute,' she said. 'We've got to change then catch the bus.'

'Sorry you can't come, Adam.' Catriona took his hand while Barbara fussed around with the flowers, primping them and settling the best blooms to the front.

'You're so like Margaret,' he whispered.

'Oh, Adam!' Catriona pleaded with her eyes. 'Please don't start that again. Margaret never married and died when she was still young; only eighteen, she was, so there's no way we're related.'

'Darling, you're getting Adam all excited,' Barbara said over her shoulder and tossed the crumpled newspaper into the bin beside the table.

'You've got to believe me,' he held on to Catriona's hand.

Barbara was first to leave and then, as if she didn't want to go from him, Catriona moved away at full arm's length before dropping Adam's hand.

'Goodbye, Adam,' she said from the door then she was gone.

On the ceiling, he found a tiny speck of black which marred the perfect whiteness. Maybe it had been a fly or a small dead insect but it was one little blemish, a flaw, no more than a minor doubt.

Why had Hamish Leckie not come to collect Tam Dubh?

It was in such contrast with the way he'd sought out the other dolls. ('Och, come to me, my little darlings. Have I been looking forward to meeting you.') And then at the viaduct with Richard, the doll had almost been his chief priority. First things first, Hamish had said.

Soon Adam began to find other small blemishes on the ceiling and was amazed at how many there were once you started looking for them. It must have been the initial overpowering whiteness that blotted them out, he reasoned. You didn't expect to see any but when you concentrated, there they were.

He rolled on his side and stared at the wall where the vaseful of flowers provided a bright dash of colour. Beneath them stood the bin containing the crumpled wet newspaper in which they'd been wrapped. There was a photograph on the front page showing a girl in shorts displaying a fair bit of leg. He could just make out that she was leaning on a bicycle.

Bicycle—his bicycle—cycling to the viaduct. It was almost like playing a word association game. One bicycle thought lead to another until there was a whole train of them. Hiding the bike in the long grass behind a low wall—Hamish with his utility—putting Richard into the cab—and the bicycle again.

'Adam, nip over and fetch your bike,' Hamish had said. 'Sling it in the back and we'll be home in five minutes.'

Adam remembered crossing the main road in the darkness, stepping over the low wall, groping around in the long grass then finding his bicycle.

But how did Hamish know it was there?

In the garage on that disastrous afternoon, Mrs Carter said she'd made a *couple* of telephone calls and the police had turned up; that was one call. Then her husband had arrived—two calls.

And then came Hamish Leckie.

At the viaduct, when Adam had most needed help; then came Hamish Leckie.

Two very timely arrivals. *But who sent him?*

Adam thought carefully. What did he know about Hamish Leckie? When he first arrived in town, Hamish had been in the papers; they'd done a story on him: *Falklands hero finds a quieter life in Dunarling*.

What sort of hero had he been? A sergeant in the Royal Engineers. And what was his specialty? An explosives expert. The word 'explosives' set off another train of associations. Tom Balfour, talking to the entire school:

'I'm sure you've also seen the story about the break-in down at the railway works department,' he had said. 'As part of that incident, a quantity of explosives, detonators and other material was removed.'

And later, Tom Balfour talking with his father:

'The dark garment, a boiler suit, is reeking of white ant killer, almost certainly stolen from the railway works department store.'

Mike Carter and Richard Vernon were possessed by the dolls they had taken and were each told to destroy themselves because they had failed their masters, but on the viaduct, what had Richard failed to do?

'I think the whole town's going to be on that train,' Adam's mother had said.

All fa' doon.

Chapter Twelve

Walking through town in his last century sailor's outfit, Adam felt stupid and conspicuous but he needn't have worried; the streets were almost deserted. Three pensioners, two men and a woman, waited by the clock tower for the bus to take them to their Saturday afternoon bingo session.

'You've missed it,' one of the men said to him. 'They'll all be there by now.'

'Yes, I'll have to get a move on,' Adam agreed and walked past.

'Talk about a drunken sailor,' the woman pensioner said behind her hand. 'As my Wilf used to put it, I think he's been sipping certain substances.' The others laughed.

Leaving the hospital had been easy. He'd got out of bed and splashed some of the water from the carafe on his face then put the sailor's outfit on over his pyjamas. He didn't have a comb to run through his hair but that was a detail. The corridor outside his room was long and empty and still in his groggy state, he dithered for a few seconds, not knowing which way to turn.

A woman patient came out of another room, wearing a dressing gown and slippers and carrying a transistor radio. She paused and regarded Adam's outfit briefly but if she thought it at all strange, she made no remark.

'Where can I buy batteries for this?' she showed him her radio.

'Um, there's usually a shop,' he said. 'It might be down by the main entrance.'

'Well, that's this way,' the woman said. 'Here, give me your arm, will you.' Together they made their way along the corridor and turned left and left again until they came to a counter with newspapers, magazines and assorted boxes of sweets arranged on it. Behind the counter a woman spoke on the telephone.

'Oh, I know,' she said into the mouthpiece. 'You've got to keep your wits about you, especially these days.' She didn't notice Adam.

'This is it,' the woman patient smiled her thanks and took her hand off his arm. Adam had already seen a sign pointing to the exit and within seconds he was out into the gardens, breathing lungfuls of fresh air.

The museum had a sign on it saying closed, but one of the double doors was ajar. Adam pushed it and it creaked open. The dummy sailor glowered at him from his darkened corner of the main room and in the opposite side, the blue light from the canvas cave still glowed. Adam approached the display but he already knew what he would see.

The broken pyramid of sand was there, but the four coffins containing the mandrake dolls had already gone.

'*Swith, Agley, Smeddum and Snell. Wi' agramie and ancient, honeyed words thy man's gudewife has given us oor grim charge tae make a' kinds o' mischief upon him.*'

Almost in a daze, Adam went out into the street and was sick.

In the station, he heard a transistor playing. It was the familiar Saturday afternoon sound of somebody calling a horse race and he traced the nasal monotone of the radio voice to the station master's office where Charlie Boyd sat, incongruously dressed in a top hat and tail coat, listening intently to the call of the race.

Charlie acknowledged Adam's presence at the door and held up a finger for him to be quiet until the result was confirmed.

'Damn!' he said when the brief surge of excitement from the radio got control of itself once more. 'Young Hardy, what can I do for you?'

'The train,' Adam said. 'Any way of stopping it?'

'You've missed it, son. You were supposed to go on the buses with the others.'

'No, I want to stop the train.'

'It's already left,' Charlie pointed to a brown station clock on the office wall. 'Been gone ten minutes now; it'll be here in an hour.'

'No,' Adam slumped and tried again. 'Is there a signal so you can stop it?'

'Here, aren't you supposed to be in hospital?' Charlie went on. 'Saw your Mum this morning and she told me where you were. You don't look all that good.' He became concerned and stood up and approached Adam, offering him a chair.

'No,' Adam said and backed away.

'Hey, listen lad,' Charlie put out a hand and came towards him. 'One thing's for sure, you're not supposed to be out of bed. So come on, sit here and I'll get someone.'

'You don't understand—' Adam began and turned away.

'Look, you'll be better off, Adam.' Charlie picked up the telephone and dialled three numbers while Adam turned away from him and ran along the length of the platform and out into the bright sunlight and down the ramp and then on to the line that led out to Dunarling Viaduct.

It was a lovely day for the re-enactment. The sun shone brightly and to Adam's right, the sea was blue and a light breeze tugged at his clothes as he walked. It took more than twenty-five minutes to cover the distance to the viaduct and he was finding the exertion and the constant pacing out along the sleepers to be tiring. Twice he missed his footing and on one of those occasions he slipped and fell heavily on the line and lay gritting his teeth with the pain from his ribs.

A flush of warm, dark nausea welled up over his eyes and he sat on the line and dropped his head between his legs, which he knew to be a safeguard against fainting. The dizziness passed and he got to his feet again and saw the viaduct only about a hundred metres ahead.

Hamish Leckie was in the middle of the structure, pacing back and forth along the edge of the line. He had something in his hand, something long and slender and silvery, which flashed in the sunlight as he turned at each end of the path he had allotted to himself.

It was a perfectly normal recognition, almost as if the two had met in Dunarling High Street on an ordinary Saturday morning.

'Hello, Adam,' Hamish was the first to call a greeting and his voice was calm although there was an apprehensive edge to it.

'Hi, Hamish,' Adam said and moved closer then stopped with only a few metres separating them.

'On your own, are you?' Hamish asked and then a slow smile broke out on his face. 'You *are* on your own.' Below them to the right, the waters rushed up the gorge then ebbed slowly outwards to meet the next wave crashing in from the sea. Even on the calmest of days you could be sure of some turbulence down there.

'It's a nice day,' Adam offered. It was something to say.

'Yes, lovely,' Hamish agreed shortly. He turned and looked back along the track in the direction from which the train would come. 'Lovely day for it. Bonny.'

'And what are you doing out here, Hamish?'

'I've got this,' Hamish showed him what he held in his

hand. It was a radio control unit for a model aircraft and the slender silvery aerial whipped as he moved. 'Bought it in Dunarling Sports store. It's state of the art, this one.'

'So where's your model?' Adam tried to keep his voice normal to match the way Hamish spoke.

'It's not for a *toy!*' Hamish exploded in a sudden discharge of scorn and contempt. 'I've not got a wee aeroplane on the other end of this, you sad gawkie!' He spoke in bitter, derisive words. 'Tam Dubh's little puppy, his urchin, his lickspittle servant, his wee lap-dog without his master taking him by the hand. He has sent the spawn but not the frog.' He turned away and the aerial flashed silver.

'Hamish,' Adam tried again. 'I know everything, I've seen it. Tam Dubh showed me. It's over now, the four dolls have done their work.'

'Not till the last curse be done,' Hamish said doggedly. 'Then again and again.'

'You've got to put that thing down and come back with me. Now, Hamish,' Adam persisted.

'No, it's you that's got to come with me,' Hamish turned to face him. 'Everyone's going to come with me. All fa' doon, that's my charge and I must dae my bidding.'

Adam took a step closer.

'Stay, whelp!' Hamish warned and held the radio controller out as if it were a rapier and then he calmed again and sounded almost reasonable, as if describing some rational proposal. 'The loco will come around the bend there, then it'll come on to the viaduct. It'll take it slowly but it'll not be able to stop, y'see because they don't want such a weight resting on these old timbers for too long. When it's in the exact centre, I will blow the main supports, so that's how it will be done. It's all arranged and you cannot stop it.'

'Hamish, this is madness,' Adam said. 'The dolls have possessed you, the way they did Mike and Richard.'

'Hah!' he said. 'They were bairns. But you can run if you

want to—that way!' He pointed back towards the station. 'Make a move to interfere and I'll blow the viaduct here and now.'

'You'll be killed too,' Adam said.

'Och, that's true,' Hamish cheerfully admitted. 'But I'll have served my master and that's all that matters.' He reached into his coat and took out one of the dolls and Adam saw it's face contorted with a look of evil triumph.

Contemptuously, Hamish turned his back and began pacing again and as he walked, Adam saw the other three small coffins arranged along the railway line as if they were to have a view of the final curse being put into effect.

In the distance he heard the whistle of the locomotive and Hamish heard it too and tilted his head and smiled.

'Go, whelp, if you want to,' he said. 'Save yer ain skin and tell the ones who are left all that ye know!'

Adam recalled the vision Tam Dubh had shown him, the Gypsy woman coming into the room and giving the dolls their names.

Swith, Agley, Smeddum and Snell. He knew them by heart now.

Swith had caused the fires, Agley the bus and Smeddum was the poisoner, so he was dealing with Snell; bleak, heartless Snell. Cold as the grave, Snell who had brought about the final destruction of the ship all those years ago.

He remembered how he'd been taken over by Tam Dubh and how Tam Dubh's voice had come through him and the words he had uttered at those times. He took a huge, deep breath.

'Snell,' he said and hoped it sounded the way it should. 'Stay yer hand, Snell! Thou hast neither business nor fight wi' these people. Tak yersel' awa'!'

'Thou kenst my name!' Hamish screamed in a voice that was deep and echoing. 'Tam Dubh, thou art here but canst dae naught against the fower o' us.'

Adam took a step closer to Hamish and spoke again.

'Thou hast nae business here, Snell. Awa'. Tak yersel' awa'!'

The effect on Hamish was electric. In his sudden cowering fright, he dropped the radio control unit on the footboards of the viaduct and Adam heard the plastic casing crack as it hit the rail. Hamish backed away as if in mortal fear while Adam dived on the transmitter and searched for the battery cover to make the unit inoperable.

Just as quickly, Hamish saw the deception and he jumped too and landed heavily on Adam and tried to get him in a headlock.

'So, it's tricks, is it, whelp!' They fell across the line and Adam fleetingly thought how big the rails were when you saw them at eye-level. Hamish held him down with an elbow across his throat and picked up the transmitter and feverishly tried to operate the toggle switch with his free hand but it was difficult to get a thumb to it.

Adam's right arm was doubled up behind him and he knew from the intense pain that a bone had broken somewhere while from where his head rested on the rusty steel railway line, he was conscious of a deep vibration and an almost melodic singing noise. With his free left arm, he tried to smash his fist into the side of Hamish's head but the blows were futile.

'Whelp, haud still!' Hamish snarled as Adam struggled against him.

With his free hand, Adam reached into Hamish's coat and felt a trembling there—a living thing—the doll. Snell in a hideous quiver of excitement! Adam put his hand on it; it was loathsome to the touch and brought him to the edge of nausea. He pulled it out of Hamish's coat and saw in front of him the doll's face filled with hate and loathing. The eyes were contorted in helpless rage and the mouth was a gaping, crimson hole with a vileness seeping from it.

With all his strength Adam flung the doll away from him

and raised his eyes and saw a look of sheer horror cross Hamish's face and then from somewhere far below in the gorge there came a distinct crack and Hamish dropped the controller on Adam's chest and clutched at his own head as if it too had been broken.

'Och, no,' Hamish cried and tears came as he slowly fell forward on Adam but before he made contact, Adam pulled the controller away to the left and held it at arm's length and managed to put it down as Hamish slumped on top of him, sobbing uncontrollably.

Adam eased himself out to one side and stood up and found his right arm hanging slack and the pain from it was intense as he fought to keep another dark surge of nausea from welling up. There was time to gather the other dolls one by one and throw them into the gorge where he watched them arc out and away from him before they bounced in pieces off the granite rocks below. The fragments fell into the sea and were sucked away.

The rails trembled and sang again as Adam caught hold of Hamish's coat by the neck and dragged him clear of the line just as the locomotive appeared around the bend at the far end of the viaduct.

The last thing he remembered was watching the huge headlight come at him with brown blasts of smoke above it then the dark bulk of the locomotive surged past with flashing side rods, hissing steam and the vibration of its passing shook the entire structure. He felt the heat briefly then it was away and he saw his father leaning out of the cab looking back at him. Adam waved his good hand in recognition.

As his knees buckled under him, the carriages rattled past in a blur of anonymous faces except for one he could make out as if it stood still. She looked down at him and it was Catriona.

Or it might have been Margaret.

People gathered around and he heard his father's voice.

'Careful with him!'

Hamish Leckie was there and he was talking in a distracted way.

'I don't know . . . I can't explain it.' He sounded distressed and somebody calmed him.

There was a heavy, metallic rumbling noise and through his slightly open left eye, Adam recognised it as a railway worker's trolley. They were taking him back to the station in that!

'Take it easy, son,' his father said and Adam nodded and kept nodding gently and his head began to move in time with the swaying of the trolley as they rolled it along the line towards the station, but by then Adam was past caring.

☆   ☆   ☆

His arm was broken in two places and his ribs had received a further beating so there was more pain and further confinement in bed. On Sunday morning he woke up at home with his arm in plaster and the strapping back on his ribs. For good measure, there were more hefty bruises and a couple of cuts and one of his teeth had an alarming looseness about it.

His mother came to him, pleased he was awake but surprisingly, she made no reference to the events of the previous afternoon. She enthused over the great time everyone had on the re-enactment and what a lovely sight it had been.

'We've got dozens of photos, Adam,' she said. 'We'll get them back tomorrow. A few nice ones of Catriona.' She fussed around the bedroom, picking up clothes and tutting mildly over the state of them.

'What about Hamish Leckie?' Adam said. His mother paused before answering.

'No, didn't see him there at all,' she said as if it didn't really matter. 'And how about something to eat now? Mmm?'

'Yeah, but what happened to him? After all that stuff on the viaduct? Did they get him?'

'Two poached eggs, Adam. How does that sound? Toast and tea.' She smiled and went away.

Catriona came later and he tried to get information from her.

'What happened to Hamish Leckie?' he said.

'How do you mean, Adam?'

'I mean, after all that business on the viaduct. Didn't you see me there, and him too?'

Catriona looked genuinely blank and she held his gaze without blinking and shook her head.

'Let it go, Adam,' she said. 'You've had a sort of— episode—but you're on the mend now, so your mother says.'

'It's like a conspiracy,' he said bitterly. 'You're all covering up.'

'There's nothing to cover up,' she said.

'Then how come I've got all these injuries?'

'Because you lead such a full life, Adam,' she said.

The following afternoon, he emerged from his bedroom and surprised his mother by appearing in the garden where she sat reading under the shade of a tree.

'Heavens above!' She got up and came to him. 'What are you doing out of bed?'

'I need to know,' he fended off her attempts to turn him around.

'What do you mean, Adam?' she said and let him continue to the shady spot under the tree.

'I mean I need to know about Hamish Leckie and all that stuff last Saturday.'

'Ah,' she said. 'Well, he seems to have gone away. I found out that much.'

'Where?' Adam persisted.

'How should I know?' His mother sat on the chair opposite him. 'He's a free agent.'

'Didn't anyone try to stop him?'

'How are you feeling now, dear?'

'In the dark,' he answered and looked away from her.

In the morning, before going off to the hospital, Adam's father came and found him in his bedroom, trying to tie the sling for his broken arm but using his teeth and only one set of fingers.

'Here, let me do that bit.' His father intervened and Adam let him tie the knot and adjust the sling.

'Thanks, Dad,' he said and his father inspected the plaster critically.

'Wriggle your fingers,' he commanded. Adam obliged, although it was difficult because the plaster cast kept them from moving freely.

'It's not the easiest thing I've ever done, Dad.'

'Hmm, I think I could cut a bit of that cast away,' his father said. 'I'll do it.' He had made up his mind but there was something that kept him in the room.

He paced around, inspecting Adam's books, the wall posters and the things he had on display. He flicked over the pages of the diary and then looked at Tam Dubh.

'I listened to your cassette, Adam,' he said and paused. Adam sat on the edge of his bed and fished his sneakers out from underneath.

'What did you think, Dad?'

'Um—okay. Point taken. A man has ambitions for his son. Even wants to live his life for him, you know, sometimes he wants the son to be what the father wasn't, doesn't want the son to make the mistakes he did. That sort of thing.' His father paused.

'Yes,' Adam said.

'Sometimes, ambition gets the upper hand. Takes over.'

Downstairs, Adam's mother called up to remind them she was going to town if anyone wanted a lift.

'Better go, Dad,' Adam said.

'Yes, musn't keep your mother waiting,' his father said.

'This afternoon, we'll cut a bit of that plaster cast away from your hand. Give you more room to move. We'll do it together, eh?'

'Well, you can't do it without me, Dad. Weak joke.'

'Yes,' his father laughed. 'Good one, son. It'll soon be better. Proper healing takes time. That's all.'

☆   ☆   ☆

Days passed and Adam's condition began to improve. He was on medication so he slept long and often and by late in the day, he always looked forward to Catriona's visits. Trevor Ross and Phil Hunter also dropped in to see him and the entire class contributed to a get well card, on which Ms Mullins added her own personalized comment: *Recover soon, Hardy. That's an order!* Trevor and Phil made it plain that everyone in class understood he'd had an accident on his bike, but they didn't seem curious about how or where it had happened.

There was no more news of Hamish Leckie. He was simply 'away' and despite Adam bringing it up several times, his parents refused to say where he had gone.

'I honestly don't know anything about him,' his mother said. 'He's not my patient and even if I knew, naturally I wouldn't tell you.'

'Maybe he's got a girlfriend in Melbourne,' his father suggested. 'Gone off to see her.'

'Oh, come on, Dad,' Adam said. 'What have you heard? There must be some gossip going around.' But it was obvious none of it was coming Adam's way.

Mike Carter and Richard Vernon were also away and news about them was equally scant. To make things even more mysterious there had been no mention in the papers of the events on the viaduct; it was as if nothing had happened that day. It's true, there were dozens of photos of the re-enactment in the paper with shots of well known town identities in their period costumes. Adam's father, as part of the engine crew, posed with one or two others with long serious Victorian faces, but of the danger that had faced them all there was no mention.

There was even a photo of the train crossing the viaduct on its triumphant return to Dunarling Station but there was no sign of Adam and Hamish Leckie, locked in life or death struggle.

'Maybe I imagined it all,' he said to himself when he saw that photo. But the injuries had been real enough. And the memories wouldn't go away.

☆   ☆   ☆

As time went on, Mrs Parry, with a few other volunteers, kept the museum open to the public. They worked on a roster basis to keep an eye on things but none of them seemed to know anything about Hamish Leckie. It was as if there had been a complete adult conspiracy of silence but Adam gradually began to understand they really didn't know anything.

'Someone said he'd gone back to Scotland,' one of the volunteers offered and was vague about the source of that information.

Adam's arm was still in its sling so he had to catch the bus to school and he began to drop into the surgery to get a lift home with his mother at the end of the day. It gave him an extra hour to fill each afternoon so he spent it in the museum.

On one of those visits he brought Tam Dubh back and placed him atop the pyramid of sand in the blue lit canvas cave. The notice that Hamish had printed was inaccurate since it talked about mandrake figures and now there was only one of them. Adam started up Hamish's computer and amended the original notice and printed a new one. It gave him something useful to do.

While he was engaged in this, Sergeant Balfour came into the museum.

'What's this?' he said. 'A takeover bid?'

'No, just updating things,' Adam explained. Tom read the new notice and handed it back without a word. He watched Adam slip it into the holder and crumple up the old one.

Tom Balfour appeared to linger in the museum and Adam wondered why. It was clear he had no real interest in the exhibits and yet there seemed to be something on his mind. Adam wandered into the office and sat in Hamish's swivel chair and waited. Tom walked in after him and perched on the end of the desk.

'Well,' he began. 'Quite a business, eh?' Adam sat without speaking and Tom went on. 'Before he went away, I got quite a bit out of Hamish Leckie.'

'Oh, yes.'

'He was amazingly lucid about what had happened to him,' Tom Balfour went on. 'And about you and the part you played out there on the viaduct. Both times. It wasn't his fault, of course. That's clear. It was some sort of temporary derangement.'

'Ah, so somebody's admitting something,' Adam said. 'At last.'

'I've more or less pieced things together,' Tom went on. 'A bit here, a bit there. The diary, Catriona's Bible, Hamish Leckie's own words. Quite a fantastic story.'

'Yes,' Adam said shortly.

'But too fantastic to be let loose,' Tom said. 'Weird, unsettling, disturbing; all that sort of thing. Which is why there's been a veil of silence about it and a lot of people have been doing their best to quell any public speculation. So the official story is you've had an accident on your bike, Hamish had to go back to Scotland for family reasons and Richard Vernon and Mike Carter have gone to a coaching school in Melbourne. They are actually on the mend, after a great deal of specialist treatment somewhere, hypnotherapy I think.'

'People have been evasive with me,' Adam said.

'You can understand why,' Tom Balfour went on. 'I had a word with all the editors of the local news media and they've agreed to cooperate. That way the general population just don't know much about it.'

'I couldn't get any information out of Mum and Dad.'

'That's because the ones who know have been asked to play dumb and stick to the official line. The last few days must have been frustrating for you,' Tom went on. 'You're full of what happened but it seems no one else wants to talk. We even had the army bomb disposal people out here at the dead of night, defusing Hamish's little surprises on the viaduct. They said he'd done such a professional job they'd give him an assignment anytime.' He shivered slightly. 'So, what with one thing and another it was decided to hush everything up.'

Adam picked up a paper-knife from the desk and balanced it on top of a bottle of ink and spun it but it fell off with a clatter.

'We'd like to keep it that way, Adam,' Tom Balfour said. 'No write up in the papers, no public acknowledgement of what you did, no honour, no medals, no glory.'

'Does Catriona know?'

'She knows a fair bit,' Tom said simply. 'We had a long talk. About all sorts of things. It was her idea.'

Adam smiled at that. 'You've got to work on it,' she had once advised him.

'She was already putting two and two together herself,' Adam said. 'You know, the things she found in the Bible and the way she worked everything out.'

'You two are pretty close, aren't you?' Tom went on.

'Yes,' Adam said without hesitation. 'We're very close.'

'Well, now you've got something else between you. A secret to keep.'

☆   ☆   ☆

On a bright Sunday morning he found Catriona in the small flower garden behind the shop. She sat in an untidy, overgrown summer house with a weathered cane table and two chairs as the only furniture. On the table was a yellow waterproof pouch with two strings for tying it. Catriona was writing in a notebook, figures, names and dates. When she looked up, Adam could see she had been crying.

'Hello,' he sat in the empty chair. 'I came to see you.'

'These were in the box,' she showed him some papers. 'With all the other bits and pieces, more letters, Adam Colquhoun's Bible, a lot of receipts and other stuff. But these were wrapped up as if someone collected a whole secret history and wanted to keep it safe.'

'And it made you unhappy?'

'Some of it did,' Catriona went on. 'Barbara absolutely howled when she read them.' She smiled briefly at that and added another name to the notebook.

'What's that?' Adam said.

'I've been working things out,' she answered. 'A family tree. We go back to about 1850 something. The original couple came from Scotland and their name was Walker and he was a sea captain.'

'So, what did you find that made you cry?'

'I found this for a start,' she said and passed over a yellow and fragile clipping from *The South Coast Register*.

Another *Dunarling* Tragedy

Miss Margaret Colquhoun, a survivor of the Barque *Dunarling* which last year ran aground off our coast with the loss of 49 lives, has herself died on the 3rd of April in tragic and mysterious circumstances.

Miss Colquhoun was found lying on the beach about two miles from the site of the wreck. She was in a delirious and highly distressed state and was removed to hospital where she died without regaining consciousness.

No one is able to account for Miss Colquhoun's presence on the beach at the time so her death is a complete mystery. She had been taken in and cared for by Captain and Mrs Walker, who have no children of their own.

Miss Colquhoun's funeral was arranged by Mrs Walker, in the absence of her husband who returned to his ship. The interment took place on 5th of April, thus bringing to a close this sad chapter in our local history.

'But we know she died when she was only eighteen,' Adam said. 'The date's on her gravestone in the cemetery. 1887.'

'That's not what's important,' Catriona brushed aside his comment. 'The report says the Walkers didn't have any children of their own.' She paused. 'Can't you see—they must have or we wouldn't be here; Barbara and I and all this lot.' She showed Adam the family tree she had drawn in her notebook. 'I mean, childless couples don't leave descendants.'

'Maybe they had one later in life,' Adam said.

Catriona gave him a single sheet of lined paper with a letter on it. The handwriting reminded him of Ewart McColl's.

'Or maybe it happened like this.'

Geelong
18th April, 1887

My Dear Wife,

I write to say how sorry I am at the cruel turn of events you describe in your last letter. In giving Miss Colquhoun refuge under our roof, I had thought at last we had the

*daughter we always wanted. From the description you gave
me, she seemed such a sweet, pious lass and so full of
maidenly virtue that my heart was won over and my
happiness near complete.*

*When I returned from my long absence to find Margaret
about to give birth yet still unwed, I fear my pride and
temper overcame compassion and reason which allowed me
to give vent to my churlish and un-Christian outburst.*

*I was not to know Margaret was ill from the effects of the
shipwreck and her confinement and that she would run from
the house in such torment at my intemperate words. Please,
I beg you not to consider me too harshly for I am already
in an agony of remorse, having to endure each waking
moment the consequence of my uncharitable action whilst
knowing that I will be judged for it in a Higher Court.*

Your husband,
Jos. Walker

'So that's how she died?' Adam whistled and shook his
head. 'It doesn't say where she went on the beach but I
reckon she must have tried to go back to the cave.'

'To remember the three days she spent there with Jamie,'
Catriona suggested and Adam went silent and dropped his
eyes to Captain Walker's letter again.

'And the baby must have died with her,' he said.

'This second letter explains all that,' Catriona gave him
another sheet of paper which bore a printed crest formed of
two crossed anchors and a twining rope.

Hostel for Seamen
Melbourne
30th April, 1887

Dear Mrs Walker,

*I cannot pretend your letter was welcome to me, bringing as
it did such terrible news of Margaret's death on April 3rd.*

You cannot begin to imagine my sorrow when I read your words. What should have been joyful news, the birth of our daughter, brought forth nothing but tears and anguish on my part.

As you know, I have been in Melbourne these last months, giving evidence to the inquiry into the loss of the Dunarling. *In my grief I confess to you, I did not know Margaret was to bear my child for had she told me of it, I would have returned to marry her instantly.*

We truly loved each other and would have married as soon as the inquiry is over, but now that cannot be.

I am pleased you will look after my daughter until I return and that I am to be allowed to give her a name. I choose Margaret, in memory of her young mother, who suffered so much and was so innocent.

There is nothing to be gained in putting blame on either of us. What is done is done and if there be any guilt, Margaret has paid for her part in it. For my share in this sorry event, I am paying now and will continue to pay until I die.

Shortly, the inquiry will reach a conclusion then I will return to provide for Margaret my daughter and hold her in my arms. I am due to sail on the schooner Ringrose, *leaving Port Melbourne at the end of the month.*

Yours truly,

James Ramsay

Adam was silent for a long time as he took in the meaning of the letters. Barbara came to join them in the small summer house and Adam gave her his chair and sat on the top step.

'What do you think, Adam?' she said.

'Very sad.'

'Yes, we both howled.'

'I wept, Barbara howled.' Catriona made a joke of it.

'And then we both realised we're related to Margaret and Jamie. The Walkers must have adopted their baby.'

She made another entry in her notebook.

'Adam, did Cat show you the last item?'

'I was going to,' Catriona said and passed Adam another flimsy piece of stained newsprint from *The South Coast Register*:

Tragic Loss of The *Ringrose*
7th May, 1887
News is just to hand that the schooner *Ringrose* of 234 tons has been lost with all hands.

'And so ends the story,' Barbara said when Adam looked up.

'Poor Margaret,' Catriona added.

'And poor Jamie Ramsay.' Adam carefully put the clipping on top of the two letters and sat down on the step again.

'It's been weeks since I made a Jamie Ramsay doll,' Barbara sighed and then she brightened. 'In fact you haven't done any serious beachcombing for ages, Cat.'

They were in bare feet and they walked together along the edge of the waves. Catriona had tucked her skirt up and Adam carried both of their shoes to leave her hands free to gather things from the sand.

There was a piece of brown wood, stogged in the sand at the edge of the breakers and she bent to pull it out before the waves came back; and the wind blew her hair about her face. She inspected the wood briefly then quickly tossed it back into the sea and wrung her fingers as if to shake something off. She rubbed her hand against her t-shirt and went to Adam's side again.

'Dirty, was it?' he said.

238

'No, just made my hand tingle.' She shook her fingers and smiled at him.

'Just then, with your hair like that,' Adam said, 'you looked so like Margaret.'

'I've heard you say that before,' Catriona responded, 'and I said "shh, don't talk" because I thought you were spaced out or something. You really saw her, didn't you?'

'In the cave, yes. I saw her—and Jamie too.'

'Adam, tell me about them.'

'You mean now?'

'Yes, now.'

Turning History into Fiction

For the writer of fiction, there are two beautiful things about history; firstly there is so much of it and secondly, it is there to be borrowed.

In writing this particular piece of fiction, I have woven together historical facts from my native Scotland and some from Australia, which has been my home for the last thirty-two years.

Like many new arrivals in this country, I still have firm and unshakable attachments to the place of my birth. It's not that I don't want to fit into Australia, it's just that the way I speak, think and write mark me as a Scotsman first and then as an Australian. Also, like many new arrivals, I want to keep in touch with the youthful life and memories I left behind in my first country and to do this, I sometimes read books, newspapers and travel magazines or watch television programs or listen to music with a Scottish flavour. Just occasionally, I share memories with other former Scots people.

Most writers keep a real or a mental notebook filled with ideas and notions for stories they want to write one day, just as soon as their current project is at an end. One of the ideas from my notebook was to create a story about a ship that came to Australia with a curse on it. Later, in the story, some modern young people stumble upon the thing that carried the original curse and the evil is released all over again but this time, in the town where the young people live.

This was as much as I had and the idea, being such a slight one, was well down in my list of priorities. Then I bought a copy of the *Scots Magazine* for May, 1980 and read an article about people who collect dolls and there were photographs accompanying it which depicted the more traditional type of doll, the kind that children dress up and make a fuss over. I would probably not even have read the article but for one of the photographs in it showing two rather grotesque looking little figures in coffins. The accompanying text gave an account of a strange discovery that was made in Edinburgh, in the year 1836.

It seems some boys were out looking for rabbit burrows when they uncovered a small opening in a rock; it was protected by a cone formed out of three pieces of slate each cut into a roughly triangular shape. Inside the opening, the boys found seventeen small coffins arranged in two rows of eight with one coffin a little way apart from the rest. The dolls appeared to range in age, some being quite old to judge by the amount of decay that had taken place. The doll that stood apart from the rest had only recently been put in the hole.

Boys being boys, they soon grew tired of their discovery and began throwing the coffins and the figures at each other. Only eight of the original number have survived intact and these are now on display in the National Museum of Scotland, in Edinburgh.

Each coffin was decorated with little tinplate triangles and contained a tiny figure made out of mandrake root with a hole bored through at the shoulders and a twig inserted to form the arms. The figures were dressed in cotton clothes and I have tried to preserve these details in the novel.

Apart from the *Scots Magazine* article being an interesting one, I looked at it in conjunction with the bare idea of my story—could mandrake dolls be the things that carried the original curse? At this stage, the story began to move up a few notches on my priority list as this possibility began to take shape.

I wrote to a curator of the National Museums of Scotland in Edinburgh, explained what I was about and asked for more information. I received a fascinating article by German writer and researcher, Walter Hävernick, which dealt with the origin of the dolls and provided some theories for their use. There were also copies of newspaper articles of the time, describing the original discovery as made by the boys. These gave a variety of possible reasons for the figures being buried in the way they had been found.

One of the newspapers suggested the figures were part of a seafaring superstition in which a departing sailor would leave one of these mandrake figures with his wife for safekeeping. If his ship were to be lost at sea, the sailor's wife would bury the figure and in this way, her husband would be assured a 'Christian burial' in his own country.

The newspaper the *Scotsman* presented its readers with suggestion of a more sinister motive for the tiny burials, a motive which incidentally, fitted my own fictional intention for the mandrake dolls:

> Our own opinion would be—had we not some years ago abjured witchcraft and demonology—that there are still some of the weird sisters hovering about Mushat's cairn or the Windy Gowl who retain their ancient power to work the spells of death by entombing the likenesses of those they wish to destroy. Should this really be the case, we congratulate the public, but more especially our superstitious friends, on the discovery and destruction of this satanic spell-

> manufactory, the last, we should hope, which the "infernal hags" will ever be permitted to erect in Scotland!—The *Scotsman* July 16th, 1836.

More possibilities began to show themselves.

According to Walter Hävernick, another known use for the mandrake figure was as a ship spirit—one was kept by the captain and lived in its little coffin shaped box and ate with him in the privacy of his quarters and in return, protected the ship from dangers. Amongst all of the theories, two dominant facts emerged: the dolls were seen to be linked with seafarers and secondly, their exact use was still unclear. For the purposes of my story, I had found the carriers of my curse—the mandrake dolls in their supposedly evil incarnation. I had also found a 'good guy' in the shape of another mandrake figure who had been the captain's ship's spirit.

About this time, I produced a series of radio programs for ABC Radio National entitled *Voyages*, which looked at how we got to Australia at different periods throughout our history. Two of the programs dealt with voyages on sailing ships, for which I had to carry out a great deal of research including examination of a number of diaries and first-hand accounts of incidents and hardships of the seafaring life.

Another program dealt with ships that didn't complete the voyage—in short, they ended as shipwrecks on the Victorian south coast, often with tragic loss of life. The *Loch Ard* was one such ship which met her end on 1st June, 1878 with an almost total loss of the entire ship's company, apart from two survivors, Tom Pearce, a nineteen-year-old apprentice on the ship and Eva Carmichael, an eighteen-year-old passenger.

Somehow, both managed to get off the doomed ship separately and later they met in the wild storm and found refuge in a cave where they sheltered until they were found. Alas for the romantics, they both left Australia and went their separate ways and never met again.

Armed with these two sets of historical facts, the story was now positively burning to be written. I had read so many diaries and first-hand accounts of life under sail in the middle 1800s that a diary seemed to be the ideal way to convey the events on the doomed ship. I made my diarist a middle aged Ayrshire farmer, a bachelor, who recorded faithfully the dramatic events on the ship, and sometimes wistfully, the more tender descriptions of the innocent romance of Margaret and Jamie Ramsay.

The setting for the story was obvious; the south coast of Victoria and the fictitious town of Dunarling with its nearby gorge and viaduct and museum.

In my own early days, I had made a number of steamship voyages between Britain and Australia and in 1956, the Suez canal was closed to traffic which meant that ships had to go round the cape of Good Hope. This route was called 'south about' and took ships deep into southern latitudes where the waves were big and grey and impressive. Looking back on those experiences, I am thankful my ship was a turbo electric liner of 20,000 tons and not a sailing ship of only 1,600.

Making historical borrowings depends upon the pioneering work and research done by others and so sincere acknowledgements are due. I offer my thanks to Jack Loney whose published research into the *Loch Ard* and other shipwrecks provided an enormous wealth of important detail and to Marjorie Wilson whose article published in the *Scots Magazine* of May 1980 provided the initial idea of using the mandrake figures. My thanks also to Elizabeth Wright, a curator of the National Museums of Scotland for her ready response to my request for information which included Walter Hävernick's essay *The Ghost in the Coffin*, printed in *Folk & Farm*, published by the Royal Society of

244

Antiquaries of Ireland. This and other material provided was of particular value.

Finally, acknowledgement must be made to so many voyaging diarists of the last century, published and unpublished, who travelled under steam or sail, often uncomfortably and with great personal hardship, yet managed to set down such vivid impressions of their time at sea.

David McRobbie
Pullenvale, Queensland,
September 1990

Also by David McRobbie

The Wayne Dynasty

Warning: this book is a bit funny. You should open it in private. If you read it on the bus, you might laugh your head off. Thud! Your fellow passengers will look at your headless body and frown. You'll get no sympathy from them.

If you read it in church during the sermon then you'll giggle instead of keeping a straight face.

The Vicar will look at you over the top of his glasses, other worshippers will cough and move along the pew to show you're not with them.

So be warned. The humour starts on page one and you can't get your money back if you laugh at the wrong time . . .

The adventures of Wayne Wilson and Squocka make great entertainment for anyone from nine to fifteen (old people might laugh at them too).

Waxing with Wayne

This is the second book on Wayne, continuing his adventures in a suburban world that frequently gets the better of him.

The faithful Squocka is by his side, sometimes in front, sometimes behind, but always there, in person, hanging around sort of.

Wayne copes with many relative problems, both senior and junior, he faces complications with unwanted junk, neighbours, bullies, rivals, sunburn, unrequited love and Violet Pridmore and he does it all in only ten chapters.

How can they do it for the money?

Ivan Southall
The Mysterious World of Marcus Leadbeater

Struggling with grief and loss over the death of his beloved Gramps, Marc arrives at his grandparents' house and is shocked to find it is to be auctioned the next day. Hadn't Gramps always promised that it would be his? But even this does not prepare him for the events that will transpire.

Ivan Southall has crafted a tangled and enthralling story of a boy's attempt to make sense of the complexities of the adult world.

'Marcus Leadbeater is a brilliantly focused creation . . . Southall at his best.'

Agnes Nieuwenhuizen